WHEN ALL HELL BROKE LOOSE

WHEN ALL HELL BROKE LOOSE

A PREACHER & JAMIE MacCALLISTER WESTERN

WILLIAM W. JOHNSTONE

AND J.A. JOHNSTONE

PINNACLE BOOKS
Kensington Publishing Corp.

www.kensingtonbooks.com

PINNACLE BOOKS are published by

Kensington Publishing Corp.
119 West 40th Street
New York, NY 10018

PUBLISHER'S NOTE
Following the death of William W. Johnstone, the Johnstone family is working with a carefully selected writer to organize and complete Mr. Johnstone's outlines and many unfinished manuscripts to create additional novels in all of his series like The Last Gunfighter, Mountain Man, and Eagles, among others. This novel was inspired by Mr. Johnstone's superb storytelling.

All Kensington titles, imprints, and distributed lines are available at special quantity discounts for bulk purchases for sales promotion, premiums, fundraising, educational, or institutional use.

Special book excerpts or customized printings can also be created to fit specific needs. For details, write or phone the office of the Kensington Sales Manager: Attn.: Sales Department. Kensington Publishing Corp., 119 West 40th Street, New York, NY 10018. Phone: 1-800-221-2647.

PINNACLE BOOKS, the Pinnacle logo, and the WWJ steer head logo are Reg. U.S. Pat. & TM Off.

First Printing: October 2021
ISBN-13: 978-0-7860-4757-4
ISBN-13: 978-0-7860-4758-1 (eBook)

10 9 8 7 6 5 4 3 2 1

Printed in the United States of America

Chapter 1

Santa Fe, 1852

As he sat at a table in a cantina, Jamie Ian MacCallister stretched his legs out in front of him and crossed them at the ankles. As tall as he was, as long-legged as he was, that meant he took up a considerable amount of space.

And the cantina was crowded, so . . . it was only a matter of time.

Not that causing trouble was Jamie's intention. He was just getting comfortable.

The big, shaggy-bearded man in the equally shaggy buffalo coat tripped over Jamie's feet and nearly fell. He stumbled forward a couple of steps as his three friends laughed at him.

"I didn't think you were *that* drunk, Lomax," one of them hooted.

"You need a cane to help you walk, old man?" another man gibed.

Lomax stopped, swung around, and glared at them. "It wasn't my fault! I tripped over that varmint's big clod-hoppers!"

He leveled a finger at Jamie, who ignored him and

lifted a cup of coffee to his mouth to take a sip. It was flavored with chocolate and cinnamon, making it different from the black coffee Jamie usually drank, but it was quite good and he savored the taste.

"Hey! Blockhead! I'm talkin' to you!"

Jamie glanced up and recognized the man, even though they'd never actually met. "I hear you, Lomax."

"What the hell do you think you're doin', stickin' your feet out like that so folks trip over 'em?"

"You *could* watch where you're going," Jamie suggested.

"And you could get your damn feet outta the way!" roared Lomax.

Jamie sighed and set the cup back on the table at which he sat. He straightened in the chair and pulled his legs back. "Satisfied?"

Lomax smirked. "I reckon you could say that you're sorry, too."

Jamie shook his head. "I pride myself on being an honest man."

The muleskinner's smirk turned into a scowl. "What the hell do you mean by that?"

"I mean I'm not particularly sorry." Jamie said again, "You could watch where you're going."

Lomax's face was already flushed under the thick growth of beard. It turned even redder as he stared at Jamie. He was so outraged that he couldn't find his voice for a moment. When he did, he demanded, "Do you know who you're talkin' to?"

"Matter of fact, I do," Jamie drawled. "Your name's Roscoe Lomax. You're a muleskinner. You ramrod some of the wagon trains that carry goods along the Santa Fe

Trail. Got yourself a reputation as a brawler, as well as one of the filthiest of a foul-mouthed breed."

Lomax confirmed that by spewing a string of profane, highly creative obscenities. He followed that by saying, "If you know that much about me, mister, you know that I chew up and spit out anybody who gives me trouble. Now get on your feet, you . . ." Some colorful epithets followed.

Jamie regarded the man with a mild expression, but when Lomax concluded by saying, "Stand up, damn you!", Jamie complied. He put his hands flat on the table and slowly rose to his feet.

Lomax was a big man, but it seemed like Jamie just kept rising and rising. He towered over everybody else in the cantina, and he was so muscular, so broad-shouldered in his buckskin shirt, that he seemed to loom like a mountain. His broad-brimmed, high-crowned, dark brown hat rested on thick, graying brown hair. The mustache that drooped over his wide mouth was the same shade. A rather large nose and deep-set, piercing eyes dominated his craggy face. He was in his forties, but he was weathered like a mountain, too. A sheathed Bowie knife was on his left hip, a holstered Walker Colt on his right.

One of the muleskinner's friends swallowed hard and said, "Oh, hell, Lomax, I recognize that fella now. That's Jamie MacCallister."

"I don't care if he's Andrew Jackson and Davy Crockett rolled into one," snapped Lomax. "Nobody shoots their mouth off at me and gets away with it."

"Those are some good men you're talking about," Jamie said. "I'll thank you not to sully their names by mentioning them again."

Lomax took a step toward him, sticking out his chest

and sneering. He was half a head shorter than Jamie but almost as powerfully built.

"There you go again, tellin' me what to do. I don't like it, MacCallister. And just so you know . . . you don't scare me, mister. Not one little bit."

"The feeling's mutual, then," Jamie said with a curt nod.

Despite the crowd, the cantina had fallen silent.

A few minutes earlier, a girl had been dancing while a couple of hombres played guitars. Her taunting smile, her swirling midnight hair, her lush bosom and bare shoulders in a low-cut blouse, her brown, flashing legs under the long skirt she twitched up as she danced, all had the men watching her clapping, whistling, and calling ribald encouragement.

She backed away in the silence, retreating behind the bar, and the formerly rapt audience turned its attention to the confrontation in the corner.

The man who had recognized Jamie said, "I don't know if you should be doin' this, Lomax. MacCallister's fought Injuns and all sorts o' badmen and has hisself a big ranch up in Colorado. He ain't a man to mess with."

"Well, neither am I," Lomax blustered. "Anybody with a lick o' sense knows that I'm a man to stand aside from."

One of the other men snickered and said, "Yeah, because you're liable to trip over somethin' and fall on somebody, like you damn near just did a minute ago."

Lomax whirled on that unfortunate soul, who probably wouldn't have said such a thing if he hadn't been drunk. The muleskinner lashed out with a big, knobby-knuckled fist that crashed against the man's jaw and sent him flying through the air to land on a nearby table, which collapsed under the impact and made the men who had been sitting there topple over backward in their chairs. They shouted angrily as they scrambled to their feet, grabbed the man who had fallen on the table even though the calamity hadn't been his idea, and started punching him.

Lomax's other friends yelled and charged over to help the man being assaulted. Still more of the cantina's customers leaped into the fray. The fight spread through the room like somebody had taken steel and flint and struck a spark that landed in a pile of black powder.

Lomax frowned at the sudden chaos, then turned to look at Jamie and raised his voice to declare over the uproar, "Hell, I ain't sure I want to fight you if there ain't nobody to watch, MacCallister." He jerked a hand toward the melee. "All these fools are too busy with their own scufflin' now."

Jamie leaned his head toward the table and said, "Want to sit down and have a cup of coffee with me instead?"

Lomax scratched at his beard, pushed his lips in and out as he thought about it, and after a moment he said, "Sure, why the hell not?"

A thrown chair sailed through the air toward Lomax's head. Jamie reached out, the movement smooth but almost too swift for the eye to follow, and grabbed the chair before it could strike Lomax. He set it at the table and nodded.

"Obliged," Lomax said.

Jamie looked over at the bar, caught the eye of the proprietor, who was peering nervously over the hardwood, and raised his cup, then pointed at Lomax to indicate that the man should bring coffee to both of them. A few minutes later, one of the working girls weaved her way through the fighting, yelling crowd and set a tray with two cups on it on the table in front of Jamie and Lomax.

"Hell of a note, ain't it?" Lomax said as he picked up one of the cups.

"Yep," Jamie said. He sipped from the fresh cup. "I haven't forgotten the things you called me, by the way."

"Don't expect you to. But we'll settle that later, I reckon."

Jamie nodded. They sat there and watched the brawl ebb and flow around them as they drank their coffee.

Like a wildfire, the fracas burned itself out quickly. Half-conscious men were draped over the backs of chairs or sprawled in the wreckage of tables. Puddles of booze from broken whiskey and tequila bottles soaked into the hard-packed dirt floor. Moans and groans filled the air. The cantina's proprietor stood behind the bar with both hands clapped to his mostly bald head as he looked around in dismay at the destruction and wailed, *"Aiii, Dios mio!"*

Jamie nodded toward the man and said to Lomax, "You really ought to pay that hombre for all this damage, since you're the one who started it."

"Me?" Lomax demanded. "It was your damn fault. You and your big feet!"

Jamie shook his head. "You just weren't paying attention where you were going."

Lomax gulped down the rest of his coffee and clattered the cup back onto the table. "That's it," he said as he surged to his feet. "You and me are gonna settle this once and for all, MacCallister."

"You sure about that?"

"Damn right, I'm sure! Come on, let's get to it! I'm the rippin'est, roarin'est lobo wolf on the Santa Fe Trail! I'm gonna beat you to a frazzle! I'm gonna tear one o' your arms off and whale the tar outta you with it! I'm gonna knock your head right offen your shoulders and . . ."

Jamie stood up and uncorked a roundhouse right that landed while Lomax was still flapping his jaw. The blow lifted him off his feet and dumped him on his back with his arms and legs spraddled out. He managed to raise his head and groan once before it flopped to the side. He was out cold.

"That was a mighty nice punch, Jamie," a new voice called from the cantina's doorway. "Glad I got here in time to see it."

"Thanks," said Jamie without looking around as he flexed the fingers of the hand he'd just used to wallop Lomax.

Satisfied that he hadn't broken any bones, he turned his head and then frowned as he saw a man in an army uniform walking toward him.

"I'd say it's good to see you again, Colonel, but I'm not so sure about that. You've got some sort of job that's going to keep me away from home for a while, don't you?"

"That's right, Jamie," the officer said. "I'm afraid I do."

Chapter 2

San Francisco, 1852

"Dadgum it, woman," Preacher said as he tugged at the tight collar around his neck and grimaced. "Are you tryin' to strangulate me to death?"

Colleen Grainger slapped lightly at his hand and said, "My goodness, Preacher, if you keep messing with that, you're going to ruin it. You look so dapper and handsome, all dressed up in a nice suit. And you even shaved!"

"Don't get used to it," muttered Preacher.

"What did you say, dear?"

"Nothin'. Are you about ready to go out and have dinner at this fancy eatin' place?"

"Yes, and then to Mr. Maguire's theater. The local players are putting on a production of *Hamlet*. I'm sure you'll enjoy it."

Preacher frowned. "Is there killin' in that one?"

"Yes, quite a bit."

"All right, then," the mountain man said. "I reckon it won't be too bad."

Colleen rested a hand on his freshly shaven cheek, which was so smooth that it felt strange to Preacher.

"You're just humoring me, aren't you, Preacher?" she asked, smiling.

"Nah, of course not. I want to go out and eat at the place and then see the play. It'll be, uh, enjoyable."

"Well, I still think you're lying, but it won't hurt you to soak up a little culture."

"No, ma'am," he said. "It sure won't."

But he *was* lying. He would have much rather been back at Red Mike's, the riverfront tavern in St. Louis where he had spent so many happy hours—and quite a few dangerous ones—as a younger man.

Red Mike's wasn't there anymore, though. The brawny Irishman who'd owned it had gone to live with his daughter and now spent his days in a rocking chair on her front porch.

The very thought of living like that made Preacher shudder, right down to his bones.

Colleen patted his cheek, then turned to pick up her handbag and go to the door of the hotel room. She looked mighty nice in the fancy, expensive green gown she wore, with her auburn hair piled up on top of her head like that.

She was a widow in her early forties, about ten years younger than Preacher. Her late husband had struck it rich during the Gold Rush but hadn't lived long enough to really take advantage of his new-found wealth. Colleen seemed to enjoy being rich, though. She could afford to indulge her every whim, and seldom hesitated in doing so.

The money she had didn't interest Preacher in the slightest. For him, true riches lay in clear, crisp mountain mornings, high country meadows, and peaks so tall that they looked like God His Ownself might live on them. As long as Preacher had enough money for provisions, powder, and shot, that was all he needed to reach those places where he was truly happy.

On the other hand, Colleen Grainger was one hell of a nice-looking woman and mighty pleasant company, so he could put up with fancy restaurants and going to the theater, at least for a while.

He had been in California for several months, just drifting around at loose ends after going out there with some friends, a young couple looking to make a new start. After making sure they were well established on a farm in that big valley to the south, he had taken his leave, not wanting to intrude on them.

Eventually he'd wound up in San Francisco, which had boomed like blazes in the years since the Gold Rush, and had met Colleen Grainger, who evidently had seen something she liked in a scruffy old mountain man in a buckskin shirt. They had spent considerable time together since then, all of it enjoyable.

It helped that Colleen wasn't looking for another husband—and Preacher sure as blazes wasn't looking to settle down.

He put on the short, silk top hat she had bought him to go with the fancy dark suit. It was silly looking, he thought, but she seemed to like it. They went downstairs and out through the ornate lobby of the hotel where Colleen lived.

Officially, Preacher wasn't staying there. He had an arrangement with the owner of a livery stable not far away. He was keeping Horse, his rangy gray stallion, there, and Dog, the big, wolflike cur who was his other trail partner, hung around the stable, too. The proprietor had told Preacher he could sleep in the hayloft if he wanted to. But most nights, the mountain man had been at the hotel.

Colleen had a carriage waiting. It was all dark, polished wood and gleaming brass trim. The big black horses hitched to it had brass decorations on their harness, as well.

He and Colleen would be traveling in style tonight, thought Preacher.

The driver would have opened the door for her, but Preacher was there first and helped her into the carriage. He climbed in and settled himself on the seat beside her, facing forward.

"This is cozy," she said as the vehicle began rolling through the streets toward the restaurant. She leaned against Preacher and turned her face up. He knew she expected him to kiss her, and he didn't see any harm in obliging.

Several minutes passed like that, then Colleen moved back a little and said breathlessly, "My, you certainly do know how to start off an evening in enjoyable fashion, Preacher."

"I aim to please, ma'am."

"So far, you're succeeding admirably. I'd even go so far as to say—"

She stopped short, prompting Preacher to ask, "What was that you were gonna say?"

"This isn't the way to the restaurant."

Preacher didn't think that was what she'd been about to say a moment earlier, but it didn't matter. He heard the worried tone in her voice and turned his head to look out the window on his side of the carriage.

The neighborhood through which they were passing appeared to be a mite on the squalid side, but that didn't mean anything. Areas of riches and poverty were cheek by jowl all over San Francisco, as they were in any city once it got big enough.

"Maybe the fella at the reins knows a different route," Preacher suggested.

Colleen shook her head. "No, I'm pretty sure we're going the opposite direction from the restaurant. There's no reason we should be in this part of town. It can be dangerous here."

"The driver's lost, then. I'll tell him to turn around and head back to the hotel."

As Preacher leaned over and stuck his head out the window, he heard warning bells going off in the back of his mind. For the most part, cities were treacherous, rotten places where the dangers were usually hidden, rather than being out in the open like they were in the wilderness.

At Colleen's insistence, he hadn't worn the pair of .44 Colt Dragoon revolvers he usually carried these days. The weight of the guns would have been mighty comforting right about now, he thought. But he wasn't exactly without resources—or weapons.

He had stuck a couple of small flintlock pistols in the waistband of his trousers, at the small of his back where his coat covered them. He also had a dagger hidden down the side of his boot. He'd figured what Colleen didn't know wouldn't hurt her.

Still, maybe there was nothing to worry about. Maybe the driver was just inexperienced and lost. Preacher could understand how somebody could get turned around in a place like San Francisco, with all of its narrow, twisting streets.

"Hey, mister," he called to the driver. "The lady says you're goin' the wrong way."

The man glanced back over his shoulder, then suddenly whipped the horses and sent them lunging ahead faster. The unexpected surge threw Preacher back against the seat and jolted him into Colleen's shoulder.

She cried out in surprise. "What's that lunatic doing?"

"I reckon he's up to no good," Preacher replied.

At the higher rate of speed, the carriage bounced more on every rough spot, throwing him and Colleen around. It was enough to rattle a fellow's teeth.

"What does he want?"

"Most folks probably know you've got a heap o' money," Preacher said. "My guess is that he's working with some gents who want to make you a prisoner and hold you until you turn over a big pile o' cash to them."

"I won't do it!" flared Colleen. "And they can't make me!"

Preacher didn't explain just how brutal varmints like that could be, especially when they had a woman at their mercy. Anyway, he didn't plan on allowing things to get that far.

For a second, he considered letting the driver continue on to wherever he was supposed to rendezvous with his partners, just so he could take care of them all at once, but that would be running too much of a risk with Colleen's safety. He told her, "Hang on tight," and reached for the door handle. He twisted it with one hand while he used the other to grab one of the pistols at the small of his back.

Standing up and swinging his body partially out of the carriage, Preacher pointed the gun at the driver and shouted, "Stop that team right now, you lowdown skunk!"

The man glanced over his shoulder, fear on his beefy face. He jerked on the reins and veered the running horses sharply to one side, making the carriage sway violently. Colleen cried out again as the maneuver threw Preacher far out to the side. He barely hung on with one hand and was able to keep only one foot in the carriage.

As the vehicle straightened, he recovered quickly, but

before he could bring the pistol to bear again, the driver twisted on the seat and slashed at him with the whip. The leather strands struck the back of Preacher's gun hand and left a bloody streak. The pain made him drop the gun.

"Son of a—" Preacher grated, then bit back the rest of the curse. He had another pistol, but before he could reach for it, the driver slashed at him again with the whip, aiming for his face.

Preacher flung up his bleeding hand just in time, and the whip wrapped around it instead of slashing his face. He didn't give the driver a chance to jerk it back. He pulled hard.

Lurching toward Preacher, the driver yelled in surprise and alarm. He let go of the whip, but not in time to prevent him from sprawling on the seat where the mountain man could reach him. Preacher threw the whip aside and grabbed the driver's collar.

The horses were runaways, thundering straight along the street. Preacher hesitated just a second when he saw that they were approaching a wrought iron hitching post sticking up at the side of the street then he heaved with his considerable strength and the unfortunate driver slid off the seat and tumbled from the carriage.

Preacher heard the heavy thump as the man's momentum carried him into the hitching post. He had no way of knowing how much damage the collision did to the driver, but it had to be considerable. Enough to render him no longer a threat for the time being, that was for sure.

"You all right in there, Colleen?" Preacher called to the auburn-haired widow.

"Y-yes," came back the shaky answer. "Can you stop this thing, Preacher?"

"Just what I'm about to do," he assured her. He got a

good grip with both hands on the brass rail around the top of the carriage and threw a leg up onto the driver's box. It took only a second for him to haul himself onto the seat.

The reins hissed and writhed on the floorboards like snakes. Preacher reached down and snagged them, glad he wouldn't have to jump onto the backs of the team in order to stop them. He could do that if he needed to, of course, but he was getting a mite too long in the tooth for such hijinks, he told himself.

He was just about to haul back on the reins when, somewhere behind the carriage, a gun boomed and a split second later he heard the flat, sinister hum of a pistol ball passing close beside his head.

Chapter 3

Preacher bent a little lower on the seat and turned his head to peer back over his shoulder. Four men on horseback were charging after the carriage. Muzzle flame bloomed red in the darkness as one of them fired another shot.

"Looks like we ain't stoppin' after all!" he called to Colleen. "That varmint's partners are on our trail! Grab somethin' in there and hold on tight!"

"Ohhhh!" she moaned. Preacher hoped she was just scared and not hurt.

He snapped the reins against the horses' backs and shouted at them to keep going. Not many people in that neighborhood were out on the streets at that hour, but a few pedestrians had to scramble to get out of the way of the racing carriage. From the corner of his eye, Preacher saw them glaring at him in surprise and confusion.

More shots blasted from the pursuers. At least one of them had a revolver. Preacher could tell that from the frequency of the reports.

If he'd had his Colts, he would have stopped and shot it out with the would-be kidnappers. Since acquiring a pair of Paterson Colts from the Texas Rangers some years earlier, he had practiced a great deal and become expert in their use, and he was even better with the newer Dragoons he usually carried. He would match his speed and skill with the revolvers against anyone, even outnumbered.

But he had only a single-shot pistol and the dagger with him, so it was more important that he try to get Colleen to safety.

The fact that he didn't know San Francisco all that well made that more difficult. He sent the carriage careening around corners at such a high rate of speed that a couple of times he thought it was going to turn over. Although he was able to right it each time, he didn't know if he was heading back toward the hotel or just deeper into trouble.

One of the riders had pulled ahead of the others and was getting closer. Preacher glanced over his left shoulder and saw the man thrusting a gun toward him. He ducked as the weapon roared and a cloud of smoke spurted from its barrel. The silk top hat, which improbably had stayed on Preacher's head, flew off and sailed away as the bullet struck it.

Preacher couldn't give the man another shot at him. As the pursuer struggled to thumb back the revolver's stiff hammer, Preacher reached down to his boot, plucked the dagger from it, and twisted on the seat to throw it.

The blade flew true and lodged in the man's throat. He let out a choking cry, dropped the gun, and his hands went to his throat to paw at the dagger's handle. He managed to rip it loose, but that just did more damage and caused blood to flood down the front of his shirt. He toppled out of the saddle, crashed to the street, and rolled over a couple of times before coming to a stop and not moving again.

Preacher didn't see that because the carriage was still

bucketing along at a high rate of speed, but he didn't have to see it to know he had disposed of another enemy.

Maybe that man's grisly death would be enough to make the others back off and abandon the chase.

No such luck. They shouted furiously at seeing one of their own go down and urged their horses on faster.

Preacher wheeled the carriage into another turn.

It was difficult to see where he was going. Some light spilled into the street from windows and open doors in the buildings. Here and there, a torch flickered or a lantern hanging from a post glowed. He made another turn and came into a straight stretch of road that ran between two huge buildings. Those were warehouses, he realized, having seen buildings like them on the riverfront back in St. Louis.

And up ahead . . .

"Well, hell," said Preacher.

Up ahead, he could see the tall masts of ships docked at the piers. He and Colleen were about to run out of road.

A look back told him he couldn't turn around. The three riders had already entered the stretch between the warehouses. He would be driving straight into their guns if he reversed course.

He kept going as the docks loomed closer and closer.

A narrow street ran between the warehouses and the water, Preacher saw. He would have to turn right or left and hope the carriage wouldn't overturn. People might be on some of the ships tied up at the piers, so there was a chance the pursuers would give up rather than risk trying to kill him and grab Colleen in front of witnesses.

That was only a slim hope, however. Men bold enough to kidnap a wealthy widow and hold her for ransom probably wouldn't worry a lot about witnesses.

Preacher allowed his instincts to guide him and swung the carriage into a sharp left-hand turn when they reached the waterfront. A good decision, he saw instantly. To the right, the open area between the docks and the warehouses was littered with stacks of cargo. He would have been forced to stop if he'd tried to go that way.

But he and Colleen weren't out of the woods yet. From an alley up ahead, two more riders suddenly emerged and charged toward the carriage.

Just how many of the damn varmints *were* there, anyway?

They had him in a crossfire, and he had only one bullet with which to fight back. The two men in front of him reined their horses to a halt and started firing at him. Preacher bent as low as he could on the seat to make himself a smaller target. A slug spanged off the brass trim on the carriage's roof.

Holding the reins in his left hand, he reached behind him with his right and pulled the remaining pistol, never slowing the carriage. The attackers' nerves broke first. They yanked their mounts aside.

As the carriage flashed past one of the men, Preacher was close enough to use the pistol. He thrust the gun toward the man and pulled the trigger. The pounding hoofbeats drowned out the pop from the small caliber weapon, but Preacher saw the man's head jerk as the bullet struck him. He threw his arms in the air and pitched limply out of the saddle.

The second man galloped after the carriage, and he didn't have very far to go. Preacher felt the vehicle shift and looked back to see the man hauling himself onto the roof. He'd made a daring leap from horseback to the carriage and succeeded in the risky attempt. If he had missed, he probably would have broken his neck.

He was on the roof and pulling himself closer to Preacher.

The man had the coarse, cruel features of a thief and killer. Preacher knew he had guessed right about this bunch. They were after Colleen for her money, and even if they got what they wanted, more than likely they would treat her badly.

Preacher wasn't going to let that happen.

With the other three still coming up fast behind, he couldn't stop the carriage. He looped the reins around the brass grab bar at the side of the driver's seat and turned as the man on the roof leaped at him.

Preacher got himself braced just in time to keep from going over backward as the man crashed into him. Ducking the punch that the man swung at his head, Preacher hooked a fist into the attacker's belly and felt the butt of the gun stuck in the man's waistband. The revolver must have been empty, or else the man would have just shot him off the carriage.

Despite the blow Preacher had landed, the man bulled ahead and got an arm around the mountain man's neck. They swayed back and forth on the driver's box, slugging away at each other. Preacher lowered his head and rammed it into the man's face, feeling the hot spurt of blood on his forehead as the impact crushed the man's nose. The attacker howled in pain.

Preacher managed to close his hand around the gun butt, jerked the revolver loose, and slammed it against the man's head. The man slumped but hung on stubbornly. Preacher hit him again and felt bone crunch in the man's skull, before the varmint let go and fell off the speeding carriage.

Preacher didn't have time to take any satisfaction in that triumph. A gun boomed somewhere close and the bullet passed so close to his cheek that it felt like a gust of hot air.

One of the riders had pulled up alongside the carriage, trying to draw a bead on Preacher again. That wasn't easy from the back of a galloping horse.

Preacher flipped the revolver in the air, caught it by the barrel, and slung it at the man. The gun spun through the air and smashed into the man's face with enough force to knock him back. He lost the saddle and flew off, crashing to the ground.

Preacher didn't figure that hombre would be getting up for a while, if at all. He had whittled the odds down to two to one, but he didn't have any more weapons.

Turning to face forward on the seat of the racing carriage, he saw that yet another problem was coming up quickly. The road ran out ahead, ending in a low wooden wall. On the other side were the waters of the bay. Preacher looked at the alleys between the buildings that lined the waterfront. All of them were too narrow for the carriage.

He still had room to stop, but if he did that, the two men on horseback would just come along a few seconds later and shoot him.

With no other options, he untied the reins, let them hang loose, and leaned far over the front of the driver's box to reach down and grasp the pin that connected the tongue to the carriage body. It wasn't designed to be pulled with so much weight against it, but Preacher heaved as hard as he could and it popped free.

The horses had realized they were about to run out

of space, too, and as soon as they were loose from the carriage, they turned sharply away from the water. The carriage kept moving, though, rolling straight for the edge and not slowing down.

Preacher swung down from the box and grabbed the side of the front window on that side to steady himself as he flung his body toward the open door. He landed inside the carriage, causing Colleen to gasp.

"Preacher, what—"

"No time," he said as he grabbed her. They had only seconds.

Not even that long, actually. The carriage reached the wall and still had enough momentum to tip up and over it and plummet the six feet into the bay.

Chapter 4

Preacher had dived out the open door with Colleen in his arms just as the carriage began its somersault into the water. They struck the surface a split second later and went under.

Despite the relative warmth of the evening, the bay was cold, and the weight of the clothes they wore pulled them deep.

Preacher was a strong swimmer and kept his left arm locked around Colleen while using his right arm and his legs to stroke and kick toward the surface.

They broke into the air a few moments later. Colleen gasped and choked and spluttered. Preacher knew she must have swallowed some water, but she sounded like she would be all right.

As for himself, he'd had the presence of mind to drag in a big breath as they leaped from the runaway carriage, so he was in pretty good shape as he kept them afloat. He put his mouth close to Colleen's ear and said, "Keep as quiet as you can. The fellas who are left from that bunch may be lookin' for us."

"We . . . we have to get to shore!" she said. Her teeth chattered. "It's so cold! And I can't swim!"

"Shhh," Preacher said, trying again to impress on her the need for quiet. He tried not to splash too much, but he had to put some effort into keeping them from sinking.

He heard hoofbeats and then men's voices calling to each other, not too far away. The two remaining pursuers were up there. One of them said, "How are we going to find them now?"

"They're probably dead," replied the other man. "The wreck could have killed them, and if it didn't, they drowned when that damn carriage went to the bottom."

"Now what are we gonna do?"

"We won't be able to get any money out of that woman, that's for sure." The would-be kidnapper heaved a disappointed sigh. "Who knew that fancy pants with her would turn out to be such a fighting fool?"

"He sure didn't look like it in that silly top hat." The other man's voice turned grim. "But he killed four pretty tough fellows. I wouldn't have believed it if I hadn't seen it."

"What are we going to do about the bodies?"

"Leave them where they fell. What else can we do about it?"

"The law might connect them with us. We've been seen together."

"Might be a good idea for us to leave town for a while."

Preacher hoped they would do just that. He was angry and wouldn't have minded settling up with those two, but as long as he had Colleen Grainger to look out for, it was better that they just move on.

Before that could happen, Colleen picked that moment to sneeze.

She didn't actually pick it, Preacher reflected later. The water that had gone up her nose probably was the cause. But whatever the reason, the urge had struck and she couldn't hold it back, and as the sound echoed over the water, the men on the dock exclaimed in surprise.

"She's down there in the water!" one of them said. "We need to find her. We can still cash in!"

"Oh, Preacher, I'm sorry!" Colleen wailed.

He didn't waste any time or breath trying to reassure her. Kicking strongly, he pulled at the water with his free arm and headed toward the nearest pier. If they could get underneath it, Colleen would be relatively safe for the moment, and she could hang on to one of the support crosspieces while he dealt with the two men.

Looked like he might get to settle that score after all, Preacher thought.

He heard running footsteps.

One of the men shouted, "Over there! I hear them!"

A gun blasted.

The other man yelled, "Don't shoot, you fool! You might hit the woman!"

Another strong kick sent Preacher and Colleen gliding through the water into the pitch darkness underneath the pier. Preacher felt around until he found one of the crosspieces. Thinking Colleen could sit on it and hold on to one of the vertical beams, he slid his hands under her arms and lifted her. She clutched desperately at the beam.

"Stay right there," he told her. "I'll come back and get you after I've dealt with those hombres."

"Preacher, I-I'm freezing! I don't know how long I can hold on."

In her soaked clothes, she would be even colder now that she was mostly out of the water and the wind was blowing on her. But the alternative was for them to surrender to the two men, and they sure weren't going to do that. There was no chance it would end well for either of them if they did.

"Just hang on and don't make any noise. I'll be back for you."

He took his boots off, hating to lose them, then drew in a deep breath and went under the water. He twisted out of the coat and let it go, as well. Free of those encumbrances, he was able to swim underneath another dock, found the ladder attached to it, and climbed up.

The two men weren't making any effort to be quiet. After all the shooting, it probably was too late for that, anyway. More than likely, it would be a while before any law showed up to investigate the commotion, so the men had time to search for their intended prey.

"We need a damn lantern," one of them complained as Preacher crouched behind a barrel and watched them. The man leaned over to look underneath one of the piers.

"You'd better be careful," the other man advised. "That's a good way to get shot in the face."

"Any gun he has won't be any good to him after being dunked in the bay."

"Yeah, I reckon you're right about that. Still, if it was me, I wouldn't underestimate that man, whoever he is."

Preacher's keen eyes had adjusted to the faint light available along the docks and spotted a length of board lying on the ground a few feet away. Moving with the same silent grace that had allowed him to sneak into Blackfoot camps as a young man without ever being caught, he slipped over to the board and picked it up. It would make a nice, makeshift club, he decided.

He glided like a phantom toward the two men, who were heading for the pier where Colleen was hiding. He was almost within reach of one of them when the man suddenly lifted his head and said, "Hey, do you hear something dripping?"

Preacher lunged and swung with plenty of power before the other man could answer. The board cracked against his target's head, and he knew from the soggy thud and the way the man dropped like a rock that he had crushed the varmint's skull.

The gun in the man's hand dropped to the ground as he collapsed. The other searcher turned around in response to the noise. The gun in his hand swung toward Preacher.

The mountain man scooped up the fallen weapon and dropped to one knee as his hand came up with blinding speed. Flame belched from the gun's muzzle. The second man staggered back and cried out in shock and pain as the bullet drove into his chest. His feet suddenly reached empty air, and he toppled backward into the water next to the pier, raising a huge splash.

Preacher heard a pitiful little cry from under that pier, then Collen called, "Preacher, help!"

He set the gun aside and went back into the water in a smooth dive. As he came back up, he heard Colleen flailing and splashing as she fought desperately to keep her head out of the water. A couple of swift strokes took him to her side.

"I got you," he told her as he slipped an arm around her and pulled her against him. "It's all right, Colleen. They're all dead now."

She threw her arms around his neck and clutched him as if she would never let go. Sobbing, she buried her fact against his shoulder. "Oh, Preacher . . . I . . . I slipped off . . . when that man fell in . . . I was just . . . too cold to hang on."

"It's all right," he told her again. "Let's get you out of this water. We need to get back to the hotel and dry off, otherwise you're liable to catch your death o' cold."

He took her to the ladder and helped her climb, then followed her out of the bay. The damp wind off the water chilled him to the bone, and if he felt like that, he knew it had to be even worse for Colleen. She wasn't accustomed to such harsh conditions.

Farther up the docks, Preacher had seen some coarsely woven blankets spread over the piles of cargo to protect them from the elements. Those blankets could serve the same purpose for Colleen. He put an arm around her shoulders and led her in that direction. She shivered violently. Her teeth clattered together.

He found one of the blankets and wrapped it around her, then sat her down on a crate.

"Stay here for a minute," he told her. "I'm gonna see if I can catch the horses those last two fellas were ridin'. I don't think they've had time to wander far."

"H-Hurry, Preacher. I th-think my insides . . . are going to shake apart."

He hustled along the dock and found the two horses standing at the mouth of an alley, clearly confused as to what they should do next. Using his knack for getting along with animals, he spoke to the horses softly as he approached them, not making any sudden moves. He was able to snag the dangling reins of both mounts.

Colleen looked miserable, huddling deep inside the blanket, when he got back to her.

"You're gonna have to ride astride," he said. "Sorry."

"I . . . I don't care. I just want to get warm again."

"Won't be long now," Preacher assured her, adding under his breath, "As the tavern wench said to the parson."

"Wh-what?"

"Never mind. Nothin' important."

He lifted Colleen onto one of the horses, then decided to swing up behind her instead of riding the other horse. He kept his arms wrapped around her to help her warm up more as he took the reins and nudged the horse into motion.

"How . . . how can you keep *going* like this? I mean . . . you're not a young man anymore."

"Clean livin'," replied Preacher with a grin. "As the parson said to the tavern wench . . ."

By the time they got back to the hotel, Colleen's tremors finally had subsided some. Preacher slid down from the horse's back and lifted his hands to catch her as she practically fell out of the saddle.

They got a lot of startled looks from the hotel staff and guests alike when they entered the lobby in their soaked clothes. Colleen had the cargo blanket wrapped around her. Preacher's hat and coat were gone and he had no boots.

The clerk at the desk exclaimed, "Oh, my! Mrs. Grainger, what . . . what in heaven's name happened to you?"

Preacher said, "We can explain all that later, old son. For now, we need a tub and plenty o' hot water brought up to the lady's suite just as quick as you can manage. All right?"

"Yes, of course, sir. I beg your pardon, sir, but you look like you fell in the bay!"

"That's because we did," Preacher said. "How about gettin' started on that hot water?"

"Yes!" The clerk gestured emphatically for a couple of bellmen to get busy with that task.

Preacher, with his arm around Colleen's shoulders, turned her toward the staircase. He tensed as a man stood up from the armchair where he'd been sitting in the lobby and moved to intercept them. More trouble?

Maybe, maybe not, he thought as a second later he relaxed slightly. The man wore an army uniform and had the fresh, eager look of a shavetail lieutenant about him.

"Mister . . . Preacher? Sir? I'm afraid I don't have any other name . . ."

"Preacher'll do," the mountain man said. "What do you want, son? As you can see, I'm a mite busy."

"I'm Lieutenant Milligan, sir. I'm posted at the Presidio. The post commander received a dispatch requesting that he locate and contact you on behalf of Colonel Finlay Sutton, attached to the Department of War in Washington."

"I know who Colonel Sutton is," Preacher said. "Did some work for him a time or two in the past. But whatever he wants, it's gonna have to wait. This poor lady's froze plumb half to death, at least."

He started to lead Colleen past the young officer, but Lieutenant Milligan raised a hand to stop them.

"I see that, and I apologize for my timing, sir, but my orders are to notify you that you should proceed with all due haste to a place in Colorado called MacCallister's Valley, where you will rendezvous with Colonel Sutton."

Despite the situation, Preacher didn't bull the lieutenant aside, as he'd been about to do. "MacCallister's Valley?" he repeated. "Me and Jamie MacCallister handled a little dustup down along the Mexican border a while back. What in blazes does the army want with us now?"

"I'm afraid you'll have to go to Colorado to find out about that, sir, because I have no idea." Lieutenant Milligan hesitated, then asked, "May I inform my commander

that the message is received and understood and will be
complied with?"

"Yeah, yeah, when I get around to it," said Preacher as
he stepped around the young officer and guided the still-
shivering Colleen toward the stairs. "First I got me a lady
to warm up, and that's a mite more important right now."
He glanced over his shoulder and added, "Don't you go
takin' that the wrong way, neither, you young whipper-
snapper!"

They left Lieutenant Milligan gaping up the stairs after
them.

Despite Preacher's concern for Colleen—she was his
first priority—he couldn't help but wonder what the unexpected message was going to lead to. Colonel Finlay
Sutton, though a seasoned frontier commander, was pretty
high up in the War Department these days and dealt with
important matters. And any time Preacher got together
with Jamie MacCallister, some ruckus inevitably busted
out. It seemed that trouble followed Jamie around, just like
it did Preacher.

Even though the evening hadn't gone as planned—he
hadn't had supper in a fancy restaurant or watched a bunch
of costumed players prance around on a theater stage—a
grin of anticipation stretched across the mountain man's
rugged face. As he led Colleen along the corridor toward
her suite, he said, "There, there, darlin', pretty soon
ever'thing's gonna be just fine."

Chapter 5

MacCallister's Valley, Colorado—two weeks later

"I swear, Falcon, you must've growed a foot since the last time I seen you," Preacher told Jamie and Kate MacCallister's youngest son.

"Yeah, I'm going to be as big as my pa one of these days," the blond teenager said confidently.

"Well, it's all right if you ain't." Preacher grinned at Jamie as the three of them stood beside the fence around the corral where Horse had just been put to rest after two weeks of hard riding from northern California. "It's not ever'body who can be built like a dang mountain. Your pa's so big, he's sort of a freak o' nature."

"Speaking of freaks of nature, Falcon," Jamie responded dryly, "I once knew a man who went two whole years without a bath."

Preacher frowned. "I was busy. Anyway, I fell in a river a few times durin' those two years, so I had baths. They just wasn't intentional-like."

Jamie laughed and clapped a big hand on Preacher's

shoulder. "Well, come on into the house. Kate's eager to see you again, and so is Colonel Sutton."

Preacher narrowed his eyes at his massive friend and said, "The colonel didn't get us together here for a friendly visit, much as I might like socializin' with you and your family, Jamie. What's he want?"

"I'll let him tell you about that," Jamie said as he and Preacher walked toward the big, sprawling, log-and-stone ranch house. "He's been a little tight-lipped about it with me, too."

Falcon followed them as Dog bounded on ahead. The shaggy, wolflike cur could be intimidating, even frightening, when he wanted to be, but at moments like this, full of exuberance, he was like a big, friendly puppy.

Kate, Jamie's beautiful blond wife and the mother of their brood of children, stepped onto the porch. She looked at least ten years younger than she actually was and smiled as she raised a hand in greeting to the mountain man.

"Hello, Preacher," she called. "It's so good to see you again. I was happy when Jamie told me you were going to be paying us a visit."

Preacher had first met the MacCallisters many years earlier, when Jamie and Kate were in their teens and recently married. In his wanderings from one end of the frontier to the other, Preacher had dropped in at their ranch a number of times over the years.

"And I'm mighty happy to be here," he replied as they started up the steps to the broad porch. "Even though I'm just followin' orders, you could say."

A tall, lean man came out onto the porch behind Kate. His close-cropped hair was gray threaded with silver, as was his mustache. He wore an army uniform, and his erect bearing testified that such had been his usual garb for a long time.

"If you didn't want to be here, Preacher, you wouldn't be, orders or no orders." The man grinned as he stepped forward and stuck out his hand. "I can only echo Mrs. MacCallister. It's good to see you again."

"Likewise, Colonel." Preacher gripped Finlay Sutton's hand. "Now, what in blazes is so important you had to get me and Jamie together?"

"Oh, no," Kate said before Colonel Sutton could reply. "You're not going to have that discussion standing out here. Come on inside and make yourselves comfortable in the parlor. I have a pot of coffee ready, for however long this discussion lasts."

"I hope it won't last too long," said Sutton. "The situation really isn't that complicated." His friendly expression grew solemn. "I need you to find out what happened to some unfortunate souls who disappeared five years ago."

"Inside," Kate said sternly.

A few minutes later, the three men were settled down in the ranch house's comfortable parlor. Jamie and Preacher were in armchairs flanking the massive fireplace, while Sutton sat on a divan with a heavy wooden frame. It was a masculine room, with lots of thick, dark wood, but the feminine touches Kate had brought to it lightened the mood, making it a room where either men or women could be at ease.

Falcon had wanted to sit in on their meeting, but Kate had guided him away after bringing in coffee for Jamie, Preacher, and the colonel.

"I'm gonna be having adventures of my own, one of these days," Falcon had complained as his mother was ushering him out. "You just wait and see. It may not be that awful long from now, either."

"I'm sure that's right, dear," Kate had told him with complete sincerity. "You wouldn't be your father's son if you didn't want to go off adventuring."

Sutton sipped his coffee and said, "Fine lad, that boy of yours, Jamie."

"All my kids are fine," Jamie replied. "Kate and I have been blessed, no doubt about that." He drank some of his own coffee, the china cup looking almost like a toy in his massive hands. "You've been dodging my questions until Preacher got here, Colonel, and now that he is, I'd appreciate some answers. What's so important that you had to get us together?"

Sutton sighed, then, looking like the word tasted bad in his mouth, he said, "*Politics.*"

Preacher set his cup aside on a small table and started to rise to his feet. "Reckon I'll be goin' now."

Sutton held out a hand. "Please, Preacher. Hear me out."

Preacher settled back down in the chair and said, "I want to, Colonel, but nothin' good ever comes outta Washington when the subject is politics."

"Don't you think I know that even better than you do?" asked Sutton. His voice had a hint of sharpness to it. "I have to work in that . . . that foul quagmire and find ways to do some good despite all the venality and avarice that drives the place."

"You said something about folks disappearing?" Jamie reminded him.

"That's right." Sutton looked at Preacher. "You'll listen?"

"Reckon I will," the mountain man agreed grudgingly.

"All right. Five years ago, a group of Prussian nobles came to this country for a tour of our western territory—"

Preacher was on his feet again. "I mighta knowed! Furriners!"

"What do you mean by that?" asked Sutton, looking startled by the vehemence of Preacher's reaction.

"I've had dealin's with them Prussians before. Even had a sword fight with one o' the varmints one time. And it ain't just me who's run afoul of 'em. I've heard plenty o' stories. Every time a bunch of them *Europeans* come over here, they wind up gettin' in trouble, or causin' trouble. They've durned near started more 'n one Injun war. The only thing worse for causin' trouble on the frontier than those blasted European aristocrats are the fellas who come out west wantin' to paint paintin's or write books! Damn paint daubers and word scribblers! Any time you get any o' those bunches west o' the Mississipp', all hell breaks loose!"

"Generally, that's been my experience, too," Jamie added when Preacher paused in his rant to take a breath.

Sutton nodded. "I can't deny that our visitors seem to have a habit of bad things happening to them. I think it's because they can't really conceive of how vast and danger-ous our frontier actually is. But they keep coming, and we can't very well stop them. We just have to deal with the trouble that follows them."

Preacher let out a disgusted snort, but he sat back down. "Go ahead," he told Sutton. "Like it or not, I reckon you've got me curious."

"Five years ago, a group of Prussian nobles came to the United States at the invitation of our government. The leader was a man named Peter von Eichhorn, a graf, or an earl as we call them, from one of the leading families who also possessed a lot of wealth and influence in their government. Graf von Eichhorn was what they call a Junker, a member of one of the families that's ruled that part of the world for hundreds of years."

"Let me guess," said Jamie. "Somebody in *our* government wanted to make a business deal of some sort with this fella von Eichhorn."

Sutton shrugged and said, "I don't really know. That was well before I was assigned to the War Department. But that's probably a good guess."

Preacher asked, "Is von Eichhorn the gent who went missin'?"

"Not just him. The entire party, including the American guides and helpers they had hired, along with the small army detail that accompanied them."

"The whole bunch?" Jamie said with a frown. "How many people are you talking about, Colonel?"

"Almost three dozen. Vanished without a trace."

"Where?"

"The northern Rockies. Between the Missouri River and the Canadian border."

"Blackfoot country," Preacher said. His face and voice were grim.

Jamie leaned forward and clasped his hands together between his knees. "Preacher's right, Colonel. You know what must have happened to those folks. The Indians jumped them and wiped them out."

"That's what everyone assumed," Sutton admitted. "The thinking was that they ran afoul of a Blackfoot war party—"

"Stone Bear," Preacher said.

Sutton frowned. "I beg your pardon?"

"Stone Bear," Preacher repeated. "Blackfoot war chief.

He's been raisin' hell up in those parts for years now. I've heard a heap about him. Supposed to be a mighty bad fella." The mountain man shrugged. "Can't say for sure, since I never crossed trails with him."

Jamie chuckled. "Which is the reason he's still raising hell up in that country, I expect. If you had run into him, Preacher . . . he wouldn't be."

Sutton asked, "Do you think this Stone Bear would be capable of wiping out a party of American soldiers and European nobles such as the one I've described?"

Preacher nodded. "Capable of it . . . and more than willin'."

"I agree," Jamie said. "You mentioned the Prussians had some American guides, Colonel. Do you know who was in charge of them?"

"I've seen the name. Let me think . . ." After a moment, Sutton nodded. "His name was Reese Coburn. Do you know him?"

"Heard of him," Jamie said. "I don't think we've ever met."

Preacher said, "I've run into Coburn before. Several times, in fact. Seemed like a fella who knows what he's doing. How about the army detail with them?"

"Commanded by a Lieutenant Barton," said Sutton. "That's all I know about them."

Jamie's eyes narrowed shrewdly. "Why the interest in what happened to these folks now, after all this time?"

Sutton crossed his legs and said, "A couple of months ago, a trader who operates up there in that region brought back rumors of seeing some white women who were captives of an Indian band. It was all very vague and unsubstantiated, but the stories got around and finally made their way back to Washington, where representatives of the

Kingdom of Prussia heard about them. Relations between our government and theirs have always been a little chilly ever since Graf von Eichhorn and his party disappeared. We'd like to change that, so when they sent a letter to President Fillmore asking that these new rumors be investigated, the request was passed along to the War Department"—the colonel smiled—"which is how it wound up landing in my lap."

"Even if Stone Bear and the Blackfeet have white captives, that's no reason to think they're some of those Prussians," Jamie pointed out. "Could be any pilgrims or settlers they came across and enslaved."

"I know that," said Sutton, "but my orders are to investigate anyway and determine, if at all possible, what actually happened to Graf von Eichhorn and his party. To rescue any survivors and to . . . recover any remains."

Preacher shook his head. "That's a fool's errand, if you ask me. And a good way to get killed."

"I know. That's why I decided my best chance of success . . . and of survival for myself and my men . . . was to have the best assistance possible."

"Preacher and me," Jamie said heavily.

Colonel Sutton inclined his head in agreement but didn't say anything.

Jamie looked over at Preacher. "What do you think?"

"Just said what I think. It's a fool's errand. Wasn't that long ago we tangled with a bunch of Apaches to help out the government. Now we're bein' asked to take on the Blackfeet, the only bunch that rivals the Apaches for sheer meanness."

"We're not looking to start a war," Sutton said. "If we can locate the captives, I'd rather negotiate for their release. That's the best way to find out the truth of what happened, after all. Especially if they *do* turn out to be members of von Eichhorn's group."

"Tryin' to negotiate with Blackfeet usually don't turn out too well. I'd rather do my negotiatin' with hot lead or cold steel."

Sutton shrugged. "Force is always an option, if it's absolutely necessary."

Jamie asked, "How many men are you taking up there with you?"

"I'll have approximately fifty dragoons. Plus the Prussian representatives, of course."

"Hold on," Preacher said. "The furriners are sendin' more folks up there, after already losin' some?"

"This will be a small military force. A dozen men or so."

Jamie nodded and said, "So you'll have between sixty and seventy men. That's a good-sized bunch. You're hoping the Blackfeet will think twice about attacking a group that big and will be willing to talk."

"That's the hope, yes."

"Stone Bear can muster more warriors than that," said Preacher. "If you're serious about doin' this, Colonel, you'd be better off takin' several *hundred* men."

"Which would start a war for sure." Sutton shook his head. "No, I have my orders, Preacher. I'm asking for help. But I certainly can't order you and Jamie to come along on this mission. And I'll understand completely if you say no."

The two frontiersmen looked at each other in silence for a long moment.

Then, with obvious reluctance, Preacher said, "I'm a mite curious what really happened to those folks."

"I am, too," Jamie admitted. "And the colonel here has been a good friend to us. He'll stand a better chance of finding out what he wants to know if we go along."

Smiling, Sutton said, "That's what I was hoping to hear you say, gentlemen."

Preacher held up a hand and told him, "Don't go thankin' us yet. We ain't said we're joinin' up. I want your word that if we do find any captives up there amongst the Blackfeet, we'll try to get 'em out, whether or not they're the Prussians you're lookin' for."

Sutton considered that and nodded. "That's a reasonable request. I wouldn't leave helpless prisoners in the hands of those savages." He paused. "Political expediency is one thing. Simple human decency is another."

"Politics and human decency," mused Jamie. "What's the old saying? 'And never the twain shall meet.'"

"Ain't that the truth," Preacher said. "But count me in anyway, Colonel."

"And me," Jamie said. "One way or another, we'll find out what really happened five years ago."

Chapter 6

The Rocky Mountains, 1847

"Oh, my," Countess Marion von Arnim said as she stared wide-eyed at the men wearing feathers and buckskins. "Are they tame . . . or savage?" From the tone of her voice, it was difficult to guess which answer she was hoping to hear.

"Well, now, that depends on what kind o' mood they're in, Your Countessship," drawled the man who stood beside her, leaning on his long-barreled rifle as the weapon's butt rested on the ground. "Redskins is plumb notional critters. You can't never tell what one of 'em will take it in his head to do . . . which is why you need to be ready for trouble all the time out here."

Marion looked over at him and asked, "Is that why you told your men to ready their firearms when we saw this group approaching, Mr. Coburn?"

"Yes'm, it is," Reese Coburn said. "And I'd sure be obliged to you if you'd go back with the rest of your friends until we see whether these fellas are lookin' for a fight."

The tall, lean man wore a buckskin shirt and trousers like the approaching Indians, but he didn't have any feathers in his hair and a broad-brimmed felt hat shaded his deeply tanned face. In addition to the flintlock rifle, he had a pair of flintlock pistols stuck behind his belt and a sheathed hunting knife attached to that belt. He looked like what he was: an experienced, competent, tough-when-needed-to-be frontiersman.

He had been hired to guide and protect this party of Prussian nobles behind him, and he didn't intend to let anything happen to them. A dozen good, fighting frontiersmen, plus a detail of dragoons commanded by a young lieutenant, surrounded the wagons in which the visitors were traveling.

All except for Countess von Arnim, who had climbed down from the first wagon and run up to Coburn to get a better look at the Indians.

She had been a problem from the start—disregarding his orders, not taking the dangers of the frontier seriously enough, and shamelessly flirting with him every time she had the chance, which annoyed the man she was betrothed to, Graf Peter von Eichhorn, who had organized the sightseeing expedition to America.

Under some circumstances, Coburn wouldn't have minded some rich woman from another country playing up to him, especially one as pretty as the countess. But she needed to do what she was told. She was putting herself at risk, and maybe the rest of the party, too.

When she ignored his request to rejoin the others, he put his hand on her arm and added, "You really need to go back to the wagons, ma'am."

She cast a cold glance at his hand, clearly offended at being touched by a commoner—and an American, at that! "You forget yourself, Mr. Coburn."

"No, ma'am. I remember myself real well. I'm the fella

who's bein' paid to keep you safe." Some of the same chill her words displayed found its way into his voice. "So how's about skedaddlin'?"

Marion sniffed and pulled her arm out of his grip. He let it go. She turned and walked toward the wagons.

Coburn might have heaved a sigh of relief, but he still had a bunch of potentially hostile Indians striding toward him, so his nerves weren't going to ease up just yet.

They were Blackfeet, he saw as they came closer. He recognized the markings on their buckskins and the way they wore their hair. That knowledge made his gut tighten a little more.

Thirty-some years ago, when the first white men traveled through those parts, the Blackfeet had been fairly friendly, or so the story went. Then, because of a misunderstanding, one of the men on the Lewis and Clark expedition had shot and killed a Blackfoot brave, and ever since, the whole tribe hated all white men. The mean streak within the tribe grew to a mile wide once it was roused.

But they didn't *always* kill whites on sight, and since Coburn's men and the soldiers outnumbered them— slightly—they might decide to be friendly. Coburn hoped he could parley with them. If he promised that he and his companions would be moving on quickly out of the area, maybe that would be the end of it.

He stood by himself, waiting. Most of the Indians stopped about twenty feet in front of him. One of them walked on ahead.

Coburn spoke the Blackfoot tongue fairly well and hoped he didn't sound too awkward as he said, "Greetings."

"I am Stone Bear," the Blackfoot said without any

niceties. "You trespass on hunting grounds used by my people."

"We're not here to hunt, Stone Bear. We only travel through your lands and will soon be gone."

"White men have no business here, with your lodges on wheels and your odd buffalo that pull them."

"The white men who travel in the lodges on wheels come from another country," Coburn explained. "They are not accustomed to walking."

"And they have women with them," Stone Bear said.

So you noticed that, did you, old son? thought Coburn. Well, he wasn't really surprised. This warrior didn't seem like the sort of fella who would miss much.

"They have come to see the country," Coburn said, making a sweeping gesture with his left hand to indicate their surroundings, which, admittedly, were worth looking at.

It was summer, and the high meadows were full of lush grass and wildflowers, and the rugged slopes were a deep green from the pines and firs and spruce that covered them. Streams ran bubbling and foaming over rocky creek beds, making sweet music. Snowcapped peaks stood proud and towering against skies that could not have been a clearer, more breathtaking blue. Coburn loved the high country and had ever since he had first arrived a decade earlier.

Stone Bear seemed puzzled. "Is there nothing like this where they come from?" he asked.

"From what they've told me, they have mountains, and their land is a beautiful one. But they are curious about other lands, as well."

"As long as the hunting is good, people should stay

where they are," Stone Bear said, scowling. "Especially white men."

"Maybe so," said Coburn, "but they're here, and it's my job to guide them on their way and protect them. I hope Stone Bear and his people will allow me to do that." Coburn decided to add a little to the deal. "We will share some of our salt with you."

It never hurt to give an Indian a present.

Stone Bear thought it over, then asked, "You are not staying in these hunting grounds?"

"We intend to go straight through them and will leave as soon as we can, most probably within two days."

"You will not disturb the land or kill more game than you need?"

Coburn was aware that most Indians considered whites to be shamefully wasteful.

"I give you my word we will not."

Stone Bear nodded and said, "You may pass through Blackfoot hunting grounds. You will give us salt?"

Coburn turned his head and called in English to one of his men, "Dawlish, bring me a little sack of salt." To Stone Bear, he said, "My man will bring it."

In a matter of minutes, the transaction was concluded.

Stone Bear motioned for one of his warriors to take the salt then he nodded solemnly to Coburn and said, "Leave our land in peace."

"We travel in peace," Coburn assured him.

The Blackfeet disappeared back into the trees where they had come from.

Coburn finally heaved that sigh of relief and joined the others at the wagon.

Graf Peter von Eichhorn, a tall, slender man with a thin mustache and dark hair, stood holding a pistol. "I thought those savages were going to attack us," he said to Coburn in accented English.

"I reckon they gave the idea some thought," said Coburn. "If they had outnumbered us, they sure might have."

Baron Walter von Stauffenberg, a stocky man with curly, light brown hair asked, "How do we know that was all of them? Could they not return to their village for reinforcements and then attack anyway?"

"They might, Baron," Coburn admitted, "but it ain't likely. Their chief, Stone Bear, said that we can pass through their hunting grounds as long as we don't cause any trouble. There's a good chance he won't go back on his word." He paused, then added, "One of the things Injuns don't like about whites is that we can't be trusted to stick by what we say."

Von Eichhorn sniffed. "As if I care about the opinions of a savage. At any rate, they were never any real threat to us."

"How do you figure that, Earl?" Coburn asked, using the English version of von Eichhorn's title.

"I saw not a single rifle or pistol among them. They were armed only with bows and arrows, knives, and . . . What is it you call them? Tomahawks?" Von Eichhorn sniffed. "Very primitive creatures, if you ask me."

"It's true they didn't have any guns, or weren't showin' any, but there's one thing you need to remember about them Blackfeet."

"And what, pray tell, is that?"

"If one of 'em wants to kill you, he'll sure as sin find a way to do it."

* * *

As the group got underway again a short time later, Lieutenant Clarence Barton moved his horse alongside Coburn's as the frontiersman rode in front of the party.

"You should have consulted with me before negotiating with that redskinned heathen, Coburn," the young officer said. "In fact, I should have been included in any such negotiations."

"I'm sorry about that, Lieutenant," drawled Coburn, even though in reality, he wasn't the least bit sorry. "The whole thing came up sort of suddenlike. I looked around for you but didn't spot you until after the Blackfeet were already approachin'. I figured it best to go ahead and talk to 'em, as long as they wanted to parley and not go to fightin'."

Barton might make a good officer one of these days, but he suffered from the same afflictions that plagued a lot of young lieutenants: a stiff neck and a prideful nature. Experience would take that ramrod out of his backside—if he lived long enough.

Coburn considered keeping Barton and the other dragoons alive to be part of his job. He and his men knew the ways of the frontier. If Barton would just ease off on his arrogance enough to listen to reason—

"The next time we encounter hostiles, you are to notify me before you take any action, Coburn. Is that clear?"

"Yes, sir, Lieutenant, it sure is."

Coburn was glad Barton hadn't talked to Stone Bear. Given the officer's attitude, likely it would have made things worse. Maybe a heap worse. It didn't take much to rub a Blackfoot warrior the wrong way and get him all proddy.

The wagons and riders pushed on until late afternoon without running into any more Indians. Coburn dropped back alongside Graf von Eichhorn's wagon and informed the earl that they would be making camp as soon as they came to a suitable site. Von Eichhorn nodded curtly without saying anything.

He wasn't the friendliest fella in the world. Stiff-necked, like Lieutenant Barton . . . which was maybe why Countess von Arnim, who was betrothed to him, had such a flirtatious nature, Coburn reflected. He had heard that a lot of the marriages among European nobles were arranged with political considerations in mind, not because of any attraction between the folks involved.

On a whim, Coburn slowed his horse until the next wagon in line caught up with him. Each of the vehicles had a driver assigned to it, but Baron Walter von Stauffenberg handled the reins on this one himself. He might come from noble stock, he had explained to Coburn early on. Some of his ancestors had been farmers and worked the land, so driving a wagon came naturally to him, he claimed.

Coburn had to admit that von Stauffenberg did a decent job of it. And he didn't put on a bunch of airs, like von Eichhorn.

Coburn liked the fellow. "We'll be makin' camp before too much longer, Baron." Von Stauffenberg was by himself on the seat, which came as a bit of a disappointment to Coburn.

Then the canvas flap behind the baron flicked open, and a lovely blond woman stuck her head through the opening and smiled at him. "Did you say we're stopping, *Herr* Coburn?" asked Countess Katarina von Falkenhayn.

She was the person he had hoped to see. Not only was *she* beautiful, she had treated him decently ever since they'd met, too, which was something that couldn't be said for all the Prussians. Countess Katarina always had a smile and a friendly word for him.

Coburn pinched the brim of his hat, nodded to her, and said, "Yes, ma'am, that's right. We'll make camp soon as we come across a good spot."

"I'm very glad to hear it. It will feel good to climb down from this wagon and walk around."

"Aye, it will," von Stauffenberg agreed.

He and Countess Katarina were close, but after watching them for weeks, Coburn had come to the conclusion that they were just good friends, without any romantic feelings between them. That was encouraging, even though he was level-headed enough to know the countess would never have anything romantic to do with a scruffy frontiersman like him. Still, sometimes it was nice to think that a thing was *possible*, whether it really was or not.

And he purely did admire Countess Katarina.

"Coburn!"

The shrill sound of Lieutenant Clarence Barton's voice made Coburn wince. He turned his head and saw the officer waving him forward.

"Reckon I'd better go see what the lieutenant wants," he said to Katarina and von Stauffenberg. With another respectful nod, he added, "Countess. Baron." Then he wheeled his horse and rode ahead.

He had no idea that behind him, Countess Katarina von Falkenhayn was watching him with a warm, speculative look in her expressive brown eyes.

Chapter 7

Less than half an hour later, the expedition came to a stream that ran along the edge of a meadow bordered by trees on the far side. A couple of hundred yards to the left, a rugged, rocky cliff jutted up. The creek flowed over its edge and plummeted seventy or eighty feet in a beautiful, silvery waterfall, throwing up a haze of spray and creating a small pool at its base before it began its meandering way across the countryside.

"That's beautiful," Katarina said to Walter as she sat on the driver's seat beside him. She pointed a slender, elegant finger toward the waterfall.

"Very much so," Walter agreed. He turned his head. "Gerda, Helmuth, come look at this."

The two people who had been riding in the back of the wagon, sitting on camp stools and playing a game of whist with a short, thick keg serving as a table between them, joined the two aristocrats at the front of the vehicle.

The man, slender, brown-haired, and fine-featured, pushed the canvas flap aside and leaned forward to peer out. The heavyset, auburn-haired woman shoved her way up beside him, drawing an annoyed look from him.

"What are we looking at, *mein herr*?" asked Helmuth Kurtz. He was the Baron von Stauffenberg's personal man-servant, just as Gerda Reinhardt was Katarina's maid.

"The waterfall," Walter said. "Isn't it pretty?"

Helmuth sniffed. "If you like that sort of thing, I sup-pose."

"Are we going to stop soon?" asked Gerda. "The way this wagon rocks and bounces, my insides will never stop moving around!"

Katarina laughed. It was difficult to get anything other than complaints out of those two, but they were excellent servants and devoted to their charges.

"It appears that Herr Coburn is signaling for Peter to stop," she said. "So I imagine this is where we will camp for the night."

"I can't imagine that we'll find a better place," added Walter. "A good source of fresh water, plenty of grass for the stock, and firewood to be found in those trees."

The creek was shallow and its bed rocky enough that the wagons had no trouble crossing it. The water didn't even come up to the wheel hubs.

Von Stauffenberg hauled back on the reins as the wagon in front of him slowed. The procession—four wagons, plus two dozen riders and several pack horses brought along by the American military escort—came to a halt near a brush thicket on the creek's western bank.

Coburn rode up to Walter's wagon and paused long enough to say, "We'll be makin' camp, folks. I think you'll be comfortable here."

"I think so, too, Herr Coburn," Katarina said. "Such lovely surroundings. You have done a fine job leading us here."

Coburn looked a little embarrassed by the compliment. "Thank you kindly, ma'am. I mean, Your Countessship."

"Katarina would be fine, Herr Coburn."

"Not if Peter heard it," von Stauffenberg warned with a frown on his face.

"And I reckon Lieutenant Barton would feel the same way," Coburn said. "He sets a lot of store by things bein' all properlike. No offense, ma'am."

"Of course not," Katarina assured the frontiersman. "Will you come by later? Perhaps have supper with us?"

"Maybe. I'm obliged for the invite." Coburn moved on.

Walter gave Katarina a stern look and said, "You should not toy with the poor man's affections that way. You know that he likes you."

"I'm not toying with anyone's affections," she protested. "I admire Herr Coburn and find his company interesting and pleasant."

"We both know that absolutely nothing will come of it. It cannot. Such a thing is . . . inconceivable in our circumstances."

Katarina sighed and nodded. "I know, Walter. There are no affairs of the heart for the likes of us. Only affairs of political expediency."

He patted her on the shoulder and said, "But such a life has its advantages. We are still allowed to make friends, as you and I are."

She took his hand, squeezed it, smiled, and nodded. "Indeed we are. I would hate to think of being out here in this wilderness without you at my side, Walter."

Von Stauffenberg laughed and shook his head. "What can I do in case of trouble? I'm no fighter, Katarina, you know that. We can all be thankful that Herr Coburn and his friends and the American soldiers are here to keep us safe."

So far that had been true. The expedition had encountered no trouble on the journey across the American frontier.

But suddenly, as Katarina looked at the dark, thick forest about fifty yards away on the far side of the meadow an unaccountable chill went through her.

Anything could be hidden over there in those trees, watching us right now, she thought. Any sort of wild animal . . .

Or worse.

Graf Peter von Eichhorn had brought his personal chef along on the expedition, but there were limits to what even a skilled individual could do under such primitive conditions. His name was Herbert Wessells, and he spent more time complaining than cooking.

Reese Coburn thought they actually had been eating pretty well, though. Game had been plentiful, so there was always plenty of fresh meat. They had brought along a more than adequate supply of flour and salt and beans. Wild onions grew most places they had been. What else did anybody need?

As he walked past Baron von Stauffenberg's wagon that evening, however, he smelled something new and enticing in the air. The tantalizing aroma drew him over—not that it would have taken much, since he'd already spotted Countess Katarina sitting by the fire, looking as lovely as ever in its warm glow.

"I thought you were going to join us for supper, Herr Coburn," she said with a mock pout on her pretty lips as he walked up.

"I'm sorry, Countess," he said. "I got busy tendin' to some chores, and I plumb forgot."

She shook her head. "How discouraging that an invitation from me would totally slip a gentleman's mind."

"I'm sorry," he said again, hastily. "I know I should have remembered—"

Her laugh forestalled his apology. "That is all right, Herr Coburn. I was only . . . what is it you frontiersmen say to each other? I was only joshing with you."

Von Stauffenberg, who also sat by the fire, nodded solemnly. "Katarina is a great josher."

Coburn scratched at his jaw and said, "Yeah, I, ah, reckon that's so."

"Luckily for you, mein herr," Countess Katarina went on. "Although it is too late for supper, it is *not* too late for *räderkuchen*. You will join us?"

"I, uh, reckon I would . . . if I knew what you were talkin' about."

Another laugh from Katarina, then she repeated, "*Räderkuchen*. It is a pastry from my homeland, a treat to be enjoyed after a meal. Some call them angel wings. Gerda prepares them, and they are delicious."

"Yes, ma'am, I'm sure they are, and I'd be happy to try one."

"Gerda, give Herr Coburn one of your räderkuchen."

Gerda took a pastry from a pan that was sitting on top of a Dutch oven to stay warm and walked it over to Coburn.

He took it and said, "I'm obliged, ma'am."

The pastry was light and fluffy, twisted on itself so that it actually did look a little like a pair of wings, and sprinkled with sugar, a precious commodity out in those parts so far from civilization. The thing felt so delicate that he worried it would crumble in his big, rough fingers, but he managed to get it to his mouth without any mishaps and took a bite. It tasted so good that he immediately put the rest of it in his mouth.

"That's mighty good, ma'am," he said when he had finished the delicacy. "You were right."

"Have another," Katarina invited.

"I hate to take 'em away from you."

Von Stauffenberg laughed and patted his slightly rounded belly. "Please do, Herr Coburn. Otherwise I will sit here and stuff myself with them. I cannot resist such sweet delicacies."

"Well, in that case . . ." Coburn took two more of the pastries. "Thank you, Gerda. You should be proud of yourself."

"*Danke,* Herr Coburn." The normally dour Gerda looked pleased by the compliment.

Helmuth stood up from the log where he'd been sitting and asked, "Do you require my services at the moment, Baron?"

"No, I don't believe so, Helmuth," von Stauffenberg replied.

"In that case, I shall attend to some, ah, personal matters, but I will return before you're ready to retire for the evening."

"That's fine," von Stauffenberg said, smiling. "Do whatever you need to do."

Coburn tried not to grin as the servant stalked off around the wagon and disappeared into the gathering darkness. Like Lieutenant Barton, Helmuth was a mite on the stuffy side, but other than that he seemed like a decent enough fellow. He was devoted to the baron, that was certain.

Von Stauffenberg looked at Coburn and went on. "How

long will we be crossing the territory claimed by the Blackfeet? The . . . hunting grounds . . . as their chieftain called them?"

"Probably another two or three days. It all depends on how fast we move. We can't push these teams too hard, as heavily loaded as the wagons are."

Indeed, although he wasn't going to say too much about it, it seemed to Coburn that the foreign visitors had brought half the things they must have had in those castles of theirs, back in Prussia. Von Eichhorn's wagon had an actual bed in it, although the bedposts has been removed because they were too tall for the canvas cover.

Coburn had seen immigrant wagons on the Oregon Trail piled high with goods, too. Many of the items were abandoned on the journey west, though. They were just too heavy to haul all the way to Oregon.

The situation with von Eichhorn's party wasn't quite that bad, but clearly, these nobles didn't believe in traveling light.

Von Stauffenberg looked into the dancing flames of the campfire and asked, "Do you believe the savages will honor the truce they made with you this afternoon?"

"I sure hope so," Coburn replied. "If there had been a good way to go around their territory, I would have, but they roam too far and wide for that. We would have wound up going almost as far south as Mexico!"

He was exaggerating for effect, but not much.

Von Stauffenberg had a more serious look than usual on his face as he glanced over at the countess and said, "Perhaps we should have stayed in Prussia, Katarina. There was no need for any of us to make this journey. It was only at Peter's whim—"

"Be careful, Walter," Katarina broke in, pitching her

voice lower so that it wouldn't be heard around the camp. "You know that Peter wanted to prove himself worthy of the destiny that may await him someday, and of course, those of us in his circle of friends and family had to accompany him."

Coburn frowned slightly. "Wait a minute. This is none o' my business, but from what you're sayin' . . . is the earl . . . the graf . . . gonna be the king of your country someday?"

"He is in line in the succession," von Stauffenberg answered stiffly. "There is a clear path for him to someday ascend to the throne and lead our country. Whether that ever comes about is in the hands of fate, of course, but Peter felt it best that he be prepared to assume that responsibility. He has never tested his mettle in battle, but he thought that if he were to venture into a hostile wilderness, it would demonstrate his courage."

"I reckon I understand," said Coburn, nodding slowly. "It wasn't really wantin' to know about America that brought you folks here. It was political ambition."

"I *did* want to see America," said Katarina. "I still do. It is a magnificent country, Herr Coburn. The sheer vastness of it amazes me! One could travel for weeks, even months, and never see the entirety of it."

"More like years," Coburn told her. "I've been roamin' around the frontier for a long time, and there's plenty of places I've never been." He might have said more, but at that moment, a frightened yell suddenly sounded from the direction of the trees.

That was the way Helmuth had gone, Coburn recalled, probably intending to answer the call of nature.

The frontiersman sprang to the back of the wagon, his rifle held ready in his hands. "Get inside the wagon," he snapped at Katarina, von Stauffenberg, and Gerda. "You'll be safer there in case of trouble."

The vehicle's thick side boards would stop arrows and most rifle balls, he knew. But maybe it wouldn't come to that. There was no telling what might have spooked Helmuth.

Coburn breathed a little sigh of relief when, from the corner of his eye, he saw Baron Walter von Stauffenberg helping Countess Katarina climb into the wagon. The baron, always a gentleman, even where servants were concerned, assisted Gerda, too, before scrambling up and into the vehicle himself. Coburn heard von Stauffenberg telling the women to lie down on the wagon bed, below the level of the side boards.

The servant's panic-stricken yells had roused the whole camp. Coburn's men and the dragoons scrambled to their feet and readied their weapons. When Coburn glanced over his shoulder, he was glad to see in the firelight that they were spreading out so they could defend the whole camp from attack.

Lieutenant Barton was a little out of breath, either from hurrying or from fear, as he came up to Coburn. "What is it? What's going on?"

"The baron's servant went off into the trees yonder," Coburn said. "Something's got him spooked."

"You let him go by himself?" Barton demanded.

Coburn regretted that, all right. But he hadn't thought that Helmuth would stray very far from the wagons. Coburn had figured the manservant would stop in the brush only a few yards away, instead of venturing all the way into the forest.

The moon hadn't risen, but enough starlight splashed down on the meadow for Coburn's keen eye to spot Helmuth as the man dashed out of the trees and ran toward the camp.

His arms were pumping so hard and his knees came up so high that he almost looked comical as he ran. His strident shouts didn't sound the least bit funny, though, as he cried, "Help! Help! Something's after me! I . . . I think it's a bear!"

Barton looked over at Coburn and asked, "Could it really be a bear?"

"Sure it could," the frontiersman replied. "There's plenty of the critters in these mountains. We'd better hope for Helmuth's sake that it's not a grizzly." He lifted his rifle to his shoulder and used his thumb to cock the flintlock's hammer.

If a dark shape came lumbering out of the woods after Helmuth, Coburn was ready to shoot it. Bears could move surprisingly fast, no matter how big and ungainly they appeared to be.

But then orange flame spurted from the shadows under the trees, and a heavy boom bounced back from the wooded slopes around them. Helmuth cried out and pitched forward.

And Coburn knew things were a lot worse than they had appeared a moment earlier.

The bear had never been born that could use a rifle— and that was what had just blasted poor Helmuth right off his feet.

Chapter 8

More muzzle flashes winked from the trees, looking like bright orange fireflies.

They didn't sound like fireflies, though. The ragged wave of gun-thunder that followed the muzzle flashes rolled through the valley.

"Return fire!" Lieutenant Barton cried. His voice had a shrill, hysterical edge to it as he issued the command. "Return fire!"

Reese Coburn was already doing just that. He lined his sights on the spot where he had just seen a tongue of flame lick out from a rifle barrel and squeezed the trigger. The rifle boomed and kicked against his shoulder.

In the darkness, he couldn't see whether he'd hit anything. The ambushers had all the advantage, hidden as they were in the shadows while cooking fires still lit up the camp.

"Somebody put those fires out!" Coburn shouted over his shoulder as he began reloading. "Get 'em out now!"

The baron thrust the canvas flap aside and rolled over the top of the driver's seat. He tumbled all the way to the floorboards but recovered quickly and dropped to the ground, where he snatched up an empty bucket and ran toward the creek.

He had told Countess Katarina that he wasn't a fighter and intimated that he lacked courage—but nobody could tell that as he raced through the camp while bullets hummed through the air or thudded into the vehicles.

Coburn would have liked to watch von Stauffenberg and make sure the game little fella was all right, but he couldn't take that much attention off the fight. He aimed at the muzzle flashes and triggered another round. Water splashed and sizzled behind him. Shadows wrapped around him as the campfire was extinguished.

As he reloaded, Coburn said, "That you back there, Baron?"

"*Ja,* Herr Coburn," von Stauffenberg answered.

"Good job. Now get back in the wagon."

"I will help put out the other fires—"

Coburn was lifting the rifle to his shoulder again when he heard the soggy, unmistakable thud of a lead ball hitting flesh. He lowered the gun and turned around quickly to see that von Stauffenberg had dropped the bucket and was sinking to his knees as he clutched at his left arm.

"I am hit," the baron said in a voice thin with pain.

"Damn it," Coburn muttered. "Gerda, give me a hand with the baron!"

Instead of Gerda, it was Countess Katarina who pushed through the canvas and leaped from the wagon to the ground. She caught herself on a hand and knee and cried, "Walter!"

"Blast it, ma'am, get back in the wagon!"

"Walter is my friend! I must help him."

It wouldn't help von Stauffenberg for her to get her head blown off, thought Coburn, but standing around arguing about it wasn't a good idea, either. He thrust the rifle into Katarina's hands and said, "I'll get him!", then lunged toward the baron.

Coburn bent over, stuck his hands under von Stauffenberg's arms, and hauled the man around, then started dragging him toward the wagon.

He hadn't reached it when Gerda screamed inside the vehicle. Coburn jerked his head around and saw a man in buckskins standing at the back of the wagon, aiming a pistol through the opening. He was about to shoot Gerda.

Before the stranger could pull the trigger, a rifle boomed somewhere close to Coburn's right. The would-be murderer grunted and took a couple of steps back as his arm sagged and the pistol pointed at the ground. He clapped his other hand to his chest. Dark worms of blood crawled between his fingers as the life-giving fluid leaked from the hole where he'd been shot.

He dropped the pistol and collapsed into a limp heap on the ground.

Coburn looked over and saw Countess Katarina still holding the rifle he had given her. Smoke curled from its barrel. She had just shot the man. Maybe luck, maybe unexpected skill, but either way she had dropped the varmint just in time to save Gerda's life.

Coburn pulled Walter von Stauffenberg under the wagon where the wheels would offer a little protection. Conscious but moaning in pain, blood from the wound soaked the sleeve of von Stauffenberg's coat. The bullet might have broken his arm; Coburn didn't have time to check on that.

Katarina crawled under the vehicle and handed the rifle back to Coburn. "I'll take care of him," she said. "You can use this better than I can."

"I don't know about that," he said. "That was some pretty good shootin' you just did."

The air was full of a near-continuous roar of gunfire. From the way it surrounded the camp, Coburn realized that they were under attack from all sides. Stone Bear must have rounded up more warriors, because he hadn't had that many with him during the parley that afternoon.

There was no time to ponder this unexpected treachery by the Blackfeet. As he had told Countess von Arnim, it was almost impossible to predict what an Indian would do.

Stone Bear had been clever, too, not showing any guns during the initial encounter. The constant roar of shots testified that he had plenty of them with which to arm his braves.

Coburn finished reloading the rifle and knelt beside one of the wagon wheels. He looked around for another target. Shrill whoops punctuated the gunfire. Most of the campfires had been put out, as he had ordered, but a couple of small ones still burned, casting shifting shadows. Men darted here and there. Coburn wasn't sure who to shoot at. He didn't want to kill one of the Prussians or a soldier from Lieutenant Barton's detail.

Coburn spotted Barton himself stumbling toward him. The lieutenant had a pistol in his hand but didn't appear to be interested in using it. Blood ran down the side of his face from a cut or a bullet graze on his head.

"Lieutenant!" Coburn shouted. "Over here!"

They could make a stand at the baron's wagon, he thought.

Barton didn't seem to hear him, though. Coburn called to him again. Barton turned his terrified face toward the frontiersman.

At that moment, one of the buckskin-clad shapes

loomed up behind the lieutenant. Coburn yelled a warning, but Barton didn't react in time. The man behind him crashed a rifle butt against his head and drove him to the ground.

Coburn snapped his rifle to his shoulder and fired. The man who had just struck down Barton jerked his head backward as Coburn's shot drilled him. He toppled to the side.

Coburn ran to Barton, who was moaning and moving around a little. At least he was alive. Coburn wouldn't have been surprised if the vicious blow had crushed the young officer's skull.

He reached down with his free hand, clamped it around Barton's arm, and heaved him up. "Come on, Lieutenant! We'll fort up in Baron von Stauffenberg's wagon!"

That was just going to delay the inevitable, Coburn thought grimly. Killers in buckskin were swarming through the camp, cutting down the dragoons and Coburn's men. Even if the survivors rallied around von Stauffenberg's wagon, the raiders would overrun them no matter how much resistance they put up.

Even though he knew that, Coburn wasn't the sort of man to go down without a fight. He shoved the half-conscious Barton toward the wagon, but somehow he managed to stay on his feet and keep his legs moving.

From the corner of his eye, Coburn caught sight of one of the killers aiming a rifle at him. Coburn's own rifle was empty; he hadn't had a chance to reload since shooting the man who'd tried to stove in Barton's skull. All he could do was try to dodge the shot—

Then, steel flashed in the shifting light and a tall, lean form appeared next to the rifleman. Graf Peter von Eichhorn thrust a sword into the man's side, sliding the blade between his ribs and into the heart. The killer's back arched, and even though he jerked the rifle's trigger, the barrel was pointed up and the ball whined off harmlessly into the night. Von Eichhorn ripped the sword free and slashed the dying man across the face with it, driving him to the ground.

"Von Eichhorn!" shouted Coburn. "Over here!"

The nobleman whirled around and swung the sword again, slashing the throat of an invader who had come up behind him. Then von Eichhorn bounded across the camp to join Coburn. He grabbed Barton's other arm, and the two of them dragged the lieutenant, practically carrying him between them.

Coburn's shouts must have carried to some of the other defenders. As he and von Eichhorn hauled Barton toward the wagon, he saw several of the dragoons and three of his men gathered there, firing at the attackers. Countess von Arnim was under the wagon with Katarina and von Stauffenberg, and Gerda had joined them, too. A couple of the other aristocrats were crowded under there, along with their servants.

But the situation was hopeless. Coburn wondered if it would do any good to surrender, then immediately discarded the idea. Giving up just meant dying without a fight. The Blackfeet would either kill the men out of hand or take them back to their village and torture them to death. The women would become slaves and would be doomed to short, miserable lives, even though they'd probably survive for the moment.

No, it was better to fight—

"Look out!" von Eichhorn called.

Two groups of attackers charged them, one from each side. They dropped Barton and turned to fight back to back. Coburn used his empty rifle as a club, slashing and flailing as the figures clustered around him. He heard von Eichhorn grunting as the nobleman hacked and thrust with his sword. Coburn didn't like von Eichhorn, but the man had sand, no doubt about that.

Something smashed against Coburn's head, and his knees buckled. He caught himself by leaning on the rifle. The weapon's stock was shattered from using it to brain several of the attackers. Bracing himself, Coburn dropped the rifle and yanked his knife from its sheath. He swung it back and forth, relishing the hot splash of blood on his face as he opened a man's throat.

He felt a fiery pain in his side. One of the attackers had gotten him with a blade. He swayed but stayed upright. Another devastating impact on his head sent him to his knees. A kick crashed into his jaw, driving him over backward.

As he fell, his head turned toward the wagon. He caught a glimpse of the buckskin-clad killers pulling the women from under the vehicle. He saw Countess Katarina struggling in the grip of a captor. She had gotten hold of a knife somewhere and struck wildly with it. Blood flew in the air.

A man backhanded her brutally, knocking her off her feet. Coburn tried to get up, but more kicks slammed into him.

Why didn't they just go ahead and kill him?

As he plummeted down into darkness, just before oblivion claimed him, the most horrifying thought of all screamed through Reese Coburn's brain.

They were trying to take me alive.

Chapter 9

The numbness that enveloped Countess Katarina von Falkenhayn, body and soul, was a welcome relief.

She no longer felt the aches from the beatings she had endured, although the bruises stood out plainly on her face and body.

A dull resignation filled her heart and brain, instead of the sickening terror that had held her in its grip for so long.

What could her captors do to her that was worse than what they'd already done? Kill her?

Katarina would have laughed and welcomed death from anyone who wanted to put her out of her misery.

At the same time, a stubborn spark of defiance still burned deep within her, like a single ember glowing in a pile of ashes. In all likelihood, that spark would wink out soon, but for now she kept it alive.

It was late in the day after the attack on the party of nobles and their escort. While she was fighting them, someone had struck Katarina in the head and knocked her unconscious.

When she had come to, she was draped over the burly shoulder of a man wearing a buckskin shirt.

She must have done something to give away the fact that she was awake, because the man stopped, dumped her on the ground, and kicked her in the side.

"Get up," he told her, speaking English but in guttural tones. "If you can walk, there is no need for me to carry you."

Katarina rolled onto her side, wrapping her arms around the pain where he had kicked her.

"Get up," the man ordered again. "Unless you wish more punishment."

Katarina didn't want that. Panting with the effort, she got her hands on the ground and pushed herself into a sitting position, then climbed to her knees. She stood up, staggering a few steps before she caught her balance and steadied herself.

The man grabbed her arm, put his face close to hers. In the almost pitch blackness, she couldn't make out his face, but the stench of his breath made her gag as he said, "If you try to run, I will break your leg. Try a second time, I'll break your other leg and leave you for the wild animals."

This was . . . not right, a tiny voice whispered in the back of Katarina's brain. Something didn't make sense, but in her stunned state, she couldn't figure out what it was.

The man gave her a shove and sent her stumbling ahead.

The night was dark. Katarina tripped constantly but managed not to fall, knowing she would get another kick if she went down.

After a while, the sky began to lighten with the approach of dawn. Enough so that she could see where she was going, anyway. She looked around and realized that she wasn't the only prisoner. Gerda was in front of her, also being shoved along by one of the hulking, faceless brutes, and trailing behind her, also prisoners, were Marion von Arnim and her maid Lotte and Countess Joscelyn von Tellman and her maid Ingeborg. All of them looked disheveled, brutalized, and terrified.

Katarina understood that, since she felt the same way.

She saw male captives, as well, but the men weren't walking. The raiders had felled saplings and trimmed the branches off them, then tied the men's wrists and ankles to the trunks, so they hung below the saplings like sides of beef as their captors carried them, a man in front and a man at the back of each tree trunk.

Katarina felt a surge of relief when she recognized Walter von Stauffenberg and Reese Coburn. Walter had been her friend since childhood, and she felt a great deal of confidence in Herr Coburn, even though he was unconscious and helpless at the moment. If there was a way to get them out of this horrible predicament, Coburn would come up with it.

Walter appeared to be unconscious, too, although in his stupor, he moaned from time to time. The wound in his arm had bled a great deal and soaked his sleeve. He needed medical attention, or surely he would die.

Peter von Eichhorn had been taken prisoner, also, along with Lieutenant Barton and a couple of his dragoons, making the number of prisoners an even dozen.

Were they the only survivors? Katarina had a feeling they must be. Everyone else had been slaughtered back at the camp.

Before the sun rose, the raiders stopped. The man who had been dragging Katarina along raised his voice and said, "The light is getting too strong. Bind the prisoners' hands behind their backs and blindfold them."

Katarina groaned. If she was blindfolded, she wouldn't

be able to see where she was going and she would be in danger of tripping and falling again. With her hands tied, she wouldn't even be able to catch herself.

"Don't do that," she said to her captor, who seemed to be the leader of these ruthless men. "Please."

He growled, and an instant later, his open hand cracked across her face. She cried out and would have fallen if not for his cruel grip on her arm.

Her plea did no good, either. A strip of cloth was put over her eyes and knotted painfully tight behind her head. She couldn't see a thing. Her arms were jerked behind her back and her wrists lashed together. The only thing speaking up had gotten her was that vicious blow.

It felt good to stop moving, though, while the other men carried out the leader's order. All too soon, they were tramping onward again.

The first part of that journey seemed to take an eternity. Blindfolded as she was, Katarina couldn't tell how much time had passed before they stopped again. She and the other women were allowed to sit down and rest for a few minutes. Someone held a tin cup of water to her lips. She sucked thirstily at it, but it was taken away too soon.

Katarina forced herself to listen. She heard men talking to each other, their voices too low for her to make out the words. Then something crashed through nearby brush. Wild animals?

No. Something worse. More men.

A lot of talk went on. Again, close enough for her to hear but not for her to make out the words. Katarina thought the conversation was in English, which puzzled her. Why would the Blackfeet converse among themselves in the white man's tongue? Why not speak their own language?

Someone grabbed her arm and jerked her to her feet

again. A different man said, "You go with me now." He hauled her along beside him.

She tried not to stumble, but sometimes she did. That earned her a cuff to the head or a punch to the body.

Had the prisoners changed captors? That seemed like what might have happened. She had heard that Indians sometimes traded captives from one tribe to another. According to Herr Coburn, this was all Blackfoot country through here, and the Blackfeet didn't get along much better with the other tribes than they did with white men. *Would such a trade even be possible?*

And what did it matter which band of savages held them in their power, she asked herself as despair threatened to overwhelm her.

No matter who their captors were, she and the others were doomed.

After several more hours of misery, the group came to a halt again. Someone yanked the blindfold off Katarina's face, taking her by surprise enough to startle a gasp out of her.

She found a savage, coppery, hawk-nosed face glaring at her from only a few inches away. Fear clutched Katarina's throat. Her heart slugged heavily in her chest.

At the same time, her keen brain realized that she recognized the man. He was Stone Bear, chief of the Blackfeet who had confronted the party the previous day, then promised them safe passage through the Blackfoot hunting grounds—a promise that obviously hadn't been kept.

He stared at her as if daring her to show some sign of defiance. Even though anger blazed inside her, she dropped her gaze and stood meekly with her head down. She didn't want to be slapped or kicked anymore.

Apparently satisfied, he turned her around and cut the rawhide strips binding her wrists. It was a relief to bring her arms around in front of her again.

"We go," grunted Stone Bear. He put his hand on Katarina's shoulder and shoved her.

She stumbled forward. So did the other female prisoners. The men tied to the saplings had been dropped on the ground while their blindfolds were removed. The Blackfoot warriors picked up the tree trunks again and resumed their march.

None of this made sense to Katarina, but she couldn't summon up the energy, mental or physical, to ponder the situation. She concentrated all her efforts on moving her legs and putting one foot in front of the other.

Late in the day, they had been walking for what seemed like an endless time, with only occasional and very short halts to allow the prisoners to rest. As far as Katarina could tell, Stone Bear and the other Blackfeet were made of iron and never tired.

Every stumble, every fall, every complaint brought a swift and brutal response from their captors. Once, Gerda had fallen to her knees, and the Indian walking beside her began kicking her.

Katarina had acted without thinking and sprang forward, exclaiming, "Stop that!"

Stone Bear hit her in the small of the back with a club he carried, knocking her to the ground and smashing several blows on her shoulders. All Katarina could do was cover her head with her arms and cry out in pain as the club landed.

After a moment, Stone Bear stopped beating her and jerked her to her feet again.

The other Indian had stopped kicking Gerda long enough to watch what his chief was doing, and that gave her time to scramble up. As they moved on, Katarina was glad that her action had spared Gerda at least a little pain— for now, anyway.

The male prisoners had regained consciousness during the day. Peter von Eichhorn had raged at his captors in German and English until they stopped and beat him back into insensibility. Lieutenant Barton cried and begged for mercy, but that just got him kicked. Walter had said nothing, and Katarina couldn't tell from the dazed expression on his face if he even knew where he was or what was going on.

Reese Coburn had been stonily silent, and so were the two dragoons. Katarina didn't know if they were more courageous or simply resigned to their fate.

The sun was about to dip behind a mountain in the west when they came to a Blackfoot village. Dozens of conical lodges made from some sort of animal hides were scattered along the bank of a creek.

Dogs charged out to greet the new arrivals with a chorus of strident barking. Women clad in buckskin dresses, old men, and children swarmed around the returning warriors and their prisoners. Several women came up to Katarina and poked her painfully with stiff fingers until Stone Bear roared at them and ran them off.

The smell of wood smoke and several rancid odors blended together and filled the air. Katarina felt ill as she breathed in the stench, but fought down the reaction. She didn't want to give her captors the satisfaction of seeing her get sick.

All the women were herded to one of the cone-shaped lodges, as an Indian woman pulled aside the hide flap over the entrance. More of them lined up and formed an aisle through which the prisoners had to go. The Blackfoot women clutched sharp sticks and jabbed viciously at the prisoners. Marion, Joscelyn, and the servants sobbed and screamed as they stumbled through the gauntlet.

Katarina kept stubbornly silent except for urging her companions, "Go on, get inside. They'll stop if we go inside."

She wasn't sure how she knew that, but as it turned out, she was right. The torment stopped once they were inside the lodge. All six women dropped to the bare ground in exhaustion as the entrance flap closed and shadows filled the lodge.

Katarina lay in the dimness for a while, listening to the others whimper and sob, but eventually her resolute nature forced her to roll on her side and push herself to hands and knees. Her eyes had adjusted to the gloom well enough for her to see Gerda lying a few feet away. She crawled over to her maid and sat down beside her.

"It will be all right, Gerda," she said as she put her hand on the servant's shoulder. "You'll see. We just have to remain strong—"

Gerda heaved herself up, threw her arms around Katarina, and buried her face against Katarina's shoulder as she cried and shook. Katarina held her and patted her on the back now and then, trying to be reassuring although it didn't seem to be working.

Finally, Gerda choked down her sobs enough to say,

"B-But, Countess, how . . . how can we be strong? Those savages are going to k-kill us!"

"No, they won't," said Katarina. "They would not bring us all this way simply to kill us. They could have slaughtered us back there at the camp where they attacked us."

But *had* it been the Blackfeet who attacked them, Katarina suddenly asked herself. They were the prisoners of Stone Bear and his warriors, no doubt about that, but she remembered how they had been blindfolded early that morning, as if there were something their captors didn't want them to see.

Then, later, that rendezvous had taken place, and even though Katarina hadn't been able to see what was going on, it had seemed to her that the prisoners had changed hands. They had been turned over to Stone Bear and the Blackfeet.

If that was true, who had attacked the camp and carried out the bloody slayings? Who had taken them prisoner and marched them across the wilderness?

And who, she suddenly thought, had breathed the smell of sausage in her face as he was threatening her? That was what had bothered her at the time, she realized. The smell had been all too familiar to her, and now she understood why.

"Gerda," she whispered, "it was not Indians who attacked us. *It was white men!*"

Gerda sniffled, frowned at her in confusion, and said, "But Countess, what does it matter? It is the savages who have us now!"

The servant was right, Katarina realized. What did it matter?

Their fate still lay in the brutal hands of Stone Bear and the Blackfeet.

Chapter 10

Reese Coburn wracked his brain, trying to come up with some way he could attempt an escape.

Not that he actually believed he could get away from the bloody-handed varmints who had taken them prisoner. But maybe, with any luck, he could force them to kill him quick.

It was hard to think when his head still ached so blasted much. He had been knocked out during the battle, and for a while after he'd regained consciousness, he'd had double vision, which made him sick to his stomach.

The problem with his eyes had cleared up finally, and after that, his belly gradually settled down.

His arms, shoulders, legs, and hips ached abominably, though, from supporting his weight as he was carried along, dangling from that sapling. It was a great relief every time the Blackfeet put him down, even though they just let go of the tree trunks and dumped the male prisoners roughly on the ground.

Reaching Stone Bear's village, the six white men were cut loose one at a time, then their ankles were bound again and their wrists were tied together behind their backs. They were picked up once more and carried to a lodge, where they were tossed inside unceremoniously.

Coburn had heard Stone Bear giving orders outside. Two warriors were to remain on guard at the entrance all the time, and a man would be posted at the back of the lodge in case any of the prisoners tried to crawl out like a worm in that direction.

He had to get his hands and feet loose somehow, Coburn told himself. That was the only way he could put up enough of a fight to make them kill him.

In the thickening darkness inside the lodge, Graf Peter von Eichhorn asked, "What are they going to do with us?"

Coburn said, "I reckon you know the answer to that as well as I do."

"Torture, then."

"More than likely."

That curt exchange made Lieutenant Barton start sobbing again. The young fella never was going to get that chance to become a good officer, thought Coburn. How it happened sometimes on the frontier.

"Lieutenant, you'd best get hold of yourself," Coburn told him.

"Yes," von Eichhorn added sharply. "It is unbecoming for a man of your rank to be conducting himself in such a craven manner, Lieutenant." He pronounced Barton's rank in the British fashion, *leftenant*. He had been taught English by Britishers, so his speech carried that accent.

Von Eichhorn's reprimand didn't do any good. Barton continued whimpering in terror.

The nobleman turned his head to look at Coburn and asked, "Will they torture him all the more because he is weak?"

"Well, probably not," the frontiersman admitted. "In fact, they won't consider it such good sport because he's already broken. They'll get tired of him sooner."

"And thus kill him sooner," von Eichhorn said quietly.

"Could be."

"Whereas you and I will be more stubborn, Herr Coburn, and provide them with more . . . sport . . . prompting them to take their time killing us."

"That seems pretty likely."

"So we must choose between our honor . . . and a quicker death." Von Eichhorn sniffed. "I do not know about you, mein herr, but I know which I prefer. I will never give them the satisfaction of screaming and begging for my life, no matter what sort of fiendish things they do."

"Let's just wait and see how it plays out," said Coburn, thinking that von Eichhorn's arrogant confidence might vanish pretty quickly once the Blackfeet started working on him.

Or maybe he was wrong and the Prussian would stand up to their torture. Time would tell.

Coburn turned his attention to Baron Walter von Stauffenberg. The man had seemed to be in a stupor for most of their captivity and hadn't really said anything, only letting out a few groans from time to time.

Coburn scooted over closer to him, as best he could, and said, "Baron, can you hear me? Walter?"

Von Stauffenberg shifted slightly, then moaned. It was difficult to tell in the gloom, but Coburn thought the man's eyelids fluttered a little as he tried to open them. Finally, von Stauffenberg rasped, "Herr . . . Herr Coburn?"

"I'm right here, Baron."

Von Stauffenberg said something in German. Coburn

couldn't make out any of the words. Then, "Wh . . . where are . . . ?"

"We're in Stone Bear's village. The Blackfeet have us. You've lost a lot of blood, Baron, but you need to hang on. I'm tryin' to figure out a way—"

"Do not listen to the man, Walter," von Eichhorn broke in. "There is no reason for any of us to hold out false hope. We are doomed. It is only a matter of time until we die."

That callous declaration made Barton wail even louder.

Coburn turned his head to glare at von Eichhorn and said, "Damn it, mister—"

The hide flap over the lodge's entrance was swept aside. Twilight had settled over the village, but it was still bright enough for Coburn to recognize Stone Bear as the chief strode into the lodge.

Stone Bear regarded the prisoners coldly. "You will be given food and water. Do not try to escape."

"You expect us to believe anything you say," said Coburn, "after you promised us safe passage through Blackfoot hunting grounds and then attacked us?"

"My people did not attack you," Stone Bear responded with a scowl. "I kept my word." He paused, then added, "I made no promises about not bartering for you once you were already prisoners."

Based on everything he had observed that surprising statement actually agreed with a vague theory that had begun to form in Coburn's mind. The existence of a second group of enemies would explain the blindfolds and the mysterious rendezvous that had taken place earlier that day. "Who did you barter with?" he asked.

Stone Bear shook his head and declared, "That does not concern you. You are in the hands of the Blackfeet now.

My hands. The spirits have delivered you to me, and I will deal with you as I see fit."

One of the dragoons surprised Coburn by speaking up for the first time. "Hey! Injun!"

Stone Bear turned toward him. "You speak to me?"

"Damn right I do, you filthy redskin heathen."

Coburn said, "Take it easy—"

The dragoon ignored him, saying, "Come on over here, you dirty savage, and I'll tell you exactly what I think of you. You want to hear, Injun?"

Stone Bear stepped over to him. With a terrified expression on his face and tied the way he was, the other dragoon tried to edge away as best he could.

"What do you have to say to me, white man?" asked Stone Bear.

"Lean over here," the dragoon urged. "I'll tell you."

Instead of bending, Stone Bear hunkered on his heels next to the dragoon.

More words spewed from the man's mouth—obscene, outlandish, and probably physically impossible suggestions. He followed them by jerking his shoulders up off the ground and craning his neck to bring him closer to Stone Bear. He spat as hard as he could, the white gob flying through the air to land on the chief's cheek.

Stone Bear flicked the spittle away, pulled a tomahawk from the loop at his waist, raised his arm, and brought the flint head down in a powerful stroke. The blow landed on the dragoon's forehead with a crunch of bone and split his skull open, killing him instantly.

And more than likely, that was exactly the result the dragoon had sought, thought Coburn. He was dead, and nothing the Blackfeet could do would hurt him anymore.

Judging by the angry look on Stone Bear's face, the chief

had realized the same thing and was upset with himself for giving in to the violent urge that had come over him. He wrenched the tomahawk free from the dead dragoon's brain and stood up. Blood and gray matter dripped from the weapon.

"This man was a fool," he said. "He threw away a chance to live."

"What chance?" von Eichhorn asked. "We all know you plan to torture us to death."

Slowly, Stone Bear shook his head.

"The pledge I made did not keep me from accepting you as prisoners and bringing you here, once you were already taken," he said. "But even so, honor demands that you be given a chance to redeem your lives."

Coburn's heart started to beat faster. "How do you figure that?"

"Tomorrow," Stone Bear said, "each of you will fight one of my warriors. Prevail, and you will live. But if you are defeated, you will either die in battle or, if you yield, will be burned at the stake." A grim smile curved his mouth. "So rest while you can, white men. Tomorrow, you will fight for your lives."

Chapter 11

MacCallister's Valley, 1852

Once the decision was made that Jamie and Preacher would accompany Colonel Finlay Sutton on his quest to find out what had happened to the Prussian expedition five years earlier, they wasted no time in getting ready to set out on the journey. The three men, along with the small detail that had served as Colonel Sutton's escort on his trip to Jamie's ranch, would depart the next day and head for Fort Laramie, where they would rendezvous with the rest of the dragoons as well as the party of Prussians going with them.

Not surprisingly, Falcon asked if he could go along, too.

"You wouldn't let me go with you when you and Preacher headed south to the border country earlier this year," the youth said. "You claimed it would be too dangerous."

"And it was," said Jamie. "Didn't I tell you about all the trouble Preacher and I ran into down there?"

"Sure you did." Falcon's eyes shone with excitement. "I wished I could have been there with you. I could've given you a hand."

Jamie grunted. "Or gotten yourself killed, more likely, and then what would your ma have thought of me for letting that happen? Shoot, boy, I wouldn't have been able to come home for fear of being scalped!"

"Are you saying this trip's going to be just as bad?"

Sitting in an armchair with his long legs stretched out in front of him on the other side of the parlor, Preacher drawled, "We're talkin' about messin' with the Blackfeet. To my way of thinkin', yeah, they're as bad as the Apaches. Probably worse. Did I ever tell you about the time they—"

"Yes," Jamie and Falcon said in unison.

Preacher chuckled. "Well, it's a good story."

"Anyway," Jamie continued, "you're not going, Falcon, and don't even think about trailing us because you figure we won't send you back. I'll deliver you back here myself if I have to. It's been five years since those folks disappeared. A few more weeks aren't likely to make much difference now."

"One of these days I'll have adventures of my own," Falcon muttered. "You just wait and see."

"I will," Jamie said patiently. To be honest, he didn't believe it would be too many more years before Falcon was off having those adventures he talked about. The youngster was eager to leave the nest.

Falcon was older already than Jamie had been when he started learning how to survive on the frontier. Of course, that hadn't been his own choice. The Shawnee war party that had attacked his family's farm had had something to do with Jamie Ian MacCallister growing up in a hurry . . .

The next morning, with bags and baskets of Kate's delicious home cooking to give them a good start on their way, the eight men, sixteen horses, two pack mules, and one dog left MacCallister's Valley and started toward Fort Laramie.

Until a few years earlier, Jamie and Preacher both knew, it had been a trading post called Fort John. Then the army had bought it and transformed it into a military outpost, the farthest one west. Soldiers stationed there protected immigrants on the Oregon Trail and tried to keep the Indian threat under control.

They had been successful in that, to a certain extent, but Preacher doubted if anybody would ever succeed in controlling the Blackfeet. He said as much to Jamie as they rode along with Colonel Sutton on a beautiful late summer day, out in front of the party of dragoons.

The officer said, "Surely you don't mean we'll have to wipe out the entire tribe in order to pacify them."

"Based on all the dealin's I've ever had with the varmints, I wouldn't rule it out," said Preacher. "I ain't sure they're capable of anything other than hatin' and wantin' to kill all of us. Of course," he mused, "to their way of thinkin', they're in the right. They were willin' to be friendly, startin' out. It was a white man who shot one of them and made 'em all enemies."

"But good heavens, that was forty years ago!" Sutton exclaimed. "And from what I've heard of the story, it was just a tragic misunderstanding."

"That's as may be," said Jamie, "but the Blackfeet don't see it that way. We were in the wrong, they were in the right, and that's the way it'll always be."

"And that justifies them committing all sorts of atrocities and murdering hundreds, if not thousands, of innocent men, women, and children in the decades since then?"

Jamie's broad shoulders rose and fell in a shrug. "I'm

not defending them, Colonel, just telling you how they think . . . as much as a white man can grasp it."

"Well . . . I hope we don't have to wipe them all out in order to achieve peace. That would be a terrible thing."

Preacher and Jamie nodded in agreement.

Later that afternoon, when the group had stopped at a creek to let the horses and men rest for a short time, Preacher sauntered over to Jamie, tugged at his earlobe, and rasped his thumbnail along his beard-stubbled jawline.

"I know when there's something on your mind, Preacher," Jamie said to the mountain man. "Spit it out."

Preacher took that literally, turning his head to spit on the ground before he said, "We got us a shadow, back there on the trail behind us."

Jamie nodded and said quietly, "Yeah, I know. I spotted him a ways back, probably about the same time you did."

"You reckon it's that boy of yours, even though you warned him about not doin' that very thing?"

"It's possible," Jamie said. "Falcon's stubborn as he can be."

"Comes by it honest, don't he?" Preacher asked, grinning.

"Yeah, he sure does. His mother's the stubbornest woman I ever met."

"That ain't *exactly* what I meant."

Jamie chuckled. "I'll admit, I've been called mule-headed a few times myself." He grew more serious. "But if that's Falcon back there, I'm going to tan the boy's britches before I take him back home."

"You're really gonna do that?"

"I said I was, didn't I?"

Preacher didn't respond to that. He didn't have to. He

understood Jamie's response. Both of them were men who said what they meant and meant what they said.

"There's another thing to consider, though," Preacher went on. "What if that fella *ain't* Falcon?"

"Then we have somebody on our trail, and I don't like mysteries."

"Neither do I. What say I circle around a mite and then drift back a ways? Whoever the varmint is, I ought to be able to come up on him without him knowin' about it."

Jamie didn't doubt that. Preacher's reputation for stealth was unparalleled, from one end of the frontier to the other.

"If it's Falcon, he'll hang back and keep an eye on us but not close in until he figures we've gone far enough that I *won't* turn back. But if it's not, whoever it is would likely be watching us closely enough to see you veer off. You'll need to get ahead of us by at least half a mile before you start swinging back around."

Preacher nodded. "That's my plan."

"If it's *not* Falcon," Jamie said, "it might be a good idea not to kill him if you don't have to. I wouldn't mind asking him why he's following us."

"I'll take him alive," the mountain man promised, "if he'll let me."

The two frontiersmen walked over to Colonel Sutton and quickly explained the situation to him, so he would know why Preacher was leaving the group.

"I don't understand," Sutton said with a frown. "Why would anyone be following us? There's nothing about our mission to warrant such a thing."

"That's what I figure on findin' out, Colonel," said Preacher. "The rest of you just carry on and leave things to me and Dog."

"I trust you, of course. Good luck, Preacher."

"Probably be after dark before I get back, so don't go to worryin' if I don't show up for a while."

Once the party was mounted again and continuing on their way, Preacher gradually pulled out in front on Horse. Dog bounded ahead. The other riders would shield them from the view of the follower.

When Preacher judged he had gotten far enough ahead of the rest, he angled the stallion toward a stand of trees that grew close to the route he was following. In a matter of moments, Preacher, Horse, and Dog had vanished into the trees.

He followed a course through the heavy growth for at least half a mile, then turned back in the direction he, Jamie, and the others had come from. He didn't go as far, perhaps a quarter of a mile, before turning yet again and closing in on the main trail.

When he reached a clump of boulders a hundred yards west of the trail and big enough to hide Horse and Dog, he reined in and swung down from the saddle. Preacher told them to stay and knew they would.

He took off his hat, hung it on the saddle, took a spyglass from his saddlebags, and climbed a big slab of stone. It angled enough that he was able to stretch out just below the top of it. Cautiously, he stuck his head up where he could see the trail and waited.

He hadn't been there more than five minutes when a rider came in sight, plodding along at a deliberate pace while leading a pack horse behind him. Preacher extended the spyglass and put the lens on the lone rider.

The man's face sprang into focus through the glass. Preacher knew instantly that it was *not* Falcon MacCallister following them. The hombre was considerably older, although with the shaggy black beard covering a lot of his face, it was impossible to say how much older. He had a felt hat with a broad, floppy brim crammed on the back of his head. A thatch of dark hair stuck out from under it. He wore a long coat made from buffalo hide, and underneath it was a buckskin shirt criss-crossed by bandoliers of ammunition for the Sharps rifle he carried. With his rugged, formidable looks, he didn't seem to be the sort of gent anybody would want dogging their trail.

He also struck Preacher as a man who would put up a fight rather than allow himself to be taken prisoner.

They'd just have to see about that.

Preacher slid back down the rock and tucked the spyglass away, then mounted up and set out to follow the follower. He stayed well back and used every trick he knew—which were considerable—to keep the man from spotting him on his back trail.

As far as Preacher could tell, the fella never even checked to see if anybody was behind him. That was confidence—or carelessness.

Jamie and Colonel Sutton knew not to expect him back until after nightfall, so he didn't get in any hurry. He didn't close in on his quarry until the sun had set and shadows had started to gather. Letting his instincts guide him, Preacher reined Horse to a stop, slid down from the saddle, and told the stallion to stay put.

"Come on, Dog," he said quietly to the big cur. The two of them drifted off into the thickening gloom like phantoms.

Preacher dropped to one knee in some brush as he heard something moving around up ahead. A man spoke, but no one answered. More than likely, the hombre was talking to his horse. Men who spent a lot of time on the trail often did that.

Preacher had his hand on the back of Dog's neck. He leaned over and whispered in the big cur's ear, "Hunt."

Dog moved off through the brush, as silent as a shadow.

Preacher waited patiently for Dog to return. That didn't take long. Dog appeared out of the night and nudged his shoulder, then turned to head back the way he'd come from. Preacher followed, equally silent.

A few minutes later, he carefully parted some brush and peered through the opening. The moon hadn't come up yet, but millions of stars had winked into life in the sweeping ebony sky overhead, providing enough light for his keen eyes to see the black-bearded man sitting on a log. A few yards away, the saddle mount and pack horse cropped at the grass.

Preacher could tell by the sounds the man was making that he was chewing on some jerky. Not a very satisfying meal, but better than nothing. Preacher supposed the man didn't want to build a fire for fear of giving his presence away to the group he was following.

The fella probably would have given a lot for a cup of coffee right now, thought Preacher. So would he. Jamie and Sutton and the others would be brewing up a pot in their camp, and it almost seemed like Preacher could smell it.

Preacher pushed that thought aside and shifted in the brush until he was behind the man. Then he slid the right-hand Colt Dragoon out of its holster, looped his thumb over the hammer, and straightened from his crouch as he stepped out of the brush. The sound of him cocking the gun was loud in the night.

"Just sit right where you are, friend, and this here Dragoon don't have to go off," he told the man on the log.

Chapter 12

The man sat up a little straighter, but other than that, he didn't move.

"Take it easy, *friend*," he said, using the same word Preacher had but making it sound even more insincere. "You don't want that gun goin' off by accident."

"If it goes off, it won't be no accident," Preacher assured him. "How about stickin' your hands up?"

"Sure, sure." The man complied with the order. His voice was a little thick and muffled, probably because of the piece of jerky he still had in his mouth.

"Now stand up and turn around."

The man did so. As he faced Preacher, he chewed a couple of times and then swallowed. "You've plumb ruined my supper, you know."

"I don't figure I'll lose any sleep over it. Who in blazes are you, mister, and why are you ridin' this trail?"

Preacher didn't say anything about Jamie, Colonel Sutton, and the other soldiers ahead of them. There was a slim chance this man *hadn't* been following them and was, instead, just a lone pilgrim headed in the same direction.

If that turned out to be the case, there was no need to give him any details about the rest of the party.

"The way you sound, you must consider this trail your own private property," the man returned in surly tones. "That ain't the way it works, mister. I got as much right to be here as anybody el— Son of a buck! Is that a wolf?"

Dog had moved up alongside Preacher and pressed against the mountain man's leg. A low, menacing growl came from the big cur's throat.

"Well, I can't rightly say. Bound to be some wolf blood in him, I reckon. You want to see just how wild and untamed he is?"

"Keep that filthy damn beast away from me," the stranger blustered. He moved back a step, even though Preacher hadn't told him to. Clearly, the sight of Dog had raised a deep, instinctive fear in him.

"You'd best answer my questions, then," Preacher said. "Who are you, and what are you doin' here?"

Just for emphasis, he nudged Dog slightly with his leg, prompting the big, shaggy cur to growl again and lean forward. Dog knew how to play his part well.

Maybe too well, because the man's nerve suddenly snapped. Instead of babbling the answers Preacher wanted, he let out a harsh, incoherent yell and dived over the log at the mountain man in a mixture of rage and panic.

In that split second, Preacher remembered the promise he'd made to Jamie about bringing the prisoner back alive. That caused him to aim high. The Dragoon's thunderous boom should have struck fear into any man, but this one was too far gone to be thinking straight. He went low, tackled Preacher around the thighs, and drove him over backward.

Preacher clubbed at the man's head with the heavy

revolver, but the fella jerked aside so the blow landed on the back of his left shoulder. He dug a knee in Preacher's stomach and got his right hand on the mountain man's face. He didn't mind fighting dirty as his fingers clawed at Preacher's eyes.

Dog snapped and snarled, darted in and then back out without biting because Preacher and his opponent began rolling over on the ground and the big cur couldn't get a good bite of the enemy. Preacher slashed with the Colt again and the barrel thudded against the man's head, but it didn't seem to do much damage. It didn't slow the varmint down, that was for sure. He continued kicking and punching and gouging. In that buffalo coat, it was like trying to fight a big, hairy, stinking whirlwind.

When they stopped rolling, the stranger was on top again, and had clamped his right hand around Preacher's throat while his left grabbed Preacher's wrist to keep him from striking again with the gun. The man was big and powerful and pinned Preacher's gun hand to the ground. He bore down on Preacher's throat with all his strength.

But the odds were against him. Dog's jaws closed on the back of his neck. The man screamed as Dog hauled him backward off Preacher.

Preacher rolled to hands and knees and then surged to his feet. A few yards away, Dog snapped at the man, who was still screaming as he flailed his arms around, trying to protect his face and ward off the big cur.

"Dog!" Preacher snapped. "Guard!"

Dog stopped biting and backed off a couple of steps, but his teeth were still bared and he almost quivered with the desire to tear into the man again. A low, continuous growl came from his throat.

"Settle down!" Preacher told the man. "He ain't gonna hurt you . . . for now."

The man stopped screaming, but he was breathing heavily as he pushed himself up on one hand and held out the other hand toward Preacher. That hand trembled as the man said, "Keep . . . keep that devil away from me!"

"He won't bother you none, unless I tell him to. Which is exactly what I'm fixin' to do if you don't tell me what I want to know."

"Fine! My name's Lomax! Roscoe Lomax."

The name was vaguely familiar to Preacher, although he was certain he and this fella had never crossed paths before. He sorted through his memories for a moment, then frowned and asked, "You a bullwhacker?"

"That's right. I've been out and back on the Santa Fe Trail a heap of times."

Preacher nodded. "I recall hearin' stories about you. They wasn't what you'd call good ones, neither."

"Some folks are just jealous of me," muttered Lomax. "On account of me bein' the best damn bullwhacker on the Santa Fe, and a hell-roarin' he-bear when it comes to fightin' and drinkin' and sparkin' the gals!"

"Spare me the boasts, old son. Tellin' me your name is only half of what I asked you. I'm still waitin' to hear what you're doin' in these parts."

"Ain't I got a right to be where I want to be? Ain't this still a free country?" Lomax's voice rose angrily, but he shrank back a little as his tone prompted a louder growl from Dog. "But I reckon it won't do no harm to tell you. I'm lookin' for a man named MacCallister. Jamie MacCallister. And actually, I ain't really *lookin'* for him, because I know where he is." Lomax inclined his head in the direction where Jamie, Colonel Sutton, and the others would be camped for the night. "He's up yonder a ways, travelin' with some soldiers."

"What do you want with MacCallister?"

"Now, damn it, that's my business. Wolf or no wolf!"

"I'm makin' it my business," Preacher said in a flat voice, "because Jamie MacCallister's a good friend of mine. And it just so happens . . . I'm part of the same bunch he is."

That appeared to surprise Lomax. "Oh. At first I thought you was a highwayman, or somethin' like that."

"Not hardly."

"Then who are you? I reckon that's a fair question, since you asked the same of me."

"They call me Preacher," the mountain man said.

Even in the darkness, he could tell that Lomax's eyes got bigger. "Preacher," the man repeated. Then, with a note of pride in his voice, he went on. "Yeah, I've heard stories about *you*, too. And I was about to whip you. I would have, if that wolf-dog hadn't butted in."

"Son, I was just gettin' warmed up. There's a good chance Dog saved your life by tacklin' you when he did, otherwise I might've forgot Jamie asked me to bring you back alive."

"MacCallister wants me?" Lomax sounded both confused and surprised.

"He wanted to know who was followin' us, and why. And so do I. So tell me your business with Jamie."

Lomax regarded him for a long moment, then said vehemently, "No, sir! No, sir, I won't. What I got to say, I'll be sayin' to Jamie MacCallister his ownself, nobody else. If that ain't good enough, just . . . just go ahead and shoot me! I'd rather die that way than bein' mauled to death by some vicious critter."

Preacher stood there in silence as the seconds ticked by. Finally, he said disgustedly, "Nobody's gonna shoot you, and I ain't gonna sic Dog on you . . . yet. If you're that bound and determined to talk to Jamie, I reckon that's what he'd want. Throw your saddle back on your horse and let's get outta here."

"You're gonna take me to MacCallister?" Lomax sounded like he couldn't believe it.

"That's right. But I'll have a gun on you the whole time, and if you try any dirty tricks, I'll blow a hole clean through you."

"No tricks," Lomax promised. "I just want to say what I've come to say . . . and then we'll see what happens."

Chapter 13

"Hello, the camp!" Preacher called a short time later as he and Roscoe Lomax approached the spot where Jamie and the others had stopped for the night. They had built a small fire, and Preacher actually did smell coffee, as well as bacon, instead of just imagining it. The mingled aroma reminded him of how long it had been since he'd had anything to eat.

Lomax rode in front of him. Preacher hadn't tied the bullwhacker's hands, but he still held the Colt Dragoon with the barrel resting on the saddle's pommel. The revolver was ready for instant use if Lomax tried anything fishy.

So far, the man had cooperated, once Preacher agreed to take him to Jamie. Maybe he actually was telling the truth about having something to say to the big frontiersman.

"That you, Preacher?" Jamie called back in response to the mountain man's hail.

"Yeah, I'm comin' in. And I've got another fella with me, so don't shoot him unless I say so!"

A booming laugh came from Jamie. "I reckon we can do that. Come ahead."

Preacher nudged Horse into motion again. "Go on, Dog," he told the big cur. Happily, Dog raced on into camp.

"I still don't see how you can travel with a critter like that," Lomax groused.

"A lot of folks might say the same to me about ridin' with you," Preacher shot back.

Lomax muttered something Preacher couldn't make out as they rode up to the circle of flickering yellow light cast by the campfire. Jamie, Sutton, and the dragoons were all on their feet, waiting to see who Preacher had brought with him.

When Jamie laid eyes on the visitor, he exclaimed, "Lomax!"

"So you do know this hombre," said Preacher.

"I know him, all right, I just never expected to see him again. Or at least not so soon." Jamie scowled at Lomax. "The last time I saw him, he was out cold on the floor of a cantina in Santa Fe. I was the one who put him there."

"Yeah, but before that, we had a drink together, remember?" Lomax said.

After a second, Jamie shrugged and nodded. "I suppose we did." The grim cast of his rugged face relaxed a little. "As I recall, we spent that time watching everybody else in the cantina whaling the tar out of each other."

"Yeah, it was a pretty good brawl."

"A brawl that *you* started."

"If you hadn't had your big ol' feet stuck out in the way—" Lomax stopped short, drew in a deep breath, then asked, "All right if I get down off this horse?"

"Go ahead," said Jamie. "It goes against the grain to turn visitors away from a fire, even someone like you."

Lomax and Preacher both swung down from their saddles. Colonel Sutton motioned for a couple of his men to take care of the horses. Jamie stalked forward, planted his feet firmly, and hooked his thumbs in his gunbelt as he confronted Lomax. "Now, what was that you were saying about somebody's big old feet?"

Lomax grimaced and said, "I'm sorry about that, Mac-Callister. My temper just got the best of me for a second there. That's a never-endin' struggle for me." He paused, then went on. "I know it was my fault for not watchin' where I was goin' that night, and I wanted to say as much. That's why I followed you up here . . . to tell you I'm sorry for that ruckus we had down in Santa Fe."

Jamie looked like he couldn't believe what he was hearing. He stared at Lomax for several long seconds, then squinted his eyes and cocked his head a little to the side. "You're trying to tell me that you came all this way just to *apologize*?"

"That's right," Lomax stated, and the defiant expression on his face looked like he was daring anybody to cast doubt on his motive. "I knowed you had a big ranch in Colorado, so I headed there first, only before I could ride in and speak my piece, I spotted you leavin' with these here soldier boys." The bullwhacker waved a big hand at the dragoons. "That got me curious. I wondered where you were goin', so I decided to trail along for a while and see." The broad shoulders rose and fell in the buffalo coat. "I didn't have nowheres else I had to be. I work when I feel like it, and just then I felt like indulgin' my curiosity."

The story was just odd enough to be true, thought Preacher. Jamie looked like he couldn't make up his mind whether to believe it or not.

After a moment, Jamie shook his head. "There's got to

be more to the story than that, Lomax. If you want me to believe that you didn't follow us intending to cause trouble, you're going to have to tell me more. What convinced you that you were in the wrong and ought to apologize?"

"Reckon I could have some coffee first, and maybe a little somethin' to eat?" asked Lomax. "I had a cold camp, back there where Preacher jumped me, and jerky and water ain't a very satisfyin' supper."

The group had plenty of supplies, so Preacher wasn't surprised when Jamie's natural Western hospitality came to the surface again. "Yeah, go ahead and sit. Preacher, you need to eat, too."

"Just what I had in mind," the mountain man said.

The rest of the men resumed their supper as Preacher and Lomax joined them around the fire. Once they had cups of coffee and plates of bacon, beans, and biscuits, Jamie said, "All right, Lomax, let's have the story."

Lomax swallowed a mouthful of food, washed it down with a swig of coffee, and then said, "When you walloped me, MacCallister, you came mighty close to killin' me."

Jamie frowned. "You were out cold, but I didn't think I hit you hard enough to do any real damage." He grunted. "Especially considering how hard that head of yours is."

"Yeah, my skull's pretty thick," Lomax agreed with a chuckle. "Problem is, when I fell down, I landed on the back of my head, and the floor of that cantina was even harder. My pards hauled me out of there, and I didn't come to for more 'n a day."

"Is that the truth?" Jamie asked, his frown deepening.

"I got no reason to lie about it. And when I did wake up, I was still outta my head for another three or four days. My friends had jobs waitin' for 'em on a wagon train headin' back up the trail to St. Louis, but they paid a gal name of Mirabel to look after me. You might remember her. She was dancin' in that cantina."

"I remember her," Jamie said with a solemn nod. "She nursed you back to health?"

"That's right. It took a while before I was able to get my brain workin' right again. Durin' that time, I . . . I kept thinkin' I was back in the past, growin' up in Ohio and then headin' west to make my fortune." Lomax's voice had taken on a hollow tone while he was talking, and although he stared into the fire, he seemed to be looking at something a million miles away.

"I don't know if you've ever thought back over all the things you've done in your life," he went on. "It was even worse 'n that for me. I wasn't just rememberin' all those times. It was like I was livin' 'em all over again. And let me tell you, it weren't pleasant. I've done some things—" His voice choked off, and for a long moment he couldn't continue.

Silence hung over the camp, broken only by the faint crackle of flames in the campfire and the quiet noises made by the horses as they shifted around on their picket ropes.

"I always liked to boast about what a hell-roarin' he-wolf I am," Lomax finally went on. "But I've done some mighty cowardly things. I've turned my back on friends and other folks who needed me. I've made promises I knowed good and well I wasn't gonna keep. I hurt folks who didn't deserve it. When you get right down to it, I was a sorry, no-good son of a gun. Ain't no other way to say it. And there I was, experiencin' all that in my head again, only this time I saw it all clear as day, without makin' any excuses for what I done, and . . . and it shook me clear to my bones, MacCallister. It purely did. I ain't sayin' I'm the worst fella to ever come down the pike. I reckon I ain't, but I ain't good, neither, and when I finally come out of it and realized where I was and what'd happened, I figured I had to at least try to make some things right, even though there ain't no way I can ever square up accounts for the rest o' my life. And the place to start was with you. Tellin' you I'm sorry for that fight I started. I'm hopin' you'll forgive me."

Considering the sort of man he was, it was a long speech, possibly the longest Lomax had ever made in his life that didn't include any of the drunken boasting he had talked about. To Preacher's ears, it had sounded heartfelt and sincere, too. Lomax was probably capable of spinning a yarn to trick somebody, but Preacher didn't believe that was the case here.

Jamie had started out looking very skeptical, too, but he seemed to grow more convinced the longer he listened. The silence dragged out for several seconds after Lomax finished, but then Jamie said, "You just want me to forgive you?"

"Yep. That'll be a start, anyway."

"But it was just a blasted cantina brawl!" Jamie exclaimed. "I've been mixed up in dozens of them. If you hadn't started it, there's a good chance something else would have. Feeling guilty about something like that is no reason to go traipsing over hundreds of miles of frontier."

"Maybe not for most folks, but it seemed to me like what I ought to do," Lomax said stubbornly. "If you don't want to accept my apology—"

"Hold on, hold on. I never said I wouldn't accept your apology. I'm still just surprised by it, that's all." Jamie shook his head. "The idea that you'd just up and get religion never crossed my mind, Lomax."

"It ain't so much religion. Nobody appeared to me and told me to start doin' good or anything like that, like in the story about Moses and the bullrushers or whatever they was."

Colonel Sutton ventured, "I believe it was a burning bush in which the Lord appeared to Moses—"

"I said I didn't recollect exactly what the story was, remember?" snapped Lomax, then immediately looked contrite again. "Beggin' your pardon, Colonel. Like I said, I still have a problem with this short temper o' mine. But I'm workin' on it. I give you my word on that."

Jamie said, "Well, for what it's worth, I forgive you for your part in that brawl, Lomax. Now maybe you should forgive me for clouting you like that, if it nearly killed you."

"You ain't to blame for that, MacCallister. It was all my own doin'. I don't hold no grudges against you, not a blamed one."

"That's good to know," Jamie responded dryly.

Lomax looked around at the group and said, "So tell me . . . where are you fellas bound for?"

Jamie glanced at Sutton, who said, "It's not a secret."

"We're headed for Fort Laramie first to meet up with some other folks," Jamie told Lomax. "Then on up into Blackfoot country to look for some people who disappeared there five years ago."

"Disappeared five years ago in Blackfoot country?" repeated Lomax. "Well, hell, MacCallister. They're bound to be a long time dead by now!"

"That's pretty much what we figure, too, but we have to be sure."

"They must've been mighty important folks."

"To some people, I suppose," Jamie said.

After all that talking, Lomax went back to his supper, hungrily polishing off the rest of his food and slurping down the coffee still in his cup. With that done, he sat back on the rock he had chosen for his seat and let out a loud belch.

"Careful," Preacher said. "The Blackfeet'll hear us comin'."

"Won't matter," Lomax said. "You can't go skulkin' around their territory without them knowin' about it. They won't take kindly to it, neither. I never had any dealin's with 'em since most of my time's been spent down in the Southwest, but I've heard plenty of stories. No matter what you do, there's a good chance you boys are headed straight into trouble." He paused. "Which makes me feel kinda foolish over what I'm fixin' to ask you, but I'm gonna do it anyway."

"What's that?" asked Jamie.

Preacher had a feeling he already knew the answer, and the big bullwhacker confirmed that a second later.

"Can I come with you?" Lomax asked.

Chapter 14

After what had happened in Santa Fe, and knowing Roscoe Lomax's reputation, Jamie was reluctant to let the bullwhacker join their group, no matter how genuinely contrite Lomax appeared to be. He believed that most men deserved a second chance, however, so he talked it over with Preacher and Colonel Sutton, the three of them moving over next to the horses to have their discussion out of earshot of the men around the fire.

"What about it, Jamie?" Sutton asked. "Is this man trustworthy?"

"I don't know, Colonel. He has a reputation as a trouble-maker, but maybe he's changed."

"He's a fightin' man, I can tell you that much," said Preacher. "When the two of us tangled, I had my hands full. He claimed he would've beat me if Dog hadn't jumped into the fracas, and I don't believe that for a second. But he's tough, ain't no doubt in my mind about that."

"If we run into trouble up there in Blackfoot country," Sutton mused, "it might not hurt to have another good fighting man on our side."

Jamie nodded slowly. "There's that to consider. We're going into an unknown situation, but one thing we *do* know is that the Blackfeet won't welcome us with open arms. Lomax is right about that."

"It's up to you," the colonel said. "I don't want to do anything that you don't agree with or that makes you uncomfortable. We'll send the man packing, if you want."

Jamie thought about it for a moment longer, then said, "No, I'm willing to take a chance on him."

"You should be the one to tell him, then."

The three of them went back to the campfire. Jamie gave the bullwhacker a hard stare for a few seconds and then said, "All right, Lomax. Consider yourself one of us. You can come along on the mission if you want to . . . as long as you don't cause any problems."

A grin creased the man's face under the bushy beard. "I'm much obliged to you, MacCallister," he said. "I reckon comin' along and helpin' out is the best way for me to prove to you that I meant what I said about bein' sorry."

"Just keep a tight rein on that temper of yours," Jamie advised. "Where we're going, being hotheaded is a good way of getting in trouble."

"Or gettin' dead," Preacher added.

The party reached Fort Laramie three days later. The outpost was located within a large bend of the Laramie River, so that the stream bordered it on the east, west, and south sides. Only a short distance downstream, the Laramie flowed into the larger North Platte River.

That confluence of waterways meant it was a good location for a trading post. That had led the famed fur traders Robert Campbell and William Sublette to establish Fort

William at this spot, a stockade-type fort constructed of thick logs. Over time, the log stockade had been replaced by even thicker, sturdier adobe walls with several castlelike guard towers spaced around the perimeter.

Eventually the place had been renamed Fort John, and when the army took it over a few years later, it had become Fort Laramie with the addition of new buildings for stables, a blacksmith shop, officers' and soldiers' quarters, a bakery, a guardhouse, and a powder magazine to house and support the fort's garrison. It was an impressive post.

As Jamie, Preacher, and the others rode toward it, Lomax frowned and pointed to the conical hide lodges scattered around the outside of the fort. "Those are redskin tepees, ain't they?" he asked. "I hope the Injuns livin' in 'em are friendly."

"It ain't likely they'd be settin' right next to an army fort if they was hostile, is it?" Preacher said.

"No, I reckon not." Lomax's shaggy brows drew down in a frown. "I just don't trust redskins, that's all."

"You don't like dogs, neither, but I don't hold that against you . . . too much."

Jamie explained, "There was a big peace treaty council here last year. A lot of different tribes attended . . . the Lakota Sioux and the Cheyenne, the Shoshone and the Crow, and some of the smaller tribes. They all smoked the pipe and promised to keep the peace, and so far they've done it. Several times a year, they come in to trade with the army and with each other."

"Not the Blackfeet, though," Lomax said.

Jamie shook his head. "No. The Blackfeet haven't smoked the peace pipe."

"And I wouldn't hold my breath waitin' for 'em to do it, neither," Preacher put in.

Grave-faced men with feathers in their hair and blankets draped around their shoulders watched as the party rode past the lodges. The Indian women and children hung back, but they were interested in the newcomers, too. Dogs capered around and barked, although they all kept their distance from the big, wolflike cur that paced alongside Horse.

Lomax scowled at the Indian dogs, his dislike for the animals obvious. None of them came close to him, either, which was a good thing, Jamie reflected. Lomax might have kicked at them and stirred up resentment and trouble.

The watch towers still remained. Jamie knew the soldiers on guard duty should have spotted them approaching. One of the dragoons carried an American flag on a staff and rode right behind Jamie, Preacher, and Colonel Sutton, so the occupants of Fort Laramie would know they were friends.

The old adobe stockade was still there, too, although a number of other buildings were scattered around it and a large parade ground was directly in front of it. Colonel Sutton's party rode around the parade ground and went through the stockade's open gates. Inside were the buildings housing the fort's headquarters, the officers' quarters, and the sutler's store.

Entering the large courtyard inside the walls, they saw not only quite a few American troops but also a dozen or so men dressed in dark blue jackets trimmed with bright red collar and cuffs, white trousers, and tall leather helmets made even taller by the metal spikes that topped them. They were easy to tell apart from the American dragoons with their flat black caps, blue trousers, and no bright red decorations. Jamie recalled what the colonel had said about representatives of the Prussian military accompanying them on their mission, and he supposed those fancy-dressed fellows must be part of that group.

Preacher drawled under his breath, "What in blazes is a circus doin' all the way out here on the frontier?"

"I'd appreciate it if you'd keep comments like that to yourself, Preacher," Sutton said. "I'm not overly fond of being saddled with that bunch, but since we are, we might as well try to get along with them."

Preacher chuckled and said, "You know me, Colonel. I get along just fine with durned near ever'body. I'm a peaceable man."

Jamie grinned when he saw the look on Sutton's face at that bold-faced statement from the mountain man. Then he grew more serious as he asked, "Who's that fella?"

He nodded toward the headquarters building, where a tall, brawny man in one of the fancy red and blue uniforms had just stepped out onto the porch. He towered over the shorter, stockier American officer beside him, presumably the commander of this post.

"I don't know," Sutton said in reply to Jamie's question, "but by his attitude and the fact that he's with Colonel Wheeler, I suspect he's the commander of the Prussian delegation."

Soldiers, American and Prussian alike, drifted toward the headquarters building to get a better look at the newcomers. Jamie, Preacher, and Sutton reined to a stop.

Sutton turned in his saddle to call to the dragoons with him. "You men are dismissed, once you've seen to your horses and the pack animals."

Jamie looked at Lomax and said, "You go with them and give them a hand."

The bullwhacker nodded in agreement.

Jamie, Preacher, and Sutton dismounted and turned

their reins over to an orderly who hurried forward to take them.

Preacher said to the young soldier, "Careful of this stallion, son. He's friendly enough, as long as you don't give him any reason to get annoyed with you."

"How will I know if he's annoyed, sir?"

"Oh, he'll let you know," said Preacher. He turned to the big cur. "Dog, stay with Horse."

The orderly eyed Dog and Horse warily, obviously wondering what he had gotten himself into by volunteering. He led the horses out of the stockade toward the stables. Dog padded along beside them.

With Colonel Sutton leading the way, Jamie and Preacher followed him up the steps and onto the broad porch. Sutton traded salutes with the American officer, then said, "Colonel Wheeler, allow me to present Jamie Ian MacCallister and Preacher. Men, this is Colonel Alonzo Wheeler, the commanding officer of Fort Laramie."

Colonel Wheeler's gray hair and beard and weathered face testified that he was a long-time veteran of command. He stuck out a hand to shake with Jamie and said, "Welcome to Fort Laramie, Mr. MacCallister. Needless to say, I've heard of you. You've rendered invaluable service to the army on numerous occasions in the past."

"I try to help out the country when I can," Jamie said as he clasped Wheeler's hand.

"And, ah, Preacher," Wheeler went on as he turned to the mountain man. "A legend among the Indians and the frontiersmen, and that goes without saying as well."

"You know what legends are, Colonel?" Preacher asked as he shook hands with the officer. "Tall tales that get told well enough some folks start to believe 'em."

Wheeler chuckled. "Are you saying you *haven't* had all the thrilling exploits attributed to you?"

"Well, no . . . but some of 'em might've been the least little bit exaggerated."

Jamie laughed and said, "Don't believe him, Colonel. He's done everything they tell stories about, and more."

The other man on the porch cleared his throat impatiently.

Wheeler said, "Of course, Baron, I beg your pardon. Gentlemen, I'd like you to meet Baron Adalwolf von Kuhner."

The Prussian stepped forward, stood rigidly at attention, and clicked the heels of his high-topped black boots together. He bowed slightly, not much more than a token movement of his head that tipped the spiked helmet toward them. Jamie didn't know if the baron expected them to bow in return to him, but he hoped not, because that wasn't going to happen.

Colonel Sutton took the lead, giving Baron von Kuhner a salute, which the Prussian returned stiffly. Then Sutton extended his hand and said, "It's an honor to meet you, Baron."

For a second, Jamie thought von Kuhner was going to ignore the colonel's hand. Then he grasped it and said, "I look forward to joining you on this expedition, Colonel."

The man's voice was harsh and guttural, almost as if he had a mouthful of gravel. He spoke English fluently enough, but with a fairly thick accent.

Von Kuhner was around forty, Jamie estimated, with a florid, heavy-jawed face. Under the tall helmet he wore was no sign of hair. Evidently he was completely bald. Or, given his age, maybe he shaved his head. Jamie had never seen the appeal of that, but some men seemed to like it, especially Europeans.

Sutton turned and gestured toward Jamie and Preacher. "These two men are coming with us as guides and experts on dealing with the Indians."

Von Kuhner's eyes narrowed. "They are not soldiers?"

"No, they're civilians, but they've worked with the army on many occasions. This is Jamie MacCallister, and the other fellow is known as Preacher."

Von Kuhner stared at Preacher and snapped, "You have no other name?"

"Oh, I reckon I've got a name. A couple of 'em, in fact. I wasn't born bein' called Preacher. But that's what I've gone by for a heap o' years now, so it'll do."

With a contemptuous grunt, von Kuhner said, "Very well. It means nothing to me what you are called."

The Prussian hadn't offered to shake hands with either of them once he found out they were civilians, Jamie noted. Somehow, that didn't bother him overmuch.

Von Kuhner turned back to Sutton and said, "Now that you are here, Colonel, we will waste no time in departing on our expedition, *ja?*"

"We should be able to leave first thing in the morning," Sutton replied. "We can sit down with you this evening and go over our proposed route."

Von Kuhner waved away that offer. "There is no need. Whatever you and these . . . gentlemen . . . believe best will be how we proceed. I simply wish to reach the area where my countrymen met their fate with all due speed and put an end at last to the annoying speculation about what tragedy might have befallen them."

Jamie spoke up. "You understand, Baron, it's a big country up here. We only have a very general idea of where they were headed. It may take us a while to track them down."

"And to tell the truth," said Preacher, "there's a good chance we won't ever find out for sure what happened to 'em. Sometimes the frontier just sorta swallers folks up."

"That is unacceptable," barked von Kuhner. "We will find the truth and put an end to the rumors that persist in my country that Peter von Eichhorn may still be alive."

With that, he nodded curtly to the two officers, went down the steps, and stalked away from the headquarters building. Jamie wasn't sure where the baron was going, but he wasn't particularly sorry to see him go.

"So that's who we got to go off into Blackfoot country with," Preacher mused as he watched von Kuhner depart.

"That's right," Sutton said. "Wishing now that you hadn't agreed to come along, Preacher?"

"No, no," said the mountain man. "I was just wonderin' who was gonna be the biggest problem we have to deal with, Stone Bear or ol' Baron Stick-up-his-rear-end there."

"I've never run into Stone Bear," said Jamie, "but I've got a hunch it's going to be a pretty tight race."

Chapter 15

Jamie, Preacher, and Colonel Sutton ate supper that evening with Colonel Wheeler in the post commander's quarters, then headed back over to Wheeler's office to discuss the plans for the expedition.

As he'd indicated earlier, Baron von Kuhner didn't join them for either the meal or the discussion afterward.

"The baron stays to himself for the most part," Wheeler said as the four of them walked along the edge of the parade ground toward the headquarters building.

"A mite stuck-up, is he?" said Preacher.

"I don't know if that's it . . . well, yes, that's what it amounts to," Wheeler admitted. "He's what they call a Junker. Some sort of nobility, I guess you'd call it, and many of the men in that class serve as army officers. He doesn't really associate with us or his own men, except for a man named Becker, who's his . . . sergeant, I suppose you'd call it. I don't know what the Prussian word for that rank is." Wheeler shook his head. "Von Kuhner's attitude isn't something that makes much sense to Americans like us, who regard pretty much everybody as equal, but those folks over in Europe really go in for it."

"I hope such arrogance and corruption never infests our country," Sutton said.

"Amen to that," Jamie agreed. "But it's too pretty an evening to think about that."

Even though, officially, the season was still late summer, the air had an autumn crispness to it. As Jamie drew in a deep breath, he told himself that they wouldn't have a lot of time to waste once they headed north. Within a month or so, six weeks at the most, the weather might change. Winter would be filtering into the north country. A sudden blizzard would be unlikely, but such a thing couldn't be ruled out entirely.

Tonight, however, was beautiful, just as Jamie had said. The sky was clear, and millions of stars were visible overhead in a dazzling carpet laid across the heavens.

The four men paused as they came up to the headquarters building and saw someone sitting on the steps.

"Who's there?" Wheeler asked.

The man on the steps stood up and took off his broad-brimmed hat. Jamie had recognized him already from the smell of the shaggy coat the man wore.

Roscoe Lomax said, "It's just me, Colonel. Want to talk to MacCallister for a second."

"All right. We'll see you inside, Jamie."

The two officers went up the steps and into the building.

Preacher lingered and asked, "Want me to hang around for a spell, Jamie?"

"No, that's all right," Jamie told him. "Lomax isn't going to make any trouble. He gave his word on that. Isn't that right, Lomax?"

"It sure is," the bullwhacker declared.

Preacher nodded and said, "All right, then." He followed Sutton and Wheeler into the building.

"What do you want, Lomax?" Jamie asked.

"Thought I might see if you'd come over to the sutler's store with me. I wouldn't mind buyin' you a drink, now that we're back in what passes for civilization out here."

"I appreciate that, but I have to talk to the colonels and Preacher for a while. Why don't you go on, and maybe I'll be over there later."

Lomax nodded. "All right, but don't forget. I owe you a drink."

Jamie wanted to tell the man that he didn't owe him anything. He had come to believe that Lomax genuinely wanted to set things right between them, but sometimes he carried it farther than necessary.

Jamie just said, "See you later," then headed inside. Lomax drifted off toward the sutler's store, which was as much a saloon and gambling den as it was a mercantile.

When Jamie had joined the others in Colonel Wheeler's office, Colonel Sutton stood at a map hanging on the wall and used the tip of his index finger to trace the blue line representing the Missouri River.

"The Prussians were traveling by wagon and horseback," he said, "but they followed the river for the most part, anyway. There were reports of them being seen here." He tapped a spot on the map. "But that's the last place they were that we know of. Somewhere beyond that, they disappeared."

Jamie said, "You mentioned there have been reports of white captives among the Blackfeet, Colonel. Where do those reports come from?"

Sutton moved his finger over to an area some fifty or sixty miles west of the spot he had just indicated. "We've been told by two different individuals that captives were seen in this region. This is right in the middle of the area used by Stone Bear's band as their hunting grounds."

"Are the fellas who brought that word trustworthy?" asked Preacher.

Sutton looked at Colonel Wheeler, who said, "Both men are fur trappers. You're aware that the fur trade is merely a shadow of what it once was, I'm sure."

Preacher nodded. "Yeah, I haven't bothered goin' after furs for the past five or six years. Not enough money in it to make it worth all the trouble."

"Most of the trappers have given up, and the ones who persist at it have to take quite a few chances and venture into areas that aren't very safe, such as this one where Stone Bear and his people roam."

"Trappin' was always great sport," said Preacher, "but it was never exactly safe."

"No, of course not. The profession was always fraught with risks, I realize that. But these days, it's even worse. Men still do it, however. The two who brought in the relevant reports are well known to me. You may be acquainted with them, too, Preacher. Their names are Severs and Perry."

The mountain man nodded and said, "Yeah, I know 'em. I'd say they're honest. And level-headed enough that it ain't likely they'd just make up some story about seein' captives amongst the Injuns."

"That's what I think, too. However, we're talking about the Blackfeet. Those men weren't able to get too close. They didn't want the Blackfeet to spot *them*."

"Can't blame them for that," said Jamie. "What did they claim they saw?"

"Women who appeared to be white," Wheeler replied. "Blond women."

"But no men?" Sutton asked.

Wheeler shook his head. "No, just the women. But if some of the women from the Prussian expedition survived, some of the men could have, as well."

"That ain't damned likely," Preacher said. "They might've kept the women as slaves, but any of the men who got took prisoner instead of bein' killed outright was likely tortured to death or burned at the stake within a few days of bein' captured."

Sutton nodded solemnly. "We're aware that's a strong possibility, Preacher, but our orders are to investigate anyway and determine the truth if we can."

"Oh, I ain't sayin' we shouldn't go have a look around. It could be Stone Bear's holdin' some of them Prussian gals. If he is, and if we can get our hands on 'em, they ought to be able to tell us what happened."

"That's our best bet," Jamie agreed.

"So here's what we're going to do." Sutton moved his finger on the map to rest on Fort Laramie, where they were. "We'll head northwest from here and follow the shortest route to the area where the captives were seen. We should be able to cover that distance in a week or so, which ought to give us time to locate the prisoners, free them from the Blackfeet, and return here before the weather starts to get bad. With any luck, my men and I can take word back to St. Louis, along with any prisoners we recover, before winter sets in on the plains."

"You'll be cutting it close if you do," Jamie warned. "Honestly, it would be better to wait until spring to start on a mission like this."

"I know," Sutton replied, "but that wasn't what my orders from the War Department said. Our government wants to cooperate with the Prussian government and move ahead with this mission as quickly as possible."

"Our boys in Washington City oughta tell them furriners to go climb a stump," Preacher said. "It ain't our job to take care o' the rest of the world."

Sutton and Wheeler looked at each other, and Sutton shrugged.

"Whether we agree with you or not, Preacher, that's not our place to say. We have our orders, and we'll do our duty."

"And Preacher and I will live up to the promise we made, Colonel," Jamie said. "If those white prisoners are up there with the Blackfeet, we'll find—"

Before he could continue, rapid footsteps sounded in the outer office and a soldier appeared in the open doorway. The youngster came to attention and saluted, then blurted out, "Begging your pardon, Colonel, but the sergeant of the guard wishes to report that, uh . . . all hell's breaking loose at the sutler's store!"

Chapter 16

Lomax sat at a table in the rear corner of the sutler's store with a bucket of beer in front of him. He'd guzzled down half of its contents so far but hadn't felt much of an effect from the bitter brew.

Whiskey had a lot more kick, but he didn't want anything muddling his brain. When he was drunk, he had a much harder time controlling his temper, and he was determined to prove to Jamie MacCallister that he was a changed man.

So, no brawls tonight, Lomax told himself solemnly as he picked up the bucket and took another swig from it . . . even though he had been on the trail for a long time, and it sure would have felt good to cut loose his wolf and howl for a spell.

Lomax wasn't sure how long the foreign fella had been standing beside the table before he finally glanced up and realized the man was there.

"You want something?" Lomax asked in a surly tone. He might be trying to walk the straight and narrow these days, but even so, he took an instinctive dislike to the hombre as soon as he laid eyes on him.

The man wore the Prussian uniform, but the crimson collar was loose and he didn't have one of those funny-looking spiked helmets on. He wasn't particularly tall, but he was barrel-chested and broad-shouldered and had long arms. His bullet-shaped head sat on a short, thick neck, and his close-cropped hair was almost colorless. His nose had been broken at least a couple of times in the past and healed crookedly, so that it was little more than a mis-shapen lump of flesh in the middle of his face.

Judging by the way the man swayed slightly, he'd been drinking already . . . and was a lot drunker than Lomax was.

The man pointed a short, fat finger at Lomax and rasped, "You are . . . buffalo?"

Lomax glanced down at the shaggy garment he wore and said, "Yeah, it's a buffalo coat. What's that to you?"

The man shook his head and said, "*Nein, nein.* You are buffalo, *ja?*" He put his hands to his head and stuck his index fingers straight up. "*Wo ist der* horns?"

"What the hell are you sayin'?" Lomax demanded. "You think *I'm* a buffalo?"

"*Ja, ja!*" The man made a face, pinched his nose with the thumb and forefinger of his left hand, and shook his head. "*Sie stinken!*"

Lomax didn't have to speak the foreigner's lingo to know that he'd just been insulted. He started to stand up, then remembered his promise to Jamie that he wouldn't start any trouble. With an effort, he bit back the angry curses that wanted to spring to his lips and said, "I reckon it's true, I do smell a mite like a buffalo. Be hard not to, wearin' this coat and all."

"*Ja.*" The Prussian nodded. He reached for the bucket of beer. Lomax started to grab it away from him, then shrugged and pulled his arm back. "Sure, if you want a drink, go ahead," he told the man with a magnanimous wave of his hand.

"Du brauchst ein Bad," the Prussian said as he picked up the bucket.

"No savvy," Lomax said as he shook his head. "I don't know what you said, old son."

Frowning in concentration, the man said haltingly, "You . . . need . . . *ein bad* . . . a bath!"

With that, he turned the bucket up and dumped what was left of the beer over Roscoe Lomax's head, then guffawed and tossed the empty bucket back on the table.

All thoughts of controlling his temper vanished instantly from Lomax's brain. Like a beer-dripping rocket, he came up out of his chair and tackled the Prussian, wrapping his arms around the man's waist and ramming a shoulder into his midsection.

Lomax drove forward with all his strength as he bellowed in rage, forcing the Prussian backward and he was unable to slow the charge.

Lomax slammed the man down on his back onto a nearby table, causing it to collapse as its legs broke. The soldiers who'd been sitting there scattered, several of them falling down in the process.

One of them was spitting mad when he got up, grabbed Lomax by the shoulder, and yelled, "What the hell do you think you're doin'?"

Standing over the stunned Prussian lying amidst the wreckage of the table, Lomax jerked out of the dragoon's grip and blistered the air with profanity. "This is what I'm doin', you damned . . ."

He added a few more obscene epithets as he swung his left fist and crashed it against the soldier's jaw. The man went down hard.

Several of his friends charged at Lomax, throwing punches of their own. For a moment, they crowded around the bullwhacker so thickly that he wasn't even visible anymore.

Men began flying backward as Lomax's malletlike fists connected with them. He flailed around him and cleared some room.

One of the attackers picked up a chair and lunged at Lomax, who ducked low, came up under the swinging piece of furniture, and grabbed hold of the chair-wielder. With a grunt of effort, Lomax heaved the man up and over his back. The man yelled as he flew through the air and slammed into several other soldiers, knocking them off their feet, as well. All of them sprawled on the rough plank floor in a tangled heap of arms and legs.

Hearing someone rushing toward him from behind, Lomax whirled around and backhanded a soldier who was about to jump him. They were still all around him.

Another man leaped on his back and yelled, "I got him! I got him!" He had gotten more than he bargained for, though.

Lomax threw himself backward and smashed the man against the wall. The soldier's arms and legs slid off Lomax's buffalo coat as he fell in a limp sprawl.

Lomax moved to the side, keeping his back close to the wall. With that side protected, he was able to ward off the attacks as the soldiers pressed in on him from the other three sides. His fists snapped out and landed with devastating force. He took some punishment, too, but seemed to absorb it without ever showing any effect from the blows that landed.

The sutler, an overweight bald man with tufts of hair sticking out of his ears, stood behind the bar and roared at the men to stop fighting, but no one paid any attention to him. He clapped his hands to his head in dismay at the damage that had been done already. And the battle didn't seem to be anywhere near over.

In fact, it was about to get worse. The Prussian who had started the fracas by dumping the bucket of beer on Lomax's head had recovered his senses. He climbed to his feet, kicked the debris from the broken table aside, and lumbered back into the fray.

Shouldering some of the American soldiers aside, the Prussian shouted what had to be curses in his native tongue as he lunged at Lomax with his arms pistoning.

A right and a left landed on Lomax's bearded jaw and snapped his head back against the wall with enough force to make stars whirl madly before his eyes. For a second, he was disoriented, and that was enough of an opportunity for the Prussian to bore in and hook a pair of punches to Lomax's belly.

Sickness welled up inside Lomax as he bent forward. He wanted to curl up around the pain but wouldn't allow himself to give in.

Grabbing the front of the Prussian's jacket and hanging on tight, he lowered his head and drove the top of it into the man's face. He probably couldn't do any more damage to the man's nose than had been done in the past, but the impact drew a howl of pain from the Prussian and made him stumble back a couple of steps.

With room for a counterattack, Lomax clubbed his hands together and swung both arms. The blow smashed into the Prussian's slab of a jaw and knocked him sideways. The man landed on his right shoulder and slid across the floor as several of his comrades from the group of

Prussian soldiers came through the door of the sutler's store. They stopped and stared at their fallen comrade.

Sounding shocked, one of them yelled, *"Teufel! Ist Feldwebel Becker!"*

Another shouted, *"Helfen sie dem feldwebel!"*

"Ja!"

Lomax didn't understand much of that grunting, but he figured the man he had just knocked down was named Becker, and one of the Prussians had just ordered the others to help him.

They all swarmed at Lomax with blood in their eyes.

Chapter 17

With longer legs, Jamie and Preacher hurried ahead of Colonels Sutton and Wheeler as they all hurried across the parade ground. Approaching the building they heard the yelling and crashing inside the sutler's store, took the steps in a couple of bounds, and charged through the open door to see a wild melee going on. Men were fighting all over the room. At first glance, most of the battles seemed between American soldiers and the visiting Prussians; the crimson collars and cuffs on the Prussian uniforms made them easy to pick out.

But here and there, American dragoons were swinging punches at each other, too, as if there weren't enough European opponents to go around and they had to hit *somebody*.

The real center of the fight, though, seemed to be a crowded knot of Prussians hammering away at an opponent Jamie and Preacher couldn't see. Whoever was in the center of that had to be getting pummeled badly.

Paused just inside the doorway, Jamie looked around the room and didn't see Roscoe Lomax anywhere. Remembering that he had told the bullwhacker to wait for him, Jamie had a pretty good idea who those Prussians had surrounded.

"Reckon we'd better give that fella a hand," Jamie said as he started toward the group of foreign soldiers.

"Yeah, he looks to be a mite outnumbered," the mountain man agreed.

They bulled their way across the room, shouldering men aside until they reached the knot of Prussians. Jamie grabbed one of the men by the shoulders and tossed him out of the way. Another Prussian turned toward them just in time to catch Preacher's fist on his chin. The man's head snapped to the side from the force of the blow, and his knees buckled. As he went down, Preacher stepped over him and seized another man's shoulder, spinning him around and crashing a punch into his face.

Meanwhile, Jamie took hold of two of the foreigners by the back of their necks and smacked their heads together, creating a dull thud. Both men collapsed, knocked out cold.

Those actions had opened a path to the man in the center of the struggle. It came as no surprise at all that Jamie recognized Roscoe Lomax. Although the bullwhacker's beard concealed most of his face, Jamie could tell that Lomax was battered and bloody—but he was grinning under all that tangled hair.

He clamped a hand over an opponent's face and a hard shove sent the man reeling away. Lomax said, "I'm sorry, MacCallister, but I didn't start this!"

"Worry about that later," Jamie said. From the corner of his eye, he caught a glimpse of a man swinging a broken chair leg at his head. He whirled, flung up his left arm to block the blow, and sunk his right fist into the man's belly, all the way up to the wrist. The attacker doubled over, dropped the makeshift club, and fell to his knees as he crossed his arms over his agonized midsection. Jamie kicked him in the chest and knocked him on his back.

Preacher traded punches with a burly Prussian, drove the man back, and then threw a perfect left-right combination that sent the man sprawling. The next instant, a chair crashed down on Preacher's back and made the mountain man stagger several steps. He caught his balance and swung around with an angry roar.

Lomax was already dealing with the Prussian who had struck that craven blow, however. The bullwhacker hammered punches into the man's face, forcing him back. The Prussian dropped the chair, and Lomax scooped it up, raised it high, and brought it down on the man's head. The chair shattered into pieces. The Prussian would be lucky if his skull hadn't done the same.

"Stop it!" Colonel Wheeler bellowed from the doorway. "Stop this fighting *now!*"

Recognizing the voice of their commander, the American dragoons still on their feet slowly responded, throwing a few more punches before they began backing off from their opponents, but keeping their fists raised, ready to resume the battle if need be.

Only one of the few Prussians left standing, a burly man with a bullet-shaped head covered by a close-cropped fuzz of hair, disregarded the order. With a snarl twisting his heavy-featured face, he moved toward Jamie, Preacher, and Lomax, who stood shoulder to shoulder waiting for him. Even though the man was outnumbered three to one, he seemed to be so caught up in his rage that he didn't care about the odds.

He stopped short when another figure appeared in the door and shouted, *"Achtung! Feldwebel Becker!"*

The Prussian practically trembled with the urge to

continue fighting, but he stayed where he was and gradually came to attention. Baron Adalwolf von Kuhner strode into the room and joined Colonels Wheeler and Sutton in glaring at the men who had been fighting. The baron was fully and neatly dressed in his uniform, with the exception of the tall, spiked helmet. Lamplight shone on his hairless skull.

"What the devil happened here?" Colonel Wheeler demanded. "Who started this brawl?"

One of the dragoons pointed at Lomax and said, "It was him, Colonel. He dumped one o' them furriners right in the middle of the table where me and my friends were drinkin'."

A couple of the American soldiers called out in agreement with that statement.

"That's a damn-blasted lie!" responded Lomax in a bull-like bellow. "That varmint right there dumped a bucket o' beer on my head!" He pointed at the man von Kuhner had addressed as Feldwebel Becker, then glanced over at Jamie.

"I'm sorry, MacCallister," Lomax added. "I tried to keep my word, I swear I did, but you wouldn't expect me to just sit still for somethin' like that, would you?"

"No, I don't reckon I would," Jamie said. "Chances are, I would've done the same thing in your position."

"I woulda done worse," muttered Preacher.

Von Kuhner walked across the room, clasped his hands together behind his back, and glared at Becker. In English, he asked, "Is this true, Feldwebel? Did you assault this . . . American?" He managed to put a sneer in his voice as he said the word, even though his lips didn't curl.

Becker looked down at the floor and said, "*Jawohl, Oberst.* I will not lie."

"You were drunk?"

"Ja."

Von Kuhner jerked his head toward the door. "Leave now," he ordered. "All of you. And do not come back here tonight." He repeated the command in German.

The Prussian soldiers on the floor climbed unsteadily to their feet. They picked up their comrades who were unconscious and dragged them out of the barroom.

Von Kuhner turned to Wheeler and said, "My apologies on behalf of my men, Colonel. Such a thing will not occur again."

"No, I expect not, since you're all leaving tomorrow," Wheeler said dryly. "It would be a gesture of good faith if your men contributed to paying for the damages inflicted here tonight." The commanding officer raised his voice so all the dragoons in the room could hear him as he went on. "Since all of *my* men who were involved are going to be paying their share."

Von Kuhner gave one of those little bows and said, "I shall attend to it, have no doubt of that." With that, he walked stiffly out of the building without looking around.

Wheeler frowned sternly at the dragoons and said, "All right, you men, I want this place cleaned up as much as you can, and you're all going to pitch in to pay for any repairs that are necessary. Don't even think about trying to duck that responsibility."

"Thank you, Colonel." The sutler still looked distraught but didn't appear to be as upset as earlier.

Wheeler said, "You know things like this wouldn't happen if you didn't allow the men to get so drunk, MacKenzie."

The sutler spread his hands helplessly. "But they like to spend their pay, Colonel. What am I to do but help them?"

Wheeler just shook his head in disgust and turned to walk out of the store.

Sutton looked at Jamie and Preacher and said, "I'll see you fellows later. We'll leave at first light."

Jamie nodded. "We'll be ready, Colonel," he promised.

Sutton followed Wheeler out, leaving Jamie and Preacher there.

Lomax said to Jamie, "I swear, I didn't mean for this to happen, MacCallister. I stayed away from the whiskey and stuck to beer so my mind wouldn't get muddled. I even took it when that foreign fella Becker stood there and out-and-out told me I stunk. I didn't do a damned thing until he dumped that bucket o' beer over my head. And then I . . . I just couldn't hold it in . . ."

"It's all right, Lomax," Jamie told him. "I'd say you had plenty of provocation for what you did." He frowned. "But are you sure you still want to come along on this expedition, knowing those Prussians will be traveling with us?"

"I said I would, and I meant it," Lomax declared with an emphatic nod. "Shoot, if I backed out now, I'd feel like I was runnin' away from trouble . . . and I've never done that in all my borned days!"

"All right, then. I reckon you'll be part of the bunch when we pull out in the morning. It might be a good idea for you to steer clear of that fella Becker as much as you can, though."

"I'll try. Can't guarantee what *he'll* do, though."

"Well, give it time, and it won't be a problem," said Preacher. "Once we get where we're goin', we'll probably be too busy fightin' Blackfeet to tangle with each other!"

* * *

The Prussian soldiers had been given bunks at one end of the barracks. The dragoons who normally occupied those bunks had been sleeping in the stables since the Europeans' arrival. That had added to the sense of friction between the two groups, although that tension hadn't erupted into violence until tonight.

After the men had turned in and snoring filled the barracks, one of the Prussians slipped out of his bunk and padded stealthily to the door. He eased it open and stepped outside with a silent grace that was unusual in a man of his bulk. Moving along the side of the barracks to the corner, he went around it into an area of deep shadow.

A voice spoke quietly in German. "Is that you, Becker?"

"Yes, Baron, reporting as you ordered."

"You realize that your actions tonight could have jeopardized our entire plan."

Becker hung his head. "My apologies. I let my distaste for the Americans get the better of me. The man just smelled so bad!" He sighed. "But of course, I will accept any punishment you wish to give me."

"No punishment," Baron von Kuhner said. He chuckled and clapped a hand on Becker's shoulder. "I understand. I despise these Americans every bit as much as you do, Sergeant. But we must cooperate with them . . . for now."

There was a note of eagerness in Becker's voice as he said, "But when we reach our destination, eh, Baron . . . ?"

"That's right, Herman. They must never find out what truly happened five years ago." Von Kuhner paused. "So when we reach our destination . . . we will kill them all."

Chapter 18

Katarina did not sleep much that first night of captivity in the Blackfoot village. Neither did the other two female aristocrats, although exhaustion had caught up at last with the servants Gerda, Lotte, and Ingeborg, and they dozed off. Countesses Marion von Arnim and Joscelyn von Tellman whimpered and tossed back and forth on the ground for most of the night.

Katarina von Falkenhayn would not allow herself to give in to such despair. No matter what happened, she vowed that she would meet it bravely.

Of course, it was easy to tell oneself that when the worst hadn't happened yet.

Along toward dawn, Marion and Joscelyn finally quieted down. Katarina figured they had fallen into terrified stupors. The same sort of lassitude claimed her as well. She didn't think she actually slept, but for a while, her brain retreated from the horrors to which she had been subjected.

When awareness began to seep in on her again, the first thing she thought about was the realization she'd had the night before that it had been white men who'd attacked their camp and took them prisoner. The guttural tones she had mistaken for those of a savage actually belonged to a white man, but one to whom English was not his native language.

Now that the terror had receded to a dull horror and she could consider everything more clearly, she decided that the accent of the man who'd forced her along so brutally had sounded very much like some of her own countrymen speaking English.

Such a thing was almost beyond belief. Why would *Prussians* attack their fellows, slaughter many of them, and turn the survivors over to the Indians?

Why, indeed?

Katarina could think of one reason: ambition. Call it what you will—lust for power, ruthlessness—some men hungered to achieve their own ends so badly that they would do anything to get what they wanted. They would kill their own countrymen and traffic with savages. They would commit murder and treason.

All in their endless quest for power.

Peter von Eichhorn was in the line of succession for the monarchy, she reminded herself. The sheer fact of his existence might be regarded as a threat to others, whether in his own family or a rival family that had an eye on grasping the throne.

Americans probably would find it absurd and unbelievable that anyone would contemplate mass murder in order to further their own ambitions, but Katarina knew such conspiracies were common in Europe. Every monarchy was full of dark secrets, including the spilling of much blood.

That might be exactly the fate that had caught up to her and her companions.

The sudden thrusting aside of the hide flap over the lodge's entrance broke into her bleak thoughts, then they were banished entirely as the tall, haughty figure of Stone Bear stepped inside.

The other women were waking up, too, and the unexpected appearance of the Blackfoot chief abruptly did away with any drowsiness that still gripped them. Lotte and Ingeborg screamed. Gerda scrambled closer to Katarina. Marion sat up and glared at Stone Bear, while Joscelyn began to sob softly, no doubt thinking that her doom had come to claim her.

"Be quiet!" Stone Bear barked at them in English. He made a slashing motion with his hand. "Women should be silent!"

Katarina put a hand on Gerda's shoulder and told her, "Stay calm. We don't know why he's here."

Gerda sniffled and said, "The savage has come to kill us all, Countess. I know he has."

"If they wanted to kill us, they could have done so many times before now."

Stone Bear said, "You are right. You will not be harmed. This morning your men battle for their lives. You will watch." He grunted. "You can even encourage them, for what little good it will do."

"What do you mean, battle for their lives?" asked Katarina. She kept her voice and her gaze level, not wanting to show anything but disdain for their captors.

Stone Bear looked equally disdainfully at her. "Do you not understand the white man's tongue, woman?"

"There are white men from many different lands, with many different tongues," Katarina snapped back at him. "But I understand English—what you call the white man's tongue—very well. You say our men will fight, but fight who? Not each other, surely."

Stone Bear looked interested for a second, as if that idea hadn't occurred to him then shook his head. "Each of the prisoners will battle one of my warriors. If any of them defeat their opponent, that man's life will be spared and he will live among us as a slave. But those who lose will die as men should, in combat."

Katarina thought about Walter von Stauffenberg and said, "One of our men cannot fight. He is injured."

Stone Bear looked at her for a long moment. She hoped that meant he was considering what she'd said. Finally, he nodded.

"You mean the one who acts as if he hears the spirits speaking in his head." The chief shrugged. "Do you ask me to spare his life?"

"I do," Katarina responded without hesitation.

"You are condemning him to life as a slave."

"That's the best he could hope for if he fought, isn't it? And you have to know that with the shape he's in, he would stand no chance of winning."

"You are right," Stone Bear admitted. "I will spare him. There is no honor in defeating a man touched by the spirits. To do so is to risk being cursed by them."

"What about Peter?" Marion suddenly asked. Judging by the look on her face, it had taken her this long to work up enough courage to speak to Stone Bear. "Is he still alive?"

"I do not know how they are called," the Blackfoot said dismissively.

"Peter is the tall man with the mustache," Katarina said, running a finger over her upper lip. "Peter von Eichhorn."

"He lives," Stone Bear confirmed. "As does the man in buckskin, and two soldiers."

She thought of Lieutenant Barton and the two American dragoons. "There were three soldiers—"

"One is dead," Stone Bear said, interrupting her. He had a look of disgust on his face, and Katarina couldn't help but wonder what had happened.

She wondered, too, which of the men had died, whether it was Lieutenant Barton or one of the dragoons who had been taken prisoner.

She would find out soon enough, she supposed, since Stone Bear had said they would serve as an audience for the desperate battles the male captives would fight today.

"Women will bring you food," Stone Bear went on. "Soon, warriors will come to bring you out. Do not try to escape. You have some worth to us as slaves . . . but we can always get more slaves."

It was pretty obvious what he meant by that, thought Katarina.

A few minutes after Stone Bear had shoved aside the hide flap and left the lodge, the women he had mentioned came in, bringing with them two large wooden bowls of some sort of bitter-tasting mush, as well as a bucket full of water from the creek. The prisoners had to share the food from the bowls and eat with their hands.

At first Marion and Joscelyn refused to lower themselves to such indignity. Even in the depths of their fear, they were conscious of their station in life. But hunger overcame that ingrained arrogance and soon they were dipping their fingers into the mush and licking the bitter stuff off of them, just like Katarina and the three servants.

They passed around the water, which tasted much better than the food. Further humiliation followed, as they had to crawl away from the others as much as they could and tend to their personal needs. The other two noblewomen began crying again at the sheer misery of it all.

Katarina felt like joining them in self-pity, but with an effort, she managed to keep herself from sinking into that morass. If she ever did, it would be difficult to get back out.

At least they didn't have it as bad as the men, she told herself. She and the other women were assured of being kept alive, as long as they didn't cause any trouble. True, they would be facing brutal, probably short lives as slaves, but at least they would survive for a while.

Katarina doubted if any of the men would live to see the sun set today.

On the other hand, Reese Coburn was a seasoned frontiersman. Was there a chance he could defeat one of the Blackfoot warriors? Katarina couldn't rule it out. And Peter at least had *some* martial experience. He had been trained in the use of the saber and the dueling foil since he was a young man.

Of course, it was doubtful either of those weapons would be used in the battle Peter would have to fight today.

The women had barely finished their unsatisfying meal when several of Stone Bear's warriors showed up, armed with lances. They looked like they would enjoy having an excuse to prod the captives with the sharp tips, so when they motioned with the weapons, the women quickly got to their feet.

"We had better cooperate with them," Katarina said in a low voice. She didn't know if any of these warriors spoke English, as their chief did.

"Of course we're going to cooperate with them," Marion said, her tone scathing. "What do you think we're going to do, Katarina? Take those spears away from them and fight?"

Joscelyn groaned and said, "Don't give her any ideas, Marion. You know how she's always been."

Katarina felt a flash of anger at that comment. It was true she'd always been a bit headstrong and accustomed to getting her own way, and she preferred pursuits that were not as vain and trivial as the other women in their circle. But that didn't give them any right to think less of her.

None of that mattered at the moment, of course. They were all slaves of the Blackfeet. That terrible fate was the best they could hope for.

She really *wouldn't* have minded getting her hands on one of those lances, though. If the men were being allowed to fight for their lives, why shouldn't she?

The warriors ushered them outside. It felt good to step into the sunlight again, although the brightness of the morning made all the women flinch a little and squint against the glare until their eyes adjusted. Surrounded by warriors, they shuffled over to a large open area near the creek where the rest of the village appeared to be congregating.

Once they stopped, Katarina looked around for Peter, Coburn, Walter, and the two soldiers. She didn't see any of them. Evidently they hadn't been brought out yet from wherever they were being held.

Not far away, a thick post was sunk into the ground. It stood about six feet tall and looked like the trunk of a small tree with all the limbs peeled off and the bark trimmed away. A shiver went through Katarina as she realized that was where the Blackfeet burned captives at the stake.

Children ran around, playing and laughing merrily, trailed by barking dogs. The Blackfoot women smiled and chattered among themselves. Men stood with their arms folded over their chests, talking solemnly, but they appeared to be enjoying themselves, too.

They were all as happy as if they were attending a *fest*, thought Katarina . . . all because they were about to watch men fight and probably die. The spilling of blood was an occasion of celebration for them, and she was horrified by their cheerful acceptance of that. She couldn't even begin to comprehend the depths of cruelty and savagery a people had to have in their hearts to glory in such a thing.

The hubbub came to an abrupt halt, and all eyes swung toward the lodges. Katarina and her companions looked in that direction, too.

Blackfoot warriors were bringing out the male prisoners, prodding them along with lances toward the bloody fate that awaited them.

Chapter 19

A short time earlier, several warriors had come into the lodge where the prisoners were being held and cut the bonds on their ankles. They had been dragged onto their feet, which were numb from being tied so tightly for so long. The Blackfeet had shoved them out of the lodge, not giving them any time for feeling to return to their feet.

That made walking pretty difficult. All the captives struggled as the warriors forced them toward a large clearing beside the creek where the rest of the villagers waited. Pins and needles bedeviled Coburn's feet, hurting like blazes. He stumbled a little as the tip of one of the Blackfoot lances jabbed him in the back but managed to stay upright and keep moving.

A wave of relief went through him as he spotted Countess Katarina among the crowd. She and the other female prisoners were surrounded by guards. They looked pretty haggard and bedraggled, but none appeared to be seriously injured.

Baron von Stauffenberg was walking beside Coburn. He swayed and staggered and looked like he was about to fall down. Coburn moved closer. He would have put an arm around von Stauffenberg to steady him, but his wrists were still tied together behind his back. All of them were still bound that way. Coburn got a shoulder against von Stauffenberg's shoulder and braced him up as best he could.

"Hang on, Walter," he muttered. "Maybe they'll let us stop in a minute."

That was exactly what happened when they reached the clearing. Warriors still surrounded them, holding lances ready to strike, but at least the prisoners got to stand still and let more blood seep back painfully into their legs and feet.

Von Stauffenberg leaned against Coburn and muttered something in his own language.

"I don't speakin' zee Dutch, Walter," said the frontiersman, "but I reckon you're right, whatever you just said."

Von Stauffenberg looked over at him wide-eyed and said, "Papa?"

Coburn could understand that. He was about to tell von Stauffenberg that he wasn't his father, then thought better of it. Instead he said, "That's right, Walter, it's me, Papa. Everything's gonna be all right."

Coburn didn't believe that for a second. The state the baron was in, there was no point in making things worse for him. If the delusion helped, then so be it.

Von Eichhorn looked around and said, "I wonder which of these savages we will be forced to fight?"

"Just look for the biggest, meanest-lookin' ones," Coburn told him. "I reckon that'll likely be them."

Von Stauffenberg said something else in German. Coburn could tell that he was asking a question of his father. As gently as he could, he said, "I don't know, Walter. But just don't forget, you'll be all right."

"Stop lying to him," snapped von Eichhorn. "None of us will be all right. You know perfectly well that so-called chief was lying to us. He doesn't intend for any of us to live. Even if we defeat his champions, he'll have us killed. Otherwise, our continued existence will be an insult to his honor."

"I ain't so sure about that," said Coburn. "You're lookin' at it from a different way of thinkin' than he is. To him, breakin' his word would be more of an insult to his honor."

Von Eichhorn glared at him. "Are you implying that a Junker lacks honor?"

"Not implyin' nothin'," Coburn replied with a shake of his head. "Just sayin' there's at least a chance ol' Stone Bear will keep his promise."

"We will see. And soon, it appears. Here he comes now."

Coburn looked around and saw Stone Bear striding toward them. Lieutenant Barton saw the chief approaching, too, and began to whimper. He knew their time was running out. The other soldier was talking fast and soft, under his breath, and although Coburn couldn't make out the words, he was pretty sure the fella was praying.

Even though he wasn't much of a spiritual man, Coburn didn't see how that could hurt anything, so he quickly muttered a prayer of his own.

Stone Bear walked past the prisoners and turned to face them. "I am a man of my word. Each of you will battle one of my warriors. Victory means you will not be killed. Defeat means you die here today, either in battle or burned at the stake . . . if you fight well enough. If you do not . . . if you show that you are a coward . . . your death will be long and painful, and you will beg for the flames."

Barton broke down and started to sob.

"Stop it, you spineless fool!" von Eichhorn told him.

"Can you not see that you are just making it worse for yourself?"

"I . . . I don't care," Barton choked out. "I don't want to die!"

"Then win your battle! But death comes to all men. The only thing that matters is how you meet it."

Coburn wasn't sure he completely agreed with von Eichhorn on that part, but the man still had a point. However, more important things were on Coburn's mind at the moment, so he spoke up. "Stone Bear, heed my words."

Stone Bear looked surprised. "You dare speak to me like that?"

"What've I got to lose?" asked Coburn as a wry smile curved his lips. "I speak to you as one man of honor to another, and I ask that you spare this man." He nodded toward Walter von Stauffenberg, who stood close beside him, bumping his shoulder occasionally as he swayed and muttered. "You can see for yourself that he's in no shape to fight anybody. He's no threat to the Blackfeet, and he likely never will be again."

"What would you have me do with him?"

"Let him go be with the women. They can take care of him."

Stone Bear smiled. It didn't make him look any less threatening.

"The yellow-haired woman who prides herself on her defiance has already spoken to me about this one." Stone Bear nodded toward von Stauffenberg. "I have agreed that he will not have to fight."

Coburn knew from the description Stone Bear had just given that the chief was talking about Countess Katarina. All the other female prisoners looked cowed, despairing, but not Katarina. Her head was still up, and as she returned

Coburn's glance across the clearing, he saw the fire burning in her eyes.

There was a woman who would never give up, he thought. A woman who would do to ride the river with . . . in another time, another place . . . if they had been different people . . .

No sense in thinking about that, Coburn told himself. He turned his eyes back to Stone Bear and said, "Thank you."

"Will you beg for your own life now?" the chief asked in a taunting voice.

"Not hardly."

"Very well. I would not have granted it, anyway." Stone Bear motioned to one of his men. "Free the white man touched by the spirits."

The warrior went over, drew a knife from a sheath at his waist, and moved behind von Stauffenberg to cut the rawhide thongs around his wrists.

Von Stauffenberg looked over his shoulder and said, "Papa?"

"He's not your papa, Walter," said Coburn. "I'm right here, remember?"

Von Stauffenberg looked at Coburn again and smiled. "Papa." His bonds fell off and his arms sagged back around to their normal position.

Coburn nodded toward the women. "Go over there, Walter. Go to those women. You see Countess Katarina? She's your friend. She'll take care of you."

"Yes, Walter," Katarina called. "Come over and join us."

Von Stauffenberg looked at her for a second, then turned back to Coburn and said, *"Auf wiedersehen, Papa."*

Coburn had picked up enough of their lingo to know what that meant. He smiled and said, "So long, Walter."

Von Stauffenberg walked over to the women, weaving a little on the way. Katarina greeted him by throwing her arms around him and holding him tightly to her.

Coburn felt a little better, knowing the countess would do everything she could for the poor fella.

That left the rest of them to face what Stone Bear had in store for them. In a way, Coburn was ready to get it over with, and the nod he gave Stone Bear indicated that.

Stone Bear wasn't going to make it easy, though. He pointed to Barton and said, "You first."

"No!" Barton cried. "No, I . . . I won't do it! You won't make me fight for your . . . your perverted entertainment!"

Stone Bear fingered the hilt of his knife. "You fight or die now."

Barton sobbed a few times, but as Stone Bear started to pull the knife out, he said, "All right! All right, I . . . I'll do what you say. I'll fight."

Stone Bear grunted. He turned, looked at his assembled warriors, and pointed to one of them. The man he chose was middle-aged, probably a veteran of many battles. That impression was confirmed when the warrior pulled his buckskin shirt over his head and revealed numerous scars on his still muscular torso.

At a nod from Stone Bear, the man who had cut von Stauffenberg's bonds moved behind Barton and sawed through the thongs around his wrists. Barton pulled his arms in front of him and hurriedly began rubbing his hands to get some feeling back into them. Tears still ran down his cheeks, but a dull look of fatalistic gloom had come over his face.

"Would you fight with knives?" asked Stone Bear. "Tomahawks? Or bare hands?"

Barton tried twice before he got out the word *knives*.

The warrior who had cut him loose stepped in front of him and extended the knife in his hand, bone handle first. Barton hesitated, swallowed hard, and then took the weapon. He wrapped his fingers around the handle, hefted it, acted like he was studying the blade and getting a feel for its balance.

Maybe he was, thought Coburn. Or maybe he was just putting it off as long as he possibly could.

"The time is now," Stone Bear said. He stepped back to give the combatants plenty of room in the open area along the creek.

Coburn saw something in Barton's eyes and suddenly knew the young officer was considering making a run for it. Barton glanced at the creek, which was shallow enough to get across easily. "Don't do it, son," Coburn warned him in a low voice. "You'd be full of arrows before you made it ten yards."

"Maybe . . . maybe that would be b-better," Barton said without looking at him.

Maybe it would be, Coburn mused. He wouldn't take that way out himself, but he had no right to tell anybody else how to spend the last few moments of life they had left. "Do what you gotta do," he said quietly.

Barton drew in a deep breath. Then, suddenly, he broke into a run. Not toward the creek, though.

With a strident yell, he charged at the middle-aged warrior waiting for him.

Chapter 20

The attack didn't really take anybody by surprise, since fighting was what they were there for, but Coburn thought Barton's opponent wasn't really prepared for the desperate speed with which the lieutenant came at him. Barton thrust out the knife, and the Blackfoot warrior had to twist aside hurriedly to avoid the blade.

Not having drawn his own knife yet, the warrior clamped both hands on Barton's arm and took advantage of the fact that the lieutenant was off balance to throw him to the ground. Barton landed hard and rolled over a couple of times.

Instead of seizing the advantage and closing in to finish Barton off, the warrior turned to face the assembled villagers and held up both arms, motioning with them as he grinned. He was really playing to the crowd, and the Blackfeet rewarded him with cheers of appreciation.

Barton forced himself to his feet and charged again.

The warrior was just waiting for that. He turned as Barton reached him, grabbed the lieutenant's wrist, and thrusting that arm up, leaned in to head-butt his opponent.

Barton reeled back several steps before catching his balance.

Looking more serious, the warrior drew his knife from its sheath and stalked toward Barton. The young officer waved the knife he held back and forth in front of him. His dark hair fell down in front of his eyes, and sweat coated his face even though the day was cool.

The warrior feinted, leaping forward and jabbing with the knife. Barton jumped to avoid the thrust, only to find that the blade was already slashing at him in a backhanded swipe. The tip raked across his chest, ripping through his shirt and drawing blood. He cried out in pain and stumbled backward.

"Compose yourself!" von Eichhorn shouted at Barton. "Your fear makes you slow and confused."

Barton didn't show any signs of even hearing the nobleman. He tried another clumsy rush that the Blackfoot warrior avoided easily. As Barton went past him, the man bent low and swiped with his weapon. Barton screamed and pitched forward, blood welling from the back of his left calf where the blade had cut him deeply.

Again, the warrior held back instead of finishing him off. Gasping and whimpering, Barton got his hands under him and tried to push himself to his feet. Hamstrung, his left leg wouldn't hold his weight, and he collapsed.

With a mocking smile, the warrior held out his empty left hand and crooked the fingers, making a beckoning gesture. The villagers roared their approval.

Anybody who figured that Indians were unemotional had never seen them tormenting an enemy, thought Coburn. "Blast it, that's enough," the frontiersman called to Stone Bear. "He can't get up. What's the point in this?"

Stone Bear didn't answer that directly. He asked Barton, "Do you wish to yield, white man?"

Barton knew what giving up would mean. He gave a desperate shake of his head and tried again to get to his feet. He made it, although his left leg dangled uselessly. He couldn't move, but he could stand and wait for the warrior to come to him. His hand shook wildly as he held the knife up.

The warrior moved in, knocked Barton's knife arm aside with no trouble, and then sliced his forearm deeply with his blade. Barton shrieked, dropped his knife, and clamped his left hand over the blood-spouting wound.

"Just finish it," Coburn said wearily.

The warrior wasn't ready to do that. He bent and picked up the knife Barton had dropped, and held it out, handle first, to the lieutenant. Barton, crying and swaying, hesitated, then reached out and took it with his left hand.

So swiftly that no one could even think about stopping him, he plunged the blade into his own throat, driving it in so hard that the bloody tip emerged from the back of his neck. As his eyes rolled up in their sockets, he toppled to the side and landed on the ground, where he quivered for a few seconds before the stillness of death stole over him.

Silence had fallen over the crowd when Barton struck the fatal blow against himself. It lasted for several seconds, then the Blackfeet erupted in laughter. It wasn't as amusing as torture, of course, but seeing a white man kill himself in sheer panic that way was still great sport to them.

Coburn looked over at the women and saw that all of them had averted their eyes from the grisly sight, even Countess Katarina. A couple of the servants doubled over and lost whatever the Blackfeet had fed them for breakfast.

Walter von Stauffenberg gazed around vacantly. Clearly, he had no idea what was going on.

The remaining dragoon looked a little pale and sick, too. Von Eichhorn stood straight and stiff, his face impassive. Coburn got the sense that he was holding a very tight rein on his emotions, though. Von Eichhorn didn't want the Blackfeet to see how deeply the atrocity had affected him.

Coburn understood that. He felt the same way himself.

Stone Bear barked orders in his native tongue. Several of the older men came forward, took hold of Barton's corpse, and dragged it away.

The middle-aged warrior who had battled the lieutenant stalked back and forth, scowling and obviously upset that he hadn't gotten to strike the fatal blow. He flung out a hand and said something to Stone Bear, then pointed at the remaining soldier.

"He wants to fight you, too," von Eichhorn said to the man. "He feels that the lieutenant robbed him of his dignity."

"I don't give a damn about that," muttered the dragoon. "He's got to be a little tired after that, and I've seen how he fights now. I figure I've got more of a chance against him."

"Perhaps," von Eichhorn agreed. "But I do not know if Stone Bear agrees with you."

Indeed, the chief had snapped something back at the warrior, who continued to argue. Finally, Stone Bear jerked his head in a nod. The warrior looked satisfied and turned toward the captives.

The dragoon didn't wait for Stone Bear to ask him which weapon he preferred. He said, "I'll take a knife."

One of the old men who had hauled off Barton's body

had retrieved that knife. At a nod from Stone Bear, the old man handed it to the dragoon, who took it without any of the fussing Barton had done over it. He stepped into the clearing, ready to confront the warrior who waited there for him.

Instead of charging wildly, the dragoon came to a stop and waited for the warrior to come to him. The Blackfoot advanced warily as he slowly weaved his knife in front of him. When he was close enough, he tried the same sort of feint he had been successful with against Barton. The dragoon didn't fall for it, and lashed out with his own blade. The warrior darted aside, untouched.

That initiated a burst of lunges and slashes from both men, that left both of them breathing hard from the effort. Even though neither of them had done any harm to the other, they drew apart, panting and glaring at each other for a long moment before the warrior sprang forward again.

The dragoon twisted out of the way and swung his knife. Angry shouts came from the onlookers at the sight of blood on the warrior's chest. The dragoon had raked a long slash across the torso that would add to the warrior's scars—if he survived.

The painful wound increased the warrior's visible fury. With his lips drawing back from his teeth, he grimaced and charged again. The dragoon leaped away and backpedaled. The warrior went after him.

Coburn saw what the soldier was trying to do. He wanted to wear out the warrior and get him mad enough to make a mistake. In a contest like this, one error was usually enough to end it. One slip, one delay in adjusting to a new angle of attack, and it would be all over. The dragoon had nothing to look forward to except a life of mistreatment and degradation, but at least he would be alive.

The crowd wasn't making nearly as much noise as the villagers sensed what was happening. They didn't want to see one of their own defeated, and they certainly didn't want one of the hated white men to emerge victorious.

Stone Bear looked on, arms crossed, no expression on his rough-hewn face.

Coburn thought the dragoon had a chance. He really did. But as the warrior puffed and wheezed, the white man got overconfident and pressed in too close.

The warrior hooked a foot behind the dragoon's left ankle and jerked that leg out from under him. With a startled yell, the dragoon fell onto his back.

He had the presence of mind to stick the knife up so that if the warrior dived on him, he would land on the blade.

The warrior struck again with his moccasin-shod foot, kicking the dragoon's wrist and sending the knife spinning away. Then and only then did the warrior leap. He rammed a knee into the dragoon's belly, pinned him to the ground, and dug the knife point into the man's chest.

But he didn't ram it home, which would have ended the fight. The warrior clamped his other hand around the dragoon's throat and held him there while he gradually, inexorably, increased the pressure on the knife. The blade penetrated a little deeper.

The dragoon let out a choked cry and started hitting the warrior in the head with his fists. He couldn't put enough power behind the blows to knock the warrior off of him. Ignoring the blows and grinning in his murderous rage, the warrior leaned closer and pushed a little harder on the knife, then a little harder . . . and a little harder . . . as inch by inch, the steel disappeared into the dragoon's chest.

Suddenly, the dragoon spasmed and his arms flung out to the sides. His legs kicked wildly. The knife point had reached his heart, Coburn knew. He wanted to look away, but horrified fascination kept him watching as the warrior, his face only inches from the dragoon's, finally bore down hard on the knife's handle.

That savage face was the last thing the dragoon saw as he jerked violently again and then died.

Chapter 21

Despite the brave façade she was trying to put up, Katarina felt like she might pass out from horror at any moment. The gruesome suicide of the lieutenant had been bad enough. The slow, methodical killing of the other soldier, after Katarina had had a glimmering of hope that the man might win his battle and therefore survive, was almost too much to endure.

With her arms around Walter's shoulders, she tightened her grip and swallowed hard. She had to be strong for his sake, if for no other reason.

She glanced at Reese Coburn. He looked as sickened as she felt. And his time was coming. He and Peter were the only male prisoners left.

The warrior who had just killed the dragoon still knelt atop the body. Stone Bear strode forward and clapped a hand on the man's shoulder, spoke to him in the Blackfoot tongue. The man pulled his knife out of the dead man's chest and stood up, looking exhausted but pleased with himself. He bent, wiped the blood from his knife on the dragoon's uniform trousers, and went to join his friends.

They gathered around him and slapped him on the back, congratulating him on his victory.

Stone Bear turned and carefully regarded Coburn and von Eichhorn, as if he were trying to decide which prisoner to send into battle next.

Von Eichhorn took that decision out of his hands by stepping forward, jutting his chin out defiantly, and declaring, "I am ready to do battle with whoever you choose, you filthy savage."

Stone Bear went over to him and regarded him with an equally arrogant look. "How would you fight, white man?"

"Well, if you were the least bit civilized, I would suggest sabers or foils or even pistols . . . but I don't suppose you have any of those things, do you?"

Stone Bear actually smiled, which surprised Katarina as she watched the tense confrontation. The chief barked something in Blackfoot to one of his warriors. The man hurried back to the village. Several minutes passed as the feeling in the air grew even more taut until the man came trotting back with a pair of scabbarded sabers in his hands.

Von Eichhorn let out a surprised exclamation in German.

Stone Bear said smugly, "The men who brought you to us had these with them. They did not want to give the long knives to me, but I told them it would be wise for them to do so."

Katarina could imagine that negotiation. It probably hadn't taken very long. The men who had attacked the camp wouldn't have wanted to antagonize the Blackfoot chief. Not if they wanted to make it out of this wilderness alive.

Stone Bear took the sabers from his warrior and turned to von Eichhorn, who reached out eagerly for one of them.

The war chief stepped back and said, "None of my men

have ever fought with long knives like these. It would not be fair to ask one of them to make such an attempt now."

"Then how about you?" von Eichhorn demanded as his lip curled in a sneer. "Perhaps you and I should duel."

"I am tempted, white man. I would like nothing better than to kill you with your own weapon." Stone Bear shrugged. "But one of my young warriors has requested that honor. He knows he will be at a disadvantage and that I would not ask it of him . . . but neither will I turn down his request."

He motioned to the crowd. A tall warrior, lean with youth, stepped out and strode forward.

Katarina thought he wasn't more than twenty years old, if that. His arms were covered with ropy strands of muscle and his face was cold with hate as he stared at von Eichhorn.

Stone Bear held out the scabbarded swords to him. The young man grasped the handle of one and pulled the blade out. He hefted the sword, then slashed it back and forth in the air. He raised it high, brought it down swiftly, then cut from side to side again.

Apparently satisfied, he nodded to Stone Bear.

The chief turned to von Eichhorn and held out the other saber. Von Eichhorn took it, raised the blade in front of his face, and bowed toward the young warrior, who just scowled at him and didn't return the bow. No one in the Blackfoot village in the middle of the untamed frontier cared anything about the protocol of fighting a duel.

Tossing the empty scabbards to the man who had brought them, Stone Bear backed off and said simply, "You will fight now."

Instantly, von Eichhorn launched his attack. He sprang forward, thrusting and jabbing with the saber. The young warrior met the attack clumsily but effectively.

At first, Katarina had believed that he would be at a huge disadvantage against the much more experienced Prussian, then she realized that the "long knives," as Stone Bear had called them, were just that: *knives*.

And the Blackfeet were expert knife fighters.

For the first few minutes, she could tell that the young warrior was struggling to adapt to the new weapon. Several times, von Eichhorn's blade came within a whisker of inflicting a serious wound. But always, the young warrior turned his opponent's sword aside or leaped out of the way at the last instant.

Von Eichhorn had the training, but the young Blackfoot had the speed, reflexes, and instincts to counteract that.

Katarina saw the frustration growing on von Eichhorn's face. She knew that he had a problem controlling his temper and tended to do rash, impulsive things when he was angered. If he gave in to that urge, it was likely he would make a mistake that could prove fatal.

"Peter, be careful!" she called to him in German. "Don't lose your head!"

"Kill him, my love!" screamed Marion von Arnim. "Gut the filthy savage!"

That was the wrong kind of encouragement, thought Katarina.

As the two fighters broke apart and put a little distance between them, von Eichhorn glanced toward the women.

"Kill him!" Marion screeched again.

Katarina saw the fury well up in von Eichhorn's eyes, fueled by the strident cries of his fiancée. She said, "Peter, no!" as von Eichhorn rushed toward the young Blackfoot again, clearly determined to put an end to the battle and vanquish his enemy.

Von Eichhorn ignored Katarina's plea and crowded in

on the warrior, hacking and slashing madly. The youth gave ground, which made von Eichhorn increase the ferocity of his attack.

The warrior didn't look desperate or afraid, and a chill went through Katarina as she realized his expression was one of cunning. He was luring his opponent into some sort of trap . . .

And von Eichhorn was falling for it completely.

So were Marion and Joscelyn and the servants, who were caught up in the battle and shouting encouragement to von Eichhorn in German. Marion started laughing gleefully, thinking that her fiancé was about to win. The sound had a hysterical edge to it.

The Blackfeet watched in near-silence, their attention rapt on the flashing, darting blades.

The young warrior stumbled. The sword in his hand sagged. With an exultant shout, von Eichhorn lunged in to strike the killing blow.

But as he did, the warrior leaped aside. Von Eichhorn couldn't check his momentum as his powerful thrust missed completely. He began to fall forward, his rush out of control.

The sword in the warrior's hand rose, the blade catching the morning sun for a split second in a brilliant flash, and then it swept down too fast for the eye to follow.

Katarina turned away and pulled Walter against her as she squeezed her eyes shut, unable to watch.

But she couldn't close her ears to the horrible sound, a dull *thunk!* combined with a slight grating noise, followed instantly by a huge roar from the crowd. Even though it was the last thing Katarina wanted to do, a seemingly inexorable force made her turn her head and open her eyes.

Graf Peter von Eichhorn's body lay belly down. His head was lying on the ground a few feet away.

Katarina clutched Walter harder. The other women stared in shock and horror, as if they couldn't quite comprehend what they had just seen.

Then Marion let out a terrible wail and fell to her knees. She screamed as she dug her fingers into her tangled dark hair and yanked on it as if she wanted to pull every strand from her head.

Her maid Lotte finally broke free of the stunned stupor that gripped her and hurried to Marion, kneeling beside her and putting her arms around the distraught countess. Joscelyn, Ingeborg, and Gerda began to cry.

"Mama?" Walter said, his voice a little muffled beside Katarina as she held him against her so tightly. "Mama, what's wrong?"

"N-Nothing, Walter," she managed to say while patting him on the back with one hand. Taking care of him was the only thing keeping her from breaking down completely.

Don't lose your head, she had warned Peter when he began attacking so rashly. Clamping her jaws together so tightly at the memory, Katarina fought to control her emotions that it was a wonder her teeth didn't crack and shatter.

The Blackfeet were still whooping gleefully, out of control with joy over what they had just seen. The celebration continued until Stone Bear raised his arms and signaled for silence. He went over to the young warrior who stood over von Eichhorn's body with the saber in his hand still dripping blood. The chief threw his arms around the young man and pounded him on the back in congratulations. Then he spoke to the young warrior.

The young warrior wiped the saber on the corpse's clothes, as the other man had done after winning his battle, then solemnly returned it to Stone Bear. Another warrior took charge of both sabers and their scabbards.

Stone Bear turned, walked over to Reese Coburn, the last male captive standing, and said, "That leaves you, white man. What is your choice?" A sneer curled Stone Bear's lip. "How will *you* die?"

Chapter 22

Only the presence of several guards standing around Coburn with lances held ready to pierce his body had held him back while von Eichhorn was fighting the deadly duel with the young Blackfoot warrior. He had felt an almost overpowering urge to rush forward, grab von Eichhorn, and try to shake some sense into the arrogant young Prussian.

But all that would have gotten him was a quick death, and Coburn knew it. Interfering with von Eichhorn's battle would have been committing suicide just as surely as Lieutenant Barton had.

So he had waited and watched in stony silence, knowing all too well how this fight was going to end, unless fate somehow intervened miraculously.

Fate had not been kind enough to do that.

Coburn looked levelly into Stone Bear's eyes and said, "I choose tomahawks."

"You have fought with them before?" Stone Bear wanted to know.

Coburn smiled thinly. "A time or two."

In fact, he had fought for his life with tomahawks on numerous occasions, although never against the Blackfeet.

He went on. "How about it, Stone Bear? You want to take me on?"

Stone Bear's smirk turned into a scowl. "Have a care," he said. "If you seek to disgrace me in front of my people, you will die screaming from torture."

"So you're sayin' you won't fight me." Coburn smiled. "Want me to ask it louder, in your lingo?"

Stone Bear didn't reply as his hand went to the tomahawk that rested in a rawhide loop at his waist. He pulled the weapon free, raised it in the air, and shouted to the villagers, who returned the cry and added some whoops of their own. Stone Bear gestured with the tomahawk in his hand. One of the other warriors drew his own 'hawk, carried it over to Coburn, and extended the handle to the frontiersman.

Smiling, Coburn took the weapon. He knew that Stone Bear wouldn't have been the chief of these people if he wasn't a formidable warrior. He couldn't take anything for granted—including the fact that Stone Bear had promised to grant the victor his life, although not his freedom, if any of them defeated their opponent.

Would Stone Bear honor that promise if *he* was the one who was defeated? How could he do otherwise without being dishonored in the eyes of his people?

If he actually killed Stone Bear, Coburn warned himself, the chief wouldn't be alive anymore to ensure that his pledge was kept. If Coburn defeated him but *didn't* kill him, Stone Bear would have a constant reminder of what had happened, and there was no telling how he would take out the resentment he was bound to feel.

Maybe it would have been better if he *hadn't* challenged the chief, mused Coburn. He had been so horrified and outraged over what had happened to von Eichhorn, though, not to mention how much Stone Bear's arrogance just flat rubbed him the wrong way, that he hadn't thought it all out.

Too late to do anything about it now. In a manner of speaking, he and Stone Bear were trapped. Neither of them could do anything except go ahead with the fight.

In that case, Coburn intended to win.

"Are you ready, white man?" asked the Blackfoot chief.

"More than ready," Coburn replied. "I've been achin' to do this ever since we first ran into you, old son." With that, he lunged at Stone Bear and swung the tomahawk. He didn't follow through on the blow but stopped short as Stone Bear leaped back to avoid it. Coburn laughed.

Stone Bear's face darkened with anger. His enemy had made him look foolish, almost cowardly. Stone Bear rushed forward, slashing back and forth with his tomahawk.

Coburn flung up his left arm and blocked Stone Bear's arm, then turned sharply and rammed his right shoulder into the Blackfoot's chest. The impact knocked Stone Bear back. Coburn chopped at his head. Stone Bear twisted aside. The tomahawk missed him, but the wooden handle slammed down on top of his left shoulder. Stone Bear grimaced in pain and swung the tomahawk at Coburn in a backhanded swipe. Coburn jumped back to avoid the blow.

Stone Bear followed and tried to kick his legs out from under him. With a nimble move, Coburn danced out of the way. Stone Bear slashed at him again. The tomahawk scraped along his ribs but didn't do any damage. With his left fist, Coburn hooked a punch to the chief's jaw that rocked Stone Bear to the side.

Coburn smashed the flat of the tomahawk's head against Stone Bear's forearm. He could have used the edge and left a significant wound, but he didn't want to kill his opponent. If he could disarm Stone Bear, the chief might declare him the victor rather than continue.

Even though Coburn's blow caused Stone Bear to drop the tomahawk, he reacted instantly and dived forward, ramming into Coburn's thighs and knocking him off his feet. As the American sprawled on the ground, Stone Bear scooped up the fallen tomahawk and whirled it high in the air before bringing it down in a strike almost too swift for the eye to follow.

Coburn's eyes followed it, though, and he rolled desperately aside just in time. He felt the tomahawk whip through the air only inches from his ear. The head struck the ground, embedding its sharp edge.

Coburn jerked his leg up and snapped his foot out in a kick that landed on Stone Bear's ribs. The chief grunted in pain and tried to grab Coburn's leg with his left arm, but it wasn't working too well because of the blow to that shoulder a few moments earlier. Coburn broke free of the clumsy grasp and scrambled a few yards away to put some room between them before he climbed back to his feet.

Breathing hard, Coburn's chest rose and fell rapidly as he watched Stone Bear stand up. The chief looked a little winded, too. Neither of them was as young as they had been, although both were still in the prime of life. But a fight like this was hard, tiring, and dangerous work.

Even so, Coburn worked up a grin and said, "Want to call it a draw?"

With an angry shout, Stone Bear charged him again.

For a fast couple of minutes, the tomahawks flashed back and forth and the men wielding them jumped and twisted this way and that. The Blackfoot onlookers roared in anticipation every time it seemed that Stone Bear was about to strike a fatal blow. They held their breath when the chief faltered and the white captive appeared to get the upper hand. The battle ebbed one way and flowed the other, and neither combatant was able to seize the advantage for more than a moment.

During one of the inevitable lulls when both men tried to catch their breath, Coburn saw from the corner of his eye that Countess Katarina and the other women had recovered a little from the sick horror that had gripped them at von Eichhorn's gruesome death. All were watching this fight avidly. Coburn couldn't afford to take much of his attention off of Stone Bear, but he thought he spotted a bit of hope in Katarina's gaze.

He didn't want to let her down. He didn't know if he would be able to do anything to help her and the other women if he survived the battle—but he sure as blazes couldn't do anything for them if he died!

Then he had his hands full again, warding off a fresh attack from Stone Bear.

For the first time, Coburn thought he detected a little desperation in the chief's manner. Stone Bear's expression was every bit as flinty as ever, but his movements were just a bit jerkier, a little rushed and not quite as crisp and swift as they had been.

Wary of letting himself get overconfident, Coburn didn't attack any more aggressively than he had been so far. He didn't want to fall into the same trap von Eichhorn had. As long as he could defend himself, it wouldn't hurt anything to let Stone Bear get even more worn out.

As if he knew the fight had to end soon, Stone Bear pressed his attack. Each man was bleeding from several scratches inflicted during the battle, but neither had suffered any serious injuries—a testament to their mutual skill with the tomahawks.

Finally, Stone Bear missed a blow completely, and the wild swing made him stumble. Coburn kicked the back of the war chief's right knee, causing that leg to buckle, and Stone Bear tumbled to the ground with his right arm outstretched.

Coburn planted a foot on that wrist, pinning the arm and the tomahawk to the ground. He bent, cupped his left hand under Stone Bear's chin, and jerked his head up. Putting the edge of his tomahawk's head against Stone Bear's throat it wouldn't take much pressure to cut deeply into the taut flesh.

The crowd of villagers had gone silent in shock at seeing their chief in such a helpless position.

Marion von Arnim shrieked, "Kill him! Kill the savage!" She added a flood of German curses or further exhortations for him to finish off Stone Bear.

Coburn leaned closer and told the chief, "Nobody ever said this had to be a fight to the death. I'd just as soon let you up and call it over and done with, old son."

Through gritted teeth, Stone Bear said, "You should . . . kill me. Sparing my life . . . will gain you nothing."

"I don't know about that. I don't trust all those other warriors to honor your word and spare *my* life if you're dead. Not to mention, I don't want them takin' out their anger at me on those women . . . and poor Walter."

"No one . . . will hurt them."

"I believe you. Like I said, it's them I don't trust." Coburn pressed a little harder with the keen edge. "What's it gonna be? If I don't have anything to lose either way, I'd just as soon cut your throat."

For a long moment, Stone Bear didn't respond. Then,

still struggling to get the words out because of his position, he said, "The fight . . . is over. You have . . . triumphed. I keep my word, white man. No one . . . will kill you . . . but you will live among us . . . as a slave."

"Deal," said Coburn. *For now*, he added to himself. No telling what the future might bring.

He pulled the tomahawk away from Stone Bear's throat and took a step back. The chief rolled onto his side and then hands and knees. He climbed to his feet and looked at his assembled followers.

In their native tongue, he called out, "The white man has won! I have given him my word that he will not be killed. From now on, he is a slave to our people and will be treated as such, as are the women." He made a slashing motion with his hand. "It is done!"

Subdued and obviously disappointed there had been no more white man's blood spilled, the crowd began to disperse. Coburn tossed the tomahawk back to the warrior who had handed it to him and walked over to Countess Katarina, who waited for him with her arm around von Stauffenberg's shoulders.

"I . . . I did not think you would win," she said quietly. "I prayed that you would, but I could not make myself actually believe it."

Coburn's heart was still beating heavily as he drew in a deep breath and smiled. "To tell you the truth, neither did I. But I figured I'd give it my best shot and see what happened."

"What *will* happen? Will they truly let you live?"

Coburn glanced at Stone Bear, who was regarding him with an expression of pure hatred.

"For now," he told Katarina. "Right now, his word means more to him than the anger he's feelin' toward me. But who knows if that'll change in the future."

"My people will come and find us," she said. "We cannot just disappear into this . . . this wilderness without someone wanting to find us. Someday help will come."

"I hope you're right, Your Countessship." He squeezed Walter's uninjured arm and gave the young man a reassuring smile. "If you are . . . it's gonna be up to us to stay alive somehow until that help gets here."

Chapter 23

Fort Laramie, 1852

By the time the sun was up, the members of the expedition were mounted and ready to go. At the head of the group, alongside Preacher and Colonel Finlay Sutton, Jamie hipped around in the saddle and studied the men behind him.

Roscoe Lomax was beside the young lieutenant, Thomas Curry, who was Sutton's second in command. Behind them, riding two abreast, were forty-eight US Army dragoons. Then came Baron Adalwolf von Kuhner, Feldwebel Herman Becker, and a dozen Prussian mounted troops. Bringing up the rear were a couple of sergeants and a pair of corporals in charge of the eight pack animals and a dozen spare mounts.

Stretched out that way along the edge of the parade ground, it was an impressive bunch. Seventy-one well-armed men setting out into the wilderness in search of . . . what?

Jamie didn't know. He didn't hold out much hope of finding any of the original group alive, but he supposed it was possible one or two of them might still be prisoners of the Blackfeet led by Stone Bear.

After the brawl in the sutler's store the previous night, he wasn't sure how smoothly things would go this morning, but other than some hard looks exchanged between the dragoons and the Prussians, nothing had happened. Lomax and Becker, especially, had traded glares, but other than that, the two men steered clear of each other.

Jamie had had another talk with Lomax and warned him to be on his best behavior. The bullwhacker promised that he would try.

Jamie faced forward again in the saddle and looked over at Sutton. "You ready to go, Colonel?"

"I don't see any point in waiting," Sutton replied. "Before we get back, we may be in a race against the weather, so we need to use our time as efficiently as possible."

"In other words," drawled Preacher, "we're burnin' daylight."

Jamie nodded in agreement, raised his arm, and waved his hand forward in a signal for the group to move out.

They rode north, and after only a short time, they came to the North Platte River. At first glance, the river wasn't a formidable obstacle. Jamie had heard it described as being "a mile wide and an inch deep." That was an exaggeration, but except in times of rare flooding, the broad stream was shallow and flowed sluggishly as it twisted across the prairie.

Fording it could be dangerous anyway, due to numerous bogs and stretches of quicksand among its many channels.

Jamie said, "Preacher, that stallion of yours always seems to know where he's going. Why don't you take the lead?"

"I was just thinkin' the same thing myself," the mountain man agreed. He moved out and let Horse have his head. Slowly, the rangy gray stallion began picking his way across the North Platte. Muddy brown water splashed and swirled around his hooves.

Jamie followed him. Colonel Sutton turned in his saddle and called to Curry, "Keep an eye on us and ride where we ride, Lieutenant. Don't allow the men to stray from that path."

"Yes, sir!" Curry turned and relayed the order to the dragoons, then started after Sutton.

Jamie didn't expect any trouble from the American soldiers. They would do as they were told. He didn't know how much the Prussians could be counted on to do the same. Von Kuhner and Becker struck him as the sort to believe they knew better than their American guides and might strike off on their own, winding up in trouble.

Von Kuhner barked orders in his native tongue, though, and the Prussian troops were just as careful as the American dragoons during the river crossing. Everybody forded the stream without any problems. Jamie and Preacher sat on horseback on a slight rise just north of the river and watched the last of the pack animals emerge from the shallow, muddy water.

"Well, they done what the baron told 'em to do," said Preacher. "Leastways, I reckon he told 'em to follow your orders. I don't savvy none o' that gruntin'."

"I don't understand much of it, either," Jamie said. "But they all made it across, and that's what I was worried about."

Preacher laughed. "You know this here is probably the easiest part of the whole trip, don't you?"

"Yeah," said Jamie. "I reckon I do."

* * *

For the first few days the expedition proceeded northward at a steady, ground-eating pace without encountering any trouble. Jamie didn't expect that good luck to last, but he would take all he could get.

It ended on the fifth day, which dawned with a cold, miserable rain falling. All the previous day, Jamie had watched the clouds drifting slowly toward them from the north. It wasn't a blue norther—too early in the season for that—or the sort of toad-strangler that could cause flooding, but it didn't take long for the steady rain to turn the ground into muddy gumbo that made the horses work twice as hard to get through it. With every step, the mud sucked stubbornly at their hooves.

The men didn't like being chilled and wet, either, and that caused tensions to run high. The two dragoons who served as cooks for the party managed to rig a cover from a piece of oilcloth that allowed them to build a small fire, but it was a constant struggle to keep the flames going while they tried to boil coffee, fry salt pork, and bake some biscuits.

They managed to slap together a skimpy breakfast, but nobody was really satisfied. The midday meal was more of the same.

While the two cooks were cleaning up, one of the Prussian soldiers walked up in a slicker, with rain sluicing off his pointed helmet, and said something in his language as he put his fists on his hips and sneered. The way he followed that by turning his head and spitting made it perfectly clear that he wasn't being complimentary.

One of the dragoons straightened from what he was doing and demanded, "What was that you said, you damn Dutchman?"

The Prussian let out another spate of German, including the word *schwein*.

The other dragoon scowled and said, "I think he's sayin' that the food we fixed ain't fit for the hogs, Jessup."

The first dragoon planted *his* fists on his hips, stuck out his chest and his chin, and crowded close to the Prussian. "Is that what you're sayin', mister? That our food ain't fit for the hogs?"

"Weg von mir, dummkopf!"

The first dragoon looked around at his comrade. "What'd he say?"

"Dunno. But if I had to guess, I'd say he called you stupid. *Dummkopf* means dummy, don't it?"

The Prussian laughed, nodded, and said, *"Ja, dummkopf! Ein verdammt dummkopf!"*

The dragoon called Jessup erupted with curses. "No damn furriner's gonna call me names!" he yelled as he swung a punch at the Prussian's face.

He moved fast enough that the Prussian wasn't able to block the blow. Jessup's fist smacked cleanly into the Prussian's face and rocked his head back, making him stagger back a couple of steps.

The Prussian caught his balance, roared something in his native tongue, and charged the dragoon who had just struck him. Jessup leaped to the side, stuck out a leg, and the Prussian stumbled over it. As the Prussian took several wild steps forward, waving his arms and trying to keep from falling, the second dragoon clubbed his hands together and smashed them down on the foreign soldier's back.

The Prussian fell hard and buried his face in the mud when he landed.

He came up sputtering and choking as he clawed at his

mouth, nose, and eyes. A man could drown in mud. He swiped it desperately away from his face as the two dragoons laughed at him.

That laughter came to an abrupt end as another bull-like bellow sounded behind him. They jerked their heads around and tried to turn, but they didn't make it in time. Another Prussian soldier, with his arms stretched out as far as he could reach on both sides, plowed into them and swept them off their feet.

More Prussians were right behind him. They pounced on the two dragoons, pinning them to the ground, hammering punches at them, digging knees into the Americans' ribs.

The fight hadn't gone unnoticed, of course. Yelling eagerly, more dragoons stomped through the mud, grabbed the Prussians, and pulled them off the two cooks. They weren't much more fond of the food the two men had come up with than the Prussians were, but they weren't going to stand by and do nothing while foreigners pounded on Americans.

The dragoons outnumbered the foreign troops four to one, and although not everyone on either side joined in the battle, it wasn't long before the overwhelming odds meant that all the Prussians who had jumped into the fight were down, being pummeled and kicked and having their faces forced into the deep mud. Lieutenant Curry and Feldwebel Becker stood on the outskirts of the fight and yelled orders for the men to stop, but no one paid any attention to them.

Preacher and Jamie arrived and waded into the melee. Jamie grabbed two of the dragoons by their collars, hauled them upright, and flung them behind him like rag dolls. A few feet away, Preacher wrapped an arm around another dragoon's neck and hauled him off the man he was trying to drown in the mud.

Dog didn't want to be left out and darted in and out of the fight, snarling and snapping but not actually biting anyone. Even so, the big cur was intimidating enough to make men let go of their opponents and scramble to get away from him.

Colonel Sutton added his voice to those of Curry and Becker as they shouted for a stop to the hostilities. Finally, the Americans withdrew, cursing and stumbling in the muck. The Prussians, their uniforms covered with the thick, sticky stuff, struggled upright and tried to get the mud out of their mouths, noses, and eyes.

Baron von Kuhner stalked over to Sutton and snapped, "The behavior of your men is abominable, Colonel! I have never seen such an undisciplined rabble."

Lieutenant Curry stiffened in outrage and began, "Now listen here, mister—"

Sutton raised a hand to silence the young officer. To von Kuhner, he said coldly, "I wouldn't start casting blame before we even know what happened, Baron. I assure you, I intend to find out, and if any of my troops were responsible for this, they'll be punished appropriately."

Von Kuhner sneered. "I would have such brawlers flogged."

"With all due respect, Baron"—Sutton's tone made it clear that not much actual respect was involved—"these dragoons aren't under your command."

"I believe the orders from your War Department said for you to assist us in any way possible. That could be interpreted as meaning that *all* of you are under my command."

"And that interpretation would be incorrect," Sutton shot back just as sharply.

The two of them glared at each other in the rain for several seconds, then von Kuhner said, "This mission cannot succeed if our men are always at each other's throats."

"Now *that*, I agree with, Baron. I assure you, I'll take steps to see that it doesn't happen again."

Off to one side, Jamie and Preacher glanced at each other. The meaning behind the look they exchanged was clear to both of them. Colonel Sutton could promise all he wanted to that such a battle wouldn't happen again . . . but neither of the two frontiersmen believed for a second that such an outcome was likely.

Jamie looked around and said quietly, "Where's Lomax? I'm a mite surprised that he wasn't in the big middle of that ruckus."

"I'm right here, MacCallister," said Lomax from behind them. He stepped around to join them. "Didn't I tell you I was gonna keep out of trouble from now on?"

"You told me," Jamie admitted.

"But you didn't believe me, did you?" Instead of being offended, Lomax chuckled. "You just hide and watch, MacCallister. You'll see that I meant what I said."

"For all of our sakes, I hope you're right." Jamie looked at the muddy figures stumbling around, getting ready to break the midday camp and push on. He shook his head in disgust at the pathetic sight.

No matter how large and well-armed this bunch was, he wasn't sure they were going to stand a chance against the Blackfeet.

Chapter 24

The rain stayed with them the rest of that day, all night, and was still coming down the next morning. Despite their best efforts, all the men were soaked to the skin, chilled to the bone, and miserable to the depths of their souls.

Colonel Sutton sought out Jamie and Preacher. "You men are more familiar with this region than I am. How long is a rain such as this likely to last?"

Roscoe Lomax, who was standing close enough to overhear the conversation, spoke up before either of the other two frontiersmen could answer. "One time down on the Santa Fe Trail at this time o' year," he said, "I seen it rain for more 'n a week solid, without ever a letup. The wagons all bogged down so bad they couldn't move, and we just had to wait it out."

Sutton looked alarmed. "Do you think the mud will get bad enough that it's impassable?"

"Probably not, since we're on horseback, not hauling wagons," said Jamie. "We can keep moving. It'll just be mighty slow going, though."

"Then you don't believe we should stay here and try to wait it out?"

"Ain't no tellin' how long it's gonna rain," said Preacher. "Might last another week, like Lomax said, or it might stop and clear off before the day's over. No way of knowin' what it's gonna do."

Sutton thought the situation over for a long moment, then nodded. "In that case, we might as well push on as best we can. We'll still be covering ground toward our destination, even if we're not going very fast."

"There'll likely be some complaints," Jamie warned the colonel.

"I don't care. It's their job on both sides to follow orders. We'll have breakfast as best we can and then prepare to move out. I'll tell Lieutenant Curry to issue the orders."

Jamie, Preacher, and Lomax all nodded.

Jamie's prediction was accurate. A lot of grumbling went on as the men got ready to move out, but by the time a lessening of the gloom suggested the sun was up, the expedition was on its way again, slowly slogging northward.

Preacher hadn't made a prediction about the weather, but he had mentioned the possibility that the rain could stop and the clouds might break up before the day was over. That was exactly what happened. By the middle of the day, the steady, sluicing rain tailed off to a drizzle. It slowed even more and finally stopped completely by the middle of the afternoon.

Not long after that, gaps began to appear in the clouds to the north, and narrow areas of blue sky were visible. The sun wasn't shining, yet, but the world began to seem like a brighter, less miserable place.

When the sun finally came out, the temperature rose quickly, growing quite warm for the season. The dampness rising from the soaked landscape made the air heavy and oppressive. Even so, everyone was so glad the rain had stopped that a sort of merriment gripped the group.

Preacher remarked on that to Jamie. "Those ol' boys may be in such a good mood they'll feel like fightin' again, just to let off some steam."

"Could be," Jamie agreed. "Or maybe the spirit of good fellowship will keep things peaceful for a while."

Preacher grunted and frowned dubiously at the idea but didn't argue.

When they made camp, the atmosphere was more like what Jamie had suggested. Particularly after the Prussians got a couple of bottles from their supplies and began passing them around, even sharing them with some of the American dragoons.

Jamie found Feldwebel Becker and asked the noncommissioned officer, "What sort of who-hit-John is in those bottles they're passing around?"

Becker frowned in confusion. "Who-hit-John," he repeated. "*Was ist los?* Do you mean, what sort of drink is it?"

"That's right."

"Ah. *Schnapps. Obstbrand.* Apple and pear brandy."

Jamie nodded. "I've heard of the stuff. I don't know how good an idea it is to let them get drunk. They'll have headaches in the morning."

Becker snorted. "They are good, strong men. Mere headaches will not bother them."

"As long as they can get up and do whatever they need to, I suppose it won't hurt anything."

"Including fight Indians?"

Jamie squinted in thought. "It'll be another week or more before we get into Blackfoot country. Of course, there's always a chance we might run across some Cheyenne or

Kiowa who feel like a scrap. Most of the tribes are busy hunting right now, so they can stock up on meat for the winter. They're not as interested in raiding and fighting at this time of year."

"It might be good to have some fighting along the way," said Becker. "My men will get . . . rusty, is that how you say it? . . . if they go too long without spilling blood."

"They'll get their chance before we're done," Jamie said confidently.

From where the men were gathered around the cooking fire, a song suddenly burst out. Jamie couldn't understand the words and figured the Prussians were singing in their own language. The song had a harsh, martial sound to it. Some of the Americans must have been picking up on it, because they joined in, even though they probably had no idea what they were singing about.

Becker walked off, and Jamie rejoined Preacher, closer to the fire.

The mountain man made a face and said, "That racket'll hurt your ears after a while. I think Dog's fixin' to start howlin' along with 'em."

"Yeah, it doesn't sound very good," Jamie said, "but at least they're not throwing punches at each other."

Hangovers were plentiful the next morning, but other than being bleary-eyed and stumbling around a little more than usual, the men were able to get up, prepare for the day, and move out as usual.

After they had been riding for a while, Lieutenant Curry rode up to the front of the column. "Colonel, one of the men on guard duty last night told me that he heard some sort of wild animals howling out on the prairie, not too far from the camp. Do you think it could have been wolves? Do we need to increase the guard at night?"

"It weren't wolves," Preacher said, shaking his head.

"I heard the same thing," Jamie said, "and I agree it wasn't wolves."

"Indians?" Sutton asked with a worried frown.

"That's right. They were scouting us out, trying to decide just how big a force we have and what they should do about it."

"Probably all that bellerin' the boys were doin' earlier in the evenin' attracted 'em," Preacher said. "Although they would've seen the fire anyway."

"Do you think they're going to attack us?" asked Sutton.

"They were considering it last night, more than likely," Jamie said. "I was ready to give the alarm if they came much closer. But they backed off and then went away."

"So they're *not* going to attack us?"

"They decided not to, but only for last night." Jamie shrugged. "Hard to say what they'll decide today or tonight, or two or three nights from now."

"Well, that's certainly nerve-racking," said Curry.

"Travelin' in Injun country usually is, Lieutenant," Preacher said.

They were still on the plains, curving gradually each day closer to the mountains that were visible as a bluish-gray line on the western horizon. Eventually, that route would take them into the Rockies, deep into the territory where the Blackfeet under Stone Bear roamed.

Before they ever got there, however, they had to pass through the region where some of the other tribes were common. Although the Cheyenne, Kiowa, Pawnee, and Sioux weren't as uniformly hostile to whites as the Blackfeet were, they were fully capable of launching an attack on the group if the mood struck them.

"Might be a good idea if a couple of scouts went on ahead a ways, just to look for signs of trouble," Preacher went on. "I nominate myself as one of 'em."

"And I'll be the other," Jamie said.

Without hesitation, Colonel Sutton said, "I'd rather you didn't do that, Jamie. It seems to me that one of you should stay here with the main body of the expedition."

Preacher grinned. "So we don't both get killed at the same time? I reckon the colonel's got a point there, Jamie."

"I'll go," Roscoe Lomax said as he urged his horse up alongside those of the other four men. "Sorry. I was back there eavesdroppin', I guess you'd say. But I've done some scoutin' before, down yonder on the Santa Fe Trail, and I've got a good eye for trouble, if I do say so myself."

Jamie looked at Preacher and asked, "What do you think?"

The mountain man shrugged. "I don't have a problem with Lomax goin' along."

"It's settled, then," Sutton said. "Lieutenant, go advise Baron von Kuhner there's a possibility of encountering hostiles and ask him to order his men to be especially watchful. I want that order passed along to our men, as well."

Curry said, "Yes, sir," and turned his horse to ride back along the column.

"If you run into anything, let us know as quick as you can," Jamie said to Preacher and Lomax. "I'm especially worried about those bluffs up there." He nodded toward a pair of low bluffs that flanked their route on either side, a couple of miles north of their current position. The gap between the bluffs was at least half a mile wide, so it wasn't really a potential trap they were riding into . . . but the bluffs would make it easier for war parties to hide and launch a two-sided flank attack against them.

"I saw 'em myself and was thinkin' the same thing you are," Preacher told Jamie. "Come on, Lomax. Let's see if we can scare up some trouble."

They urged their horses ahead of the rest of the group. Dog came along, too, of course, bounding out ahead. The ground had dried enough following the storm's passing that the mud didn't slow them down much. Soon they were able to leave Jamie and the others at least half a mile behind.

Lomax wasn't the sort to ride in silence. Since it was the first time he and Preacher had been alone together for more than a few seconds he said, "I've heard a heap of stories about you, Preacher. Back in my drinkin' and brawlin' days, I always boasted that I was a real ring-tailed roarer. I reckon you're the genuine article, though."

"Them drinkin' and brawlin' days are behind you, are they?" asked Preacher, deliberately not addressing the implication to his legendary status.

"That's what I've been tryin' to tell MacCallister. He's a pretty stubborn hombre when it comes to believin', though."

"Jamie's the sort of fella who's got to see things with his own eyes before he believes anything." Preacher looked over at Lomax as they entered the gap between the bluffs. "I'm the same way myself."

"Ain't I stayed out of trouble?" Lomax demanded, frowning. His voice had a defensive, injured tone to it.

"For a while. Keep it up."

Lomax sighed and shook his head. "What folks like you and MacCallister forget is that the rest of us are just human, with plenty o' human failin's. We ain't all like you."

"I never said I wasn't human. Shoot, even as old as I am . . . and I'm ten years older 'n Jamie, mind you . . . I get a mite too reckless sometimes. And I've sure been known to lose my temper. But I've got in the habit of tryin' to keep a tight rein on it." Preacher nodded slowly. "You'll get there, Lomax. At least, I have a hunch you will."

"Them words mean a lot to me, Preacher, especially comin' from somebody like—" Lomax stopped short, and his eyes narrowed as he turned his head to gaze toward the bluff to the east. "Thought I caught a glimpse of somethin' movin' up there," he said quietly.

Preacher was gazing toward the western bluff. "And I saw the same thing over yonder. Not much, just a little flicker of somethin'."

"Injuns?"

"Could be." Preacher nodded toward Dog. The big cur had slowed his pace. Instead of ranging well ahead of the two riders, he walked along deliberately, his shaggy head swinging from side to side.

The mountain man went on. "He smells somethin' that's got him wary. And it's on both sides of us."

"Them bluffs are hundreds of yards away. Can he really smell redskins that far off?"

"I wouldn't put it past him," Preacher said. "I've never gone wrong trustin' his instincts, neither. In fact—" He tightened his grip on Horse's reins and slowed the big stallion.

Beside him, Lomax reined in, too.

"Dog, stay," Preacher called quietly to the cur.

Dog sat, but he kept turning his head back and forth to

look at the bluffs. The hair on the back of his neck stood up, and a low growl came from deep in his throat.

After a moment, Preacher let out a soft whistle of surprise. "Would you look at that?"

"I'm lookin'," Lomax said, "but I ain't likin' what I'm seein'."

Neither did Preacher. His keen eyes had no trouble seeing the dozens of mounted figures that pushed forward until they and their ponies were poised at the edge of the bluff to the west. He saw the feathered headdresses several of the men sported, and each of the other men had a feather or two in his hair. Some held rifles with the butts resting on their thighs and the barrels pointing almost straight up in the air. Others were armed with lances or bows and arrows.

A glance in the other direction told Preacher that a force of roughly equal size had just appeared on the rim of the eastern bluff.

"Well, hell," breathed Lomax. "That don't look good. How many do you reckon there are, Preacher?"

"Fifty or sixty that we can see. Might be more than that farther back."

"So we've got 'em outnumbered by a little. Maybe. Or maybe we don't."

Preacher nodded. "Yeah. That's about the size of it."

"Why do you think they showed themselves to us like that? They could've stayed back out of sight until they were ready to jump us."

"They might be intendin' on jumpin' us. Could be they just want us to know they're there. Maybe they think we'll be scared enough to turn back."

"But we won't, will we?"

"Nope," Preacher said. "This is the shortest way to where we're goin', so I reckon we'll keep on."

"Maybe they're just showin' off," Lomax said. "But we'd better head back and tell MacCallister and the colonel anyway."

"You do that. I'll wait for you right here."

"You're gonna stay out here in front by yourself?" Lomax frowned. "I ain't sure that's a good idea, Preacher. Won't they be more likely to attack?"

The mountain man grunted. "They ain't more scared of the two of us than they are of just me," he pointed out.

"Yeah, I reckon what I said don't make much sense, does it?" Lomax lifted his reins. "All right. I'll alert the others. I don't know what MacCallister and the colonel will decide to do."

"I do. They'll keep coming, Injuns or no Injuns."

"You're probably right." Lomax wheeled his horse and galloped back toward the rest of the group.

Preacher sat his saddle calmly. It wasn't the first time he'd been in a situation such as this. Most times, you couldn't predict what was going to happen, especially where Indians were concerned. You just had to wait and see which way they were going to jump.

He looked behind him. The rest of the riders were in sight, entering the wide gap between the bluffs. He saw Lomax riding toward them. Jamie almost certainly had already spotted the Indians, so Lomax wouldn't be telling him anything he didn't already know.

The warriors on the bluffs hadn't budged. They were just sitting there and waiting.

Preacher leaned over and spat. A grin creased his leathery face. Dog growled again.

"Take it easy, old-timer. It won't be long now. I look at those Injuns and my gut tells me that all hell's about to break loose."

Chapter 25

"Who's that coming this way?" asked Colonel Sutton. He had just signaled for the column to halt when he and Jamie spotted the man galloping toward them.

"That's Lomax," Jamie replied, having no trouble identifying the bullwhacker even at that distance.

"Do you think something's happened to Preacher?"

"It's more likely Preacher sent him back with a message. And I can make a pretty good guess what it is." Jamie peered at the bluff to the east, then slowly swung his gaze back to the west. The column was far enough back that he couldn't make out any details yet, but he was sure that a large number of warriors mounted on swift, sturdy ponies waited atop those bluffs.

A few minutes later, Lomax pounded up to them and reined in. "Injuns on both sides of us, MacCallister," he reported. "Preacher says there's fifty or sixty of the red devils."

"Then we have them outnumbered," said Sutton.

Jamie said, "If you can see fifty or sixty Indians, there's liable to be that many more you *can't* see, somewhere close by."

"Yeah, Preacher said the same thing," Lomax agreed. "But he said he figured you'd want to come on ahead, anyway."

Jamie nodded. "Not much else we can do, except maybe circle a lot of miles out of the way. That would take time we can't afford, and we might just run into the same problem no matter which way we go. Better to just push on, and if there's going to be trouble, we'll get it out of the way now."

"Is there any possibility those hostiles *aren't* waiting to ambush us?" Sutton wanted to know.

"It's possible. They may just be trying to impress us with a show of force, so that we'll be more likely to keep moving and not linger in their territory."

"How likely is that?"

"Only one way to find out."

Sutton gave him a resigned nod, then turned and called to Curry, "We're moving on, Lieutenant."

"Yes, sir!" Curry barked orders at the men, who nudged their horses into motion again.

Lomax asked Jamie, "You want me to ride up yonder where Preacher is?"

"No need," Jamie replied. "We'll be catching up with him in a little while." Hoofbeats coming up behind them made him look around.

Baron von Kuhner was approaching with an angry expression on his beefy face. "What do you think you are doing?" he demanded as he drew even with Jamie and Sutton. "It appears that we are riding directly into an ambush!" He waved his arm to indicate both bluffs. "There are savages waiting up there!"

"So far they haven't made a move," Jamie said. "If we keep going, maybe they won't."

"Do you honestly believe that?"

"Well, Baron . . . there's not much else we *can* do, so I reckon worrying about whether or not we *should* is just wasted effort."

Von Kuhner glared at him, but the Prussian couldn't argue with Jamie's logic. Still scowling, he slowed his horse and fell back along the column until he was riding again at the head of his men.

"Lieutenant," Sutton called.

"Sir?" Curry asked when he joined them.

"Drop back and keep an eye on the baron and his men. He's nervous, and a nervous man makes mistakes. He might decide to fire a shot at those Indians, and we don't want to be the ones to start any hostilities. If the baron or anybody else looks like he's about to open fire, you stop them, understand?"

"Yes, sir." Curry turned his horse and trotted back along the line of riders.

Jamie said, "That's good thinking, Colonel. As long as there's even a chance we can get through this without a fight, we need to take it."

Sutton nodded, but the worried frown he wore remained on his face.

A short time later, they reached the spot where Preacher, Horse, and Dog were waiting for them. The mountain man said, "They ain't moved a lick. I don't reckon that'll last much longer, though."

"You don't think they're just trying to impress us?" Jamie asked.

"Could be. But that ain't what my belly says. It tells me they're just drawin' things out to make us more worried."

"If such is their intention," said Sutton, "then their effort has been a success!"

Jamie chuckled and said, "I reckon one way or another, we'll know pretty soon, Colonel."

He was right. Less than thirty seconds later, a shrill whoop sounded on each bluff. The line of mounted Indians suddenly surged down the slopes, which were gentle enough that the ponies were able to work up some speed by the time they reached level ground.

"Here they come!" Preacher said.

Ever since they had started the nerve-racking ride through the gap, Jamie had been looking for places where they might be able to take cover and fight off the attack. Unfortunately, the Indians had chosen well. Although a clump of rocks was about fifty yards away, and just west of it a shallow gully, the cover was adequate to protect the horses, though, and if the Indians killed their mounts and left them afoot, they would have no chance of getting out of there.

"Head for those rocks!" he called. "When you get there, get those horses down flat on the ground! Use the rocks and the gully for cover! And keep the horses down!"

The dragoons were already galloping past him as he shouted the orders. Despite their lack of experience, they were responding well to the danger and seemed to be keeping their heads.

The same couldn't be said of the Prussian troops, who milled around aimlessly for a moment even though von Kuhner and Becker were screaming orders at them. A couple of the men brought their rifles to their shoulders and fired at the Indians, unaware or not caring that the attackers were still well out of range.

Jamie rode back to them and waved his arm toward the rocks. "Move, move!" he bellowed at them. "Baron, get your men to cover!"

Von Kuhner yelled at them some more, and finally the men started riding toward the rocks. The Indians were almost in range. In fact, Jamie spotted a few puffs of powder smoke. The warriors armed with rifles were trying some long shots. That might demoralize the white men, even if the bullets never reached them.

Jamie fell back to the rear of the column, and helped the soldiers hazing the pack animals and extra mounts. The men drove the animals toward the rocks. One of the sergeants called to Jamie, "We'll never be able to save all these horses, Mr. MacCallister!"

"Save the ones you can!" Jamie told him. "And look out for yourselves, too!"

As he reined in near the rocks, he pulled out one of the new Sharps rifles sheathed in a scabbard strapped to his saddle and dropped to the ground. Turning the horse so he could rest the barrel across the saddle, he aimed toward the Indians charging from the eastern bluff.

From the corner of his eye, he saw that Preacher had had the same idea. The mountain man had drawn his own Sharps and was bracing it on his saddle as Horse stood absolutely still.

Jamie turned his attention to what he was doing and drew a bead on one of the warriors in the lead. His feathered headdress fluttering wildly as he charged, the warrior pumped a lance in the air over his head as he opened his mouth to howl a war cry.

Jamie squeezed the trigger.

The Sharps boomed and kicked hard against his shoulder. The horse flinched a little at the thunderous report, but not much. The cloud of gray smoke from the barrel cleared quickly, just in time for Jamie to see the Indian's head seemingly explode like a melon. The feathers from the headdress flew high in the air. Jamie knew that the .52 caliber ball had found its mark.

The sudden, unexpected death of one of their leaders made the Indians' charge slow momentarily. Jamie took advantage of that to reload the Sharps and glance over at Preacher. The mountain man was doing the same thing.

"Get yours?" Jamie called to him.

"Right smack through the heart, by the looks of it! How about you?"

"Blew his head off!"

Preacher nodded curtly and raised the reloaded Sharps again.

As Jamie did likewise, Colonel Sutton walked coolly among his men and called to those already dismounted and stretched out behind the rocks. "Hold your fire! Let them get closer!"

The muskets carried by the dragoons didn't have the range of a Sharps, so Sutton was right to tell his men to wait. Some of the Prussians were still firing, wasting powder and shot. Jamie didn't have time to rein them in. If von Kuhner and Becker couldn't keep their men under control, that was their problem.

He looked around and saw that most of the horses had been pulled down to the ground and were lying on their sides. Some of the dragoons had been assigned to hold the reins of several animals at the same time to keep them from rearing up and possibly bolting.

A group of men including Lieutenant Curry had taken cover in the gully and were turned so they could shoot at the Indians charging from the western bluff. Curry had them holding their fire, too, until the range was better.

Jamie and Preacher lined up their second shots and fired. Two more attackers pitched off their ponies and rolled over when they landed, ending up in limp sprawls telling they were dead.

As Jamie reloaded again, he heard a rifle ball hum through the air not far from his head. He grabbed his horse's reins and pulled the animal's head down, forcing it to lie on the ground.

As he knelt beside the horse, he called to Sutton, "They're close enough, Colonel!"

Sutton nodded and shouted, "Open fire!"

Chapter 26

Volleys roared out from the men in the rocks and those in the gully. That hail of lead swept across the flat landscape and scythed several of the charging warriors from their mounts.

Some of the ponies were hit, as well, and went down in a welter of flailing legs. Their riders sailed through the air. A few landed running or rolled and came up on their feet again, but most landed awkwardly and didn't rise.

Some even less fortunate had their ponies roll over them, breaking bones and crushing organs.

But not enough of the warriors went down to break the back of the attack. The ones who hadn't been hit continued their charge as the dragoons hastily reloaded. Some were so scared they fumbled the task, but Jamie was glad to see most of the soldiers appeared to remain coolheaded.

On one knee behind a rock, he lined up another shot, arrows began to fly through the air around him. One shaft passed close to him, less than a yard from his head. He squeezed the trigger and as the Sharps boomed, he was rewarded by the sight of a warrior sailing backward off his pony as if he'd been swatted from his seat by a giant hand.

A sudden, strangled scream made Jamie look to his left. One of the dragoons writhed on the ground with an arrow's feathered shaft sticking up from his throat. The head was buried in his neck. Blood welled out around it. The man spasmed a couple of times and then became still in death.

Jamie glanced at the gully. Preacher had joined Lieutenant Curry and some of the dragoons there. The mountain man's Sharps roared, but after the shot, Preacher didn't reload. Instead, he set the rifle aside and drew the pair of Colts he carried. The percussion revolvers thundered as he began firing them, alternating between his right and left hands.

The attackers on Jamie's side were close enough for handguns, too. He pulled out his Walker Colt, eared back the hammer, and centered the small blade sight at the end of the barrel on the chest of one of the warriors. The gun roared and bucked in his hand as he squeezed the trigger.

He didn't wait to see if his shot hit the target. He cocked the revolver again as he shifted his aim. Another shot blasted.

Pounding hoofbeats to his right forced him to twist in that direction. One of the mounted warriors thrust a lance at him. Jamie threw himself to the side, away from the lance and the pony's flashing hooves, and as he came up from the roll, he triggered again as the attacker swept past him.

Angled up, the .44 caliber slug caught the Indian under the chin, bored on up through his brain, and exploded out the top of his head, leaving a fist-sized hole in his skull. The warrior toppled backward off his racing pony and flopped to the ground a few feet from Jamie.

From the markings on the man's painted face and the decorations on his buckskins, Jamie identified him as a Sioux. Not that it really mattered at the moment which tribe was attacking the expedition, but a part of Jamie's brain took note of the knowledge anyway.

With his left hand Jamie scooped up the lance the warrior had dropped on the ground when he died, and surged to his feet, turning to face the other attackers. Another mounted warrior was nearby, trying to draw a bead on him with a rifle. Jamie lunged at the man and thrust up with the lance, driving the sharpened tip into the warrior's chest. The rifle went off as the man jerked the trigger, but the barrel was pointing up as the lance thrust made him rock backward. The shot went harmlessly into the sky, and the impaled warrior pitched off his pony, taking the lance with him.

Suddenly, yipping madly, the rest of the Sioux abandoned the fight and whirled their ponies around. They all raced toward the eastern bluff. Jamie fired the Walker again while they were still in range and saw one of the warriors fling his arms out to the side as the shot struck him between the shoulder blades. He sagged forward over the neck of his pony and then slid off.

Preacher had gotten his Sharps reloaded and blasted another of the retreating warriors off his running mount. A ragged volley came from the defenders to hurry the Indians on their way.

Jamie looked around. Feathered with arrows, three dragoons were lying motionless in death. One of the Prussian soldiers had been killed as well. Half a dozen men were wounded, but Jamie couldn't tell how serious the injuries were.

As far as he could see, only two horses had been killed in the fighting. They had gotten off lucky in that respect.

Colonel Finlay Sutton's face was drawn and haggard

as he came over to Jamie, who asked, "Are you hurt, Colonel?"

"No," Sutton replied, "but I hate to lose any men." He sighed. "It's part of being in command, but that doesn't mean I have to like it."

"No, it sure doesn't. From the looks of things, though, it could've been a lot worse."

Sutton nodded toward the Indians, who were just disappearing over the rim of the eastern bluff. "Are they going to regroup and attack again?"

"Maybe. I think there's a good chance they won't, though. We put up more of a fight than they probably expected. Your men did well, Colonel."

Baron Adalwolf von Kuhner stalked up in time to hear Jamie's last statement and demanded, "And what about my men, Herr MacCallister? How did they fare, in your expert military opinion?"

Anger welled up inside Jamie at the baron's sneering tone. Even in the aftermath of a desperate fight—a fight in which good soldiers had lost their lives—von Kuhner was arrogant and obnoxious.

Jamie controlled his temper and said flatly, "They looked a mite undisciplined to me at first, but when the Sioux got among us, they seemed to be fighting pretty well. From what I could tell." He added dryly, "I was a little busy at the time."

Von Kuhner snorted. He held his saber in his right hand, and Jamie saw blood on the blade. The baron must have fought hand to hand with some of the attackers. Jamie couldn't fault the man's courage—just his attitude.

Preacher and Roscoe Lomax walked up. Jamie was glad to see they appeared to be unhurt. He confirmed that by asking, "Did the two of you come through that little scrape all right?"

"Yeah, we managed not to get pin-cushioned with arrows like those poor varmints," Preacher replied with a nod toward the dead soldiers.

"What do you think, Preacher?" asked Sutton. "Will the Indians attack us again?"

"Not likely. We killed at least a couple dozen of 'em, along with a fair number of their ponies. Reckon there's a good chance they'll leave us alone from here on out." Preacher rubbed his beard-stubbled chin. "Word'll probably spread among the other tribes that it ain't a good idea to jump us."

Von Kuhner glowered at the Americans and exclaimed, "This is madness! Those savages have suffered a galling defeat. Their pride will compel them to attack us again and again until we are wiped out. It is the only way they can regain their honor."

Jamie shook his head slowly. "That may be the way you'd look at it, Baron, but most Indians have a different way of thinking. Their pride and honor are as important to them as to anybody else, but they're also practical. They know there aren't nearly as many of them as there are of us. I'm not talking about just this group, but about whites in general. They've figured out there's a whole heap of us, and we can just keep coming and coming no matter how many of us they kill. But they can't afford to lose a lot of warriors in a fight they may or may not win. That's why they don't attack unless they believe they stand a pretty good chance of winning."

"They attacked us today," von Kuhner pointed out, "and we defeated them."

"That's right. So now they know we're not easy pickings.

They'd rather let us go and store up the resentment they feel at being beaten. They'll take it out on some other bunch that's unlucky enough to cross trails with them in the future."

"Madness," muttered von Kuhner again.

"It's all in how you look at it."

The baron glared at Jamie a moment longer, then turned and walked back to his men.

Preacher watched him go and commented, "That fella is purely a pain to be around."

"Indeed," Colonel Sutton agreed. "But he's our responsibility, along with the mission he's on. And I suppose, since there's some daylight left, we should get on with it."

Digging graves in the still somewhat muddy ground was no easy task, but Lieutenant Curry assigned several men to the detail and it didn't take too long to lay the four dead men to rest. With no other way to leave markers, the burial detail piled rocks on the graves.

In time the disturbed earth would settle, the rocks would be scattered, and no sign would remain that four men were spending eternity there. Everyone who chose to live and work on the frontier knew such a fate might well await them someday.

Preacher and Jamie wouldn't have had it any other way, although Jamie hoped that when his time came, he could be laid to rest on his ranch back in Colorado.

While the burying was going on, the wounded men were tended to. A couple of them had fairly serious arrow wounds, but the best that could be done for them was to clean and bandage the injuries. All of them were able to ride.

Jamie had given some thought to rounding up a few of the Indian ponies left behind by the warriors who had been killed, but the ponies had raced off with the others when the Sioux called off the attack.

The fallen warriors were left where they fell. In all likelihood, their fellows would come back later to retrieve them and carry out their own ceremonies. If not, it would be a bounty for the scavengers.

Preacher stopped several of the Prussian soldiers as they were about to mutilate the dead Sioux. "Blast it," the mountain man told them. "If you want to make those Injuns mad enough to come after us again, just go ahead with what you're doin'. But you'll be damn fools if you do."

The Prussians just looked at him in confusion until Feldwebel Becker repeated in German what Preacher had said in English. Sullenly, they moved away from the bodies and left them alone. Preacher told Lomax to keep an eye on them and make sure none of them tried to sneak back and finish what they'd started.

"Guardin' dead redskins," Lomax muttered. "That ain't somethin' I ever thought I'd be doin'."

Finally, the group was ready to move out again. Everyone kept looking toward the bluffs on either side of the gap, but the Sioux didn't return. Preacher and Jamie's hunch that the Indians weren't interested in any more fighting proved to be accurate.

After several miles, the bluffs fell behind, and the riders moved northward across open plains once again. They were leaving four men behind, but the rest were still headed for Blackfoot country and the mystery and dangers waiting for them there.

Chapter 27

As Preacher had speculated that it might, word must have spread among the tribes about the battle, because as the expedition continued on its north-by-northwest route, it didn't encounter any more trouble.

On several occasions, Jamie, Preacher, and Lomax spotted Indians in the distance, and they had no doubt that scouts from more than one tribe were watching them, but no attacks took place. That was what was important.

When they reached the foothills, towering, snow-capped peaks loomed above them. Coming from a land where such mountains were common, the Prussians weren't impressed, or at least pretended not to be. More than once, though, Jamie caught them gazing around at the scenery in apparent awe.

The weather stayed good. The days were warm, the nights chilly. The rain held off. Jamie and Preacher felt the promise of winter in the air, but they agreed probably it was still a month away, Jamie estimated. Whether that would be long enough to carry out their mission and get started south again, he couldn't say.

Angling in a more westerly direction, the rescue party

skirted the northern end of a small mountain range, and traveled into an area of high valleys, lush with grass and watered by twisting streams that flowed swift and sparkling over rocky beds.

As they made camp on a hill overlooking one of those streams, Jamie told Colonel Sutton, "We're in the heart of Blackfoot territory now. Stone Bear could be anywhere around here. Preacher and I have been talking about it, and we think it might be a good idea to make our main camp here. It's probably not wise to have the whole bunch tramping around the countryside."

"Then how will we find what we're looking for?" Sutton wanted to know.

Jamie smiled and said, "You have the best scout west of the Mississippi working for you, Colonel. I'm talking about Preacher. We need to take advantage of his unique abilities."

Sutton looked a little doubtful. "I know Preacher is quite capable, but let's face it, Jamie. The man's not as young as he used to be."

"None of us are, Colonel. And I'd bet you a brand new hat that when Preacher's in his eighties, he'll still be a man to stand aside from."

Sutton rubbed his chin. "I suppose I can't really argue with that. But you're known for your scouting abilities, too."

"And I'll use 'em if I need to," Jamie said with a nod, "but for now, I think our best move is to turn Preacher loose and see what he can find."

"Sort of like a bloodhound, eh?"

Jamie chuckled. "That's one way of putting it. But I probably won't tell him you said it exactly like that."

Jamie went back to Preacher and told him the colonel agreed with the plan.

"It wouldn't hurt to fortify this hilltop a mite," the mountain man suggested. "Just in case Stone Bear comes to call while I'm out lookin' for him. He might find you before I have a chance to find him."

"Yeah, I'd had the same thought," Jamie agreed. "This wouldn't be a bad place to fort up if we had to."

Preacher reached down and scratched the ears of Dog, who was sitting beside him. "We'll start out first thing in the mornin' and keep makin' bigger circles until we strike some sign. I don't expect it'll take more 'n a few days to find Stone Bear's village. Once we do, you and me will keep an eye on it and see if we can tell whether they've got any captives there."

Jamie nodded. "Sounds like a good plan to me."

They hadn't reckoned with Baron Adalwolf von Kuhner, though. That evening, the Prussian nobleman went over to where Jamie, Preacher, and Lomax were sitting on a log, gnawing on a supper of jerky and leftover biscuits. From the look on von Kuhner's face, Jamie knew right away that the baron wasn't happy.

"Colonel Sutton tells me that we are going to camp here instead of looking for the savages and any prisoners they may have."

"That's not exactly right, Baron," Jamie said. "Preacher's going to be looking for them. We're going to wait and see if he can find them before we try anything else."

Von Kuhner slashed the air with his hand. "A waste of time! We should all be searching. We will locate our quarry sooner."

"Quarry makes it sound like we're on some sort of hunt. We didn't come up here to kill Blackfeet, although there's a good chance it may come to that. We're here to find out if they have any white captives, and if they do, we'll do our best to rescue them." Jamie paused. His voice was hard and flat as he added, "At least, that's the way I see it, Baron. Isn't that what we're after?"

"Of course, we want to free any captives we may find. But we stand a better chance of doing that if we are not all sitting here doing nothing while one man—*one* man!—searches for them."

Lomax spoke up. "Mister, that ain't just any man you're talkin' about. That's Preacher."

"And I'm sittin' right here," drawled the mountain man. "Listen, Baron, give me a few days to do a little scoutin' around. If that don't work, we'll try somethin' else. But this ain't the first time I've tackled a job like this. If Stone Bear is around here, I'll find the varmint . . . and I'll see if he's got any prisoners."

Von Kuhner glared at all three of them for a moment, then gave them a grudging nod. "Very well. But I do not have an endless supply of patience."

Lomax said, "Naw. We'd have never guessed."

For a second it looked like the baron was going to erupt in anger at that sarcastic comment, but von Kuhner turned on his heel and stomped off. Jamie gave Lomax a look and shook his head.

Lomax just grinned at him. "You've got to admit, he was sort of askin' for it."

"Yeah," Jamie allowed. "I don't reckon I can argue with that."

Guards had been posted every night of the journey so far, even while they were passing through territory where danger was unlikely to strike. Jamie and Preacher knew quite well that overconfidence was one of the most dangerous things on the frontier.

Since they had penetrated into Blackfoot territory, the guard was doubled to eight men. They were posted around the camp on the hilltop, to be relieved in three hours. Since there were three shifts, Preacher, Jamie, and Lomax each took a spot in one of the shifts, so they didn't have to rely solely on the dragoons.

Preacher was on the first shift. He sat on a rock twenty feet down the slope from the camp. Dog lay on the ground beside him, the big cur's head resting on his extended paws.

Two hours had gone by since the rest of the group had turned in for the night. The camp was quiet except for an occasional burst of snoring. All of Preacher's senses were keenly alert, radiating out from him into the night.

When trouble came, it was from the opposite side of camp. A man shouted. The sound was full of fear. An instant later, the boom of a musket followed the cry.

Preacher was on his feet instantly, swinging around with his Sharps in his hands, ready to fire. Dog was up beside him, leaning forward and growling.

"Dog, stay," Preacher ordered. He didn't go charging up the hill to see what was happening. The Blackfeet could be tricky devils. They might feint an attack at one place, only to launch their main assault elsewhere.

Besides, Jamie was up there. He would see what was going on—and deal with it.

In the camp, before the shout was more than a second old, Jamie rolled out of his blankets and came up on his feet with the Walker Colt gripped in his right fist, fully awake in the blink of an eye.

A musket roared as an orange spurt of flame gushed from the muzzle.

"A bear!" yelled the guard who had raised the alarm. "Look out! It's a bear!"

Jamie knew that was possible. Bears occasionally came into human camps in search of food. At this time of year, with winter coming on, they were even more likely to do so, as instinct drove them to pack on the fat before their long hibernation.

He charged across the camp in the direction of the yelling and the shot. He wished the guard hadn't gotten so trigger-happy. The sound of that musket going off might travel for a long distance, echoing through the mountain valleys. It was inevitable that the Blackfeet would know the party of white men had entered their hunting grounds, but Jamie would have been all right with postponing that discovery for as long as possible.

A running figure suddenly loomed up right in front of him, coming toward him out of the shadows. Jamie's reflexes made him dart aside to avoid a collision. For a big man, he was very nimble and got out of the way in time.

The shape flashed past, and even though Jamie flung out a hand and tried to grab the runner, whoever it was had too much speed. Jamie's grab found only empty air.

He called, "Hey! Stop!", but the runner never slowed down. He dashed across the camp, and as he passed the embers of the fire, enough of a glow remained to reveal a dark, hairy coat on the fast-moving figure. It was only a split-second glimpse, and then whoever—or *what*ever— the thing was, it was safely back in the shadows and headed toward the place where Preacher had taken up his guard post.

Jamie shouted, "Preacher! Coming your way!"

Down the slope, Preacher heard that, so he was ready. Or at least, he *thought* he was.

But he wasn't prepared for a shape to come flying through the air at him like some gigantic bird. It must have leaped from the top of the slope, and that huge bound carried it all the way to where Preacher stood.

Not knowing what was going on, he didn't want to shoot and tried to twist out of the way, but the thing slammed into his left shoulder and bowled him over. He tripped over Dog and fell on top of the big cur. With uncharacteristic awkwardness on both of their parts, their legs tangled and it took Preacher a couple of seconds to get back on his feet.

In that time, the escaping figure was gone, vanished into the night like a phantom.

Jamie charged down the hill. "Preacher, are you all right?"

"Yeah, just a mite discombobulated . . . and embarrassed. That was just about the fastest critter I ever saw. What in blazes was it?"

"I'm not sure, but it wasn't a bear, like that fella was yelling about. From what I saw, it was pretty skinny. And it sure didn't run like a bear. Like you said, it was mighty fast."

Several men came down the hill toward them, led by Colonel Sutton. Roscoe Lomax was close behind the colonel.

Sutton called, "Jamie? Preacher?"

"Right here, Colonel," Jamie answered.

"Is anyone hurt?"

"We're fine. How about the men in the camp?"

"Lieutenant Curry is checking on everyone now, but my

impression is that no one was injured. What in the world happened?"

"We're not sure," Jamie said. "I want to talk to the fella who raised the ruckus to start with."

Preacher glanced down at the big cur, who stood beside him growling. "Dog wants to go after that varmint. Reckon I ought to let him?"

"I'm sure Dog could track him," Jamie said, "but why don't we wait until morning so we can see what we're doing?"

"That's a good idea, I reckon." Preacher's tone of voice made it clear that he was a little disappointed not to take up the chase right away.

Jamie had a point, though. Pursuing some unknown creature into the darkness wasn't a really good idea. He looked at Preacher and asked, "You all right to finish out your shift on guard duty?"

"Me? Hell, I'm fine as frog hair. That thing knocked me down for a minute but didn't do no real damage."

"All right. Colonel, let's go see if we can find out something about our mysterious visitor."

Chapter 28

The dragoon who had raised the alarm and taken a wild shot at the strange creature was a young private named Charles Ferguson.

"Private Ferguson, tell us what happened," Colonel Sutton ordered a few minutes later as he, Jamie, and Lieutenant Curry stood near what was left of the fire.

"I . . . I don't really know, Colonel. I was standing guard, as ordered, when I thought I heard something slip past me. I was worried that somebody had gotten into the camp who didn't belong here, so I moved up the hill and had a look around. That's when I saw . . . something . . . rooting around in our supplies. I figured it was an animal and I could scare it off . . . but when I took a step toward the thing, it . . . it turned around and snarled at me. That's when I decided it was a bear, and I . . . well, I guess it spooked me. I let out a yell . . . I suppose you know what happened after that, sir."

"Yes, I do," Sutton replied. "You should have been more alert to begin with, Private Ferguson, and not allowed the intruder to get past you."

The dragoon hung his head in shame. "Yes, sir, I know. I'm sorry."

Jamie said, "Sorry doesn't count for much when you're pulling guard duty, son." His tone softened slightly as he went on. "Did you ever get a good look at whatever it was?"

"No, sir. But I could tell it was hairy, and it . . . growled at me . . . so I figured it had to be a bear."

"Have you ever *seen* a bear?"

"No, sir. Not close up. Or . . . well, not at all, if I'm telling the truth."

"Take my word for it, son, bears are a lot bigger than that thing, whatever it was. They don't usually run on two legs like that, either. Bears are a lot faster than you might think they would be, to look at them, but they run best on four legs, not two."

Sutton asked, "Could what you saw have been a man?"

"No, sir, Colonel," Ferguson answered emphatically. "Not with hair like that all over its body."

"All right, Private. Has somebody already replaced you on your guard shift?"

"Yes, sir. Lieutenant Curry told Private Jeffries to take over for me."

"Very well. Go turn in and get some rest."

"Thank you, sir." Ferguson started to turn away, then paused and added, "I'm really sorry I didn't do my duty, Colonel."

"Well, learn a lesson from what's happened, Private . . . and from whatever the lieutenant decides will be your punishment."

Ferguson swallowed hard and said, "Yes, sir."

When the young dragoon had moved off to his bedroll, Sutton said to Jamie, "What do you make of it? You're certain the intruder couldn't have been a bear or some other wild animal?"

"It wasn't a bear. I'm sure of that," Jamie replied. "And Preacher agreed with me that from what we saw, it didn't look like any other animal we've ever encountered. But it could still be an animal, I suppose. Preacher and I haven't run into *everything* that lives out here, I don't imagine."

"But there probably aren't very many beasts you haven't seen." Sutton paused, and Jamie could tell the colonel was pondering the situation. "Do you think we should go after whatever it was, in the morning?"

"The baron was already upset about staying here for a while and letting Preacher do some scouting." Jamie chuckled, but there wasn't much genuine humor in the sound. "He'll really be mad if Preacher and Dog go off hunting some sort of critter instead of Blackfeet."

"I don't really care how our Prussian guest feels about it," Sutton said. "On the other hand . . . our visitor didn't try to harm anyone, and it seemed more interested in pilfering food than anything else. I think perhaps we should do a better job of securing our supplies and carry on as planned." The colonel shrugged. "The way the creature fled, it seemed to be terrified. It probably won't come back."

"That's fine with me, Colonel." What Sutton had decided made sense, thought Jamie. But for some reason, he had a hunch they hadn't seen the last of that hairy thing.

The next morning, Dog wanted to take up the trail of the nocturnal intruder. Sitting where Preacher had encountered the thing the night before, Dog whined softly as he peered off into the distance.

"I know, old son," Preacher told the big cur, "but we got other chores to take care of today. Come on, let's see if we can find us some Blackfeet."

Dog abandoned the other goal with reluctance, but he wasn't going to disobey an order from his human trail partner. They left the camp heading west, deeper into the mountains. After they had gone a mile or so, they would swing south and make a large circle around the hill where the rest of the party was camped.

There was nothing Preacher loved more than being up in the high country on a hunt. He moved quietly, with all senses alert, not missing anything that went on around him.

The same was true of Dog. He ranged ahead of Preacher, but not with the same exuberant bounds that he demonstrated when they were out on the trail, just traveling rather than searching. He was as much of a phantom as the mountain man, drifting silently through the landscape, the great shaggy head swinging slowly from side to side as he searched for any sign of their enemies.

The cool, cloudy morning was thick with overcast but held no real promise of rain or snow, only dank gloom. Undisturbed by the almost supernaturally quiet man and dog, the wildlife was plentiful. Preacher saw deer, elk, moose, rabbits, and squirrels. Although many feathered creatures had already flown south for the winter, birds sang in some of the trees. Higher in the sky, eagles and hawks soared on wind currents.

Preacher didn't see any bears. Like Jamie, he was convinced that whatever had sneaked into their camp the night before wasn't a bear. He'd never seen a bear that could leap like that and fly through the air.

The two searchers had made their turn to the south to

begin their big circle when Dog stopped abruptly. He lifted his head. His ears pricked forward. Preacher could tell the big cur had caught an intriguing scent.

"What is it you smell, big fella?" Preacher whispered. "Blackfoot . . . or somethin' you recognize from last night?" He sniffed the air. Nothing out of the ordinary, only the familiar tang of evergreens mixed with the rich aroma of the earth. But he knew Dog's nose was a lot more sensitive than his. "Be quiet about it, Dog, but . . . trail."

The command sent Dog padding away through some brush. Preacher followed, making as little noise as he could. After a few moments, they came to a narrow game trail that twisted up a slope toward a tree-covered ridge.

They hadn't quite reached the top when something crashed through the thick undergrowth between the trees. Instinct brought the Sharps to Preacher's shoulder, but he held off on squeezing the trigger. He didn't like not knowing what he was shooting at. "Dog, hunt!" he snapped.

Dog took off, twisting through the brush and quickly disappearing. Preacher was able to track the chase by sound. Dog didn't make much noise, but whatever he was pursuing was making quite a racket and didn't care about being quiet.

Neither did Preacher. He pushed through the brush. Some of it caught and clawed at his thick buckskins, but he ignored that and pressed on.

The trail led down the far side of the ridge. The brush wasn't quite as thick where the ground leveled out again. As Preacher hurried down the slope, he caught glimpses of something running upright, like a man, but the creature's hairy pelt actually looked like a bear's.

Was it possible there was such a beast as a half-man, half-bear? The idea seemed unnatural and repugnant to

Preacher, but he had seen some mighty strange things in his life, strange enough that he hated to say anything was absolutely impossible.

He also had a few flashing looks at Dog pursuing the whatever-it-was through the brush. Dog was closing in. Preacher reached the bottom of the slope and couldn't see either of them anymore, but pushed on in the direction they had gone.

He heard Dog yelp, and his heart slugged hard in his chest. That varmint had better not have hurt Dog, he thought. He'd skin that funny-looking hide right off of it.

The sound the big cur had made had seemed more startled than pained, and Preacher saw why a few moments later as he crashed through more brush and came to a sudden halt. He was standing almost at the edge of a deep ravine a good fifty feet to the bottom, and half that wide.

Dog was at the edge, one paw resting on a narrow tree trunk that spanned the ravine like a bridge. The fallen tree was only a few inches in diameter, little more than a sapling. It barely reached to the ravine's far side.

Dog looked back over his shoulder at Preacher and whined. From the big cur's stance and his attitude, it was clear to the mountain man that whatever Dog had been chasing had scampered across that tree trunk and vanished into the trees and brush on the far side.

Preacher could also tell that Dog *wanted* to continue the pursuit, as he'd been ordered but was smart enough to know that crossing the ravine would be extremely dangerous.

"Dog, stay," Preacher said quietly. He thought Dog actually looked relieved he wasn't going to have to venture out onto that skinny little tree trunk. Dog would have done it if Preacher had told him to, of course . . . but he was just as glad not to.

Preacher listened. He couldn't hear the thing anymore. It had gone to ground somewhere over there, or it was still fleeing but trying to be quiet about it.

Either way, it appeared to have given Preacher the slip again. And that was a feeling he didn't care for.

Not one damned bit.

Chapter 29

The atmosphere in camp was tense all day while the rest of the expedition waited for Preacher to return from his scouting mission. Although relations between the dragoons and the Prussian soldiers had been rather tense from the beginning, that feeling might have eased over time if given a chance. Soldiers, no matter what their nationality, had certain things in common and sometimes bonded over those things, but the hostility of Baron von Kuhner and Feldwebel Becker toward the Americans kept that from happening.

Knowing Preacher intended to stay close enough to camp that any shots he fired would be audible, Jamie remained alert. He warned Lomax to stay ready to move out in a hurry if there were any indications the mountain man had run into trouble. "Not that Preacher can't handle just about anything himself. Especially with Dog along."

"But we wouldn't want him hoggin' all the fun, would we?" Lomax asked with a grin.

"That's right."

"Don't worry, MacCallister. I'm champin' at the bit to get back into action, too, just like you are."

Jamie would have denied that he was champing at the bit for action, but there was no point in it. That was exactly how he felt.

However, nothing happened that day.

Preacher walked into camp at dusk that evening with Dog trailing at his heels. "No sign of Stone Bear and his bunch." He got that out of the way immediately as Jamie, Lomax, Colonel Sutton, Lieutenant Curry, Baron von Kuhner, and several other of the men gathered around him and Dog.

"Are you certain you have even brought us to the right area?" asked von Kuhner.

"You can't ever guarantee where an Indian might be," Jamie told him.

"Yeah, they're plumb notional critters," Preacher added.

"But I believe there's a good chance Stone Bear is somewhere in these parts," Jamie went on. "He *should* be here. I don't know what else anybody could go on."

Von Kuhner said, "Hmmph," packing a lot of disdain and doubt into the sound.

"That ain't all, though," Preacher continued. "I had another run-in with our friend from last night."

That perked up everyone's interest.

Colonel Sutton said, "You mean the . . . bear . . . or whatever the creature was?"

"That's right. Dog caught a whiff of his scent and followed him. We got close enough to chase him for a little spell, but then he got away from us."

"It's not often anything gets away from you once you're on its trail, Preacher," Jamie said. "How'd that happen?"

Preacher explained about the ravine and the hazardous makeshift bridge spanning it. "I thought about tryin' to cross it, and if it'd been a matter of life and death, I would have, but I figured if Dog was leery about skitterin' out on that tree trunk, I ought to be, too. I ain't sure it would've held my weight."

"But that thing crossed it without any mishaps?" Sutton asked.

"I reckon. I didn't see it down in the bottom o' that ravine, and that's where it would've been if it fell. It was a far enough drop that nobody would just get up and walk away from it, especially not that quicklike. Most folks'd break their neck if they fell in there."

Jamie said, "It sounds to me like the creature *put* that tree there to use as a bridge. It probably goes back and forth there all the time."

Preacher nodded. "That's the feelin' I got, too."

"Did you get a better look at the varmint?" asked Lomax.

"A little, but still not good enough to figure out what it was. It's skinny, like Jamie said, and it runs on two legs like a man, but it's got hair all over, like a bear." Preacher rubbed his beard-stubbled chin, and after a few seconds of hesitation, went on. "I, uh, even got to wonderin' if there could be such a thing as a half-man, half-bear critter."

Von Kuhner let out a disgusted, dismissive snort. "Madness. Utter madness."

Preacher regarded him coolly. "Then I'm waitin' for your explanation, mister."

"I do not have to provide an explanation for yours to be foolish," von Kuhner argued. "Its madness stands alone perfectly well."

Jamie said, "We've got a mystery on our hands, no doubt about that, but it doesn't have anything to do with the job that brought us here. Whatever that creature is, it must roam through these parts pretty freely. We'll just have to hope it doesn't cause us any more trouble while we're trying to complete our mission."

"It sure as blazes won't stop me from goin' back out scoutin' tomorrow," said Preacher. "I'll throw a little wider loop next time. Stone Bear's out there, and I'll find the son of a gun."

The news of the mountain man's second encounter with the mysterious creature spread quickly through the camp, adding a layer of nervousness to the tension that already gripped the expedition. The creature didn't seem to be an actual threat, based on what had happened so far, but just the idea of something so odd and unknown lurking around was enough to give a man the fantods.

After supper, Jamie went over to Roscoe Lomax and said quietly, "I've got a special job for you tonight, if you don't mind doing it."

"Whatever you say," he responded without hesitation.

"That thing was after our supplies last night. Now, I don't know if it's completely wild or not, but as skittish as it acts, it must be pretty close. And it must be pretty hungry to risk coming into a camp full of men where there was a fire burning not long before."

Lomax scratched at his beard and said, "Yeah, wild animals don't act like that unless they get mighty desperate. You think it's gonna make another try for our grub tonight?"

"I think it might. That's why I'm putting you in charge of guarding the supplies."

"Fine by me," Lomax said with an emphatic nod. "You want me to kill it?"

"I'd rather catch it and find out what it is. But you do what you have to do to defend yourself."

"All right, MacCallister. You want it took alive, I'll do my durnedest."

The camp settled down for the night. The men on the first guard shift, including Jamie, took up their positions. Preacher rolled up in his blankets, with Dog stretched out on the ground beside him.

At Jamie's suggestion, Lomax waited until after darkness had descended before quietly shifting over to lie down next to the packsaddles that had been taken off the pack horses when the group made camp. In case they were being watched, Jamie didn't want anybody to know that they were taking extra precautions tonight.

Lomax spread his blankets and lay down, but he didn't go to sleep. He knew better than to think he could stay awake all night, but he wanted to remain alert for as long as he could. He was a fairly light sleeper when he needed to be. No man traveled the Santa Fe Trail with all its dangers as much as Lomax had without developing that ability.

Eventually, despite his best intentions, he began to get drowsy and let himself drift off into a half sleep.

It was a smell that woke him, a stench that made him wrinkle his nose. It took a potent scent to make him do that, since the buffalo coat he wore was pretty odiferous.

He lay absolutely still as the smell grew stronger. Something moved nearby, so quietly he could barely hear the slight sounds.

Then he heard *breathing*. Not loud, but harsh. The blasted thing was practically on top of him, he thought. Just as Jamie had suspected might happen, the creature had slipped past the sentries again, probably taking advantage of some young dragoon's inexperience. It never would have gotten by Jamie.

How it got into the camp didn't matter. Jamie wanted it *caught*. Lomax opened his eyes and turned his head slowly and cautiously. He didn't want to spook it. He knew how fast the thing was.

A tall, angular shape moved past him, almost indistinguishable in the thick shadows underneath the trees. Lomax was using those shadows to his own benefit, trusting them to conceal him as long as he didn't move. The critter didn't seem to have seen him rolled up in his blankets.

Suddenly, just as it was bending toward the stacked supplies, it stopped short. Its head came up, and Lomax heard it sniffing.

Instantly, he knew what was going on. He had smelled the creature, and the creature had just smelled *him*.

He knew it was going to bolt as it realized just how close one of the dreaded humans was.

Lomax flung aside his blankets and lunged. The creature tried to dart away, but Lomax's right hand closed around an ankle in a desperate grab. He yanked, and the intruder spilled onto the ground.

"It's here! The critter's here!" Lomax bellowed as he scrambled up and threw himself on top of the creature.

He found himself with his arms full of something that felt like a bundle of sticks wrapped in a bearskin, but it still possessed enough wiry strength to fight like a wildcat and almost tear free.

Its foul breath gusted in Lomax's nostrils, and he was gripped suddenly by a feeling of terror that it might try to bite his nose off. Despite that, he hung on and hoped that somebody would come to help him soon.

"Damn it!" he roared. "I can't hold it much longer!"

It screeched in his face, but it wasn't the mindless howl of a wild animal. It screamed what sounded like words.

"Nein! Nein!"

Chapter 30

The fact that the creature seemed to be counting at him threw Lomax for enough of a loop that his grip eased, and once again the thing almost slipped away from him. He grabbed at it and yelled, "Well, ten your own damn self!"

He knew that didn't make any sense, but if the beast was going to count at him, he'd just count right back at it.

It was going to take more than that to subdue the varmint, though. Lomax balled a fist and struck a short, sharp blow, aiming where he thought the creature's head would be. The punch landed, and though he could tell it was only a glancing blow, it packed enough force to make the thing stop fighting and go limp.

"I got him!" Lomax shouted as footsteps pounded around him and men called startled questions. "I got the critter!"

"Hang on to him," Jamie ordered. "Somebody fetch a light."

One of the dragoons stirred up the campfire embers and added kindling until the flames were leaping up again. He thrust a branch into the fire and waited until it caught then held the burning brand over his head as he walked to where

Jamie, Preacher, and a number of other men clustered around Lomax and whatever it was he'd caught.

"Step aside," Jamie told the men. "Let that fella with the torch through."

The flickering light fell over Lomax and the creature. Since the thing was still stunned, Lomax pushed himself up and rolled to a sitting position beside it, where he could grab it again quickly if it was just shamming.

"Well, I'll be damned," said Preacher. "It's a man . . . ain't it?"

"Yeah, behind all that hair and that bearskin, I think it is," Jamie said.

A gaunt, filthy face was visible behind a tangled, jutting brown beard. The beard grew so high and thick the man's closed eyes and the tip of his nose were his only visible features. He wore some sort of crude garment fashioned from a bear's hide that included a hood over his head. Strips of hide were bound around the man's feet and wrapped around his ankles and calves to serve as makeshift boots. He didn't appear too old. The beard was still brown, although it had some streaks of gray in it.

"A human being," Colonel Sutton said in a slightly awed voice.

"But not exactly a tame one," Jamie said. "The way he acts, he's as much animal as human."

Lieutenant Curry peered at the captive and asked, "Is he white or Indian?"

"White, I think. He's got so much dirt and hair on him that it's hard to say," Lomax said.

"Reckon he's crazy?" asked Preacher.

"Not so crazy he can't count," Lomax said. "He started yellin' numbers at me while we were tusslin'. Well, *one* number, anyway. Nine. What do you reckon that means?"

The guttural laugh that came from Baron Adalwolf von Kuhner startled all of them. "He was not counting. He was saying *nein*. That means no, in your primitive language. He was pleading with you not to hurt him."

"You mean he's Prussian," Jamie said sharply.

"I would assume so, yes."

"Then he must be a survivor from the group we're looking for," Sutton said with excitement in his voice. "There's no other reason a Prussian would be in this area."

Jamie looked over at von Kuhner and asked, "Did you know any of the folks in that bunch? Do you recognize this man?"

Von Kuhner shook his head. "Not at all. I was aware of the nobles who undertook the journey to this godforsaken wilderness and had met some of them briefly, but I was not well acquainted with any of them. As for this man"— von Kuhner gestured toward the captive—"I never saw him before. Perhaps he was a servant. All the noblemen would have had servants with them to attend to their needs."

"We'll have to talk with this hombre once he comes around," Jamie said. "Baron, do you mind handling the translating?"

"Of course not. I want to find out what he knows just as much as you do. If I might make a suggestion . . . ?"

"Go ahead."

"Perhaps some schnapps would revive him sooner, instead of waiting for him to wake up."

"That's a pretty good idea," Jamie said with a nod. "Go ahead."

"Becker!" von Kuhner snapped at the feldwebel. "Fetch a bottle."

"Jawohl, mein herr."

"As for the rest of you," said Sutton, "clear off and give us some room. Guards, return to your posts. The rest of you men, try to get some sleep."

After all the excitement, Jamie didn't know how well the men would sleep, especially since they knew fate might have delivered one of the people they were looking for into their hands. But within a few minutes, an open area had been cleared around the supplies. Jamie lifted the still unconscious man into a sitting position, pushed the bearskin hood off his head, and propped his back against the stacked packsaddles. He took the open bottle of schnapps Becker brought and lifted it to the man's mouth. Carefully, he trickled some of the liquor between the man's lips.

That caused a sputtering spasm as the man swallowed it. Jamie took the bottle away and steadied him with a strong hand on his shoulder. "Take it easy, old son. You're all right. We won't hurt you."

The man's eyes flew open, and his head jerked from side to side. Everyone there knew that he wanted to bolt to his feet and try to get away. Jamie held him down. The man had given Lomax a pretty good tussle, but he was no match for the strength of the massive frontiersman who gripped him.

Von Kuhner bent closer, rested his hands on his thighs, and spoke to the man in German. Jamie recognized a few of the words, but not enough to know what von Kuhner was saying.

The captive's face was so gaunt his eyes seemed sunken in deep pits. They widened as he grasped what the baron was telling him. After a moment, sounds came from somewhere under all that tangled hair. The man's voice was rusty and halting, as if he hadn't used it for a long time. He struggled to form a response to von Kuhner.

After a moment, the baron nodded and said to Jamie, "Give him some more of the schnapps."

"Don't let him have the bottle," added Sutton. "He probably hasn't had any liquor in a long, long time. It'll hit him hard, and we don't want him too drunk to talk."

Von Kuhner scowled, but he nodded and motioned for Jamie to proceed.

He raised the bottle, and although the man wrapped his own hands around it, Jamie maintained his grip and pulled it away after a couple of swallows. The man's hands, which were nothing but skin and bone, weren't strong enough to hold on.

He mumbled some more, and then von Kuhner said, "He claims his name is Helmuth. He served Baron von Stauffenberg, one of the members of the expedition."

"How in blazes did he wind up in this condition?" Jamie wanted to know. "Did the Blackfeet capture him, and he got away from them later?"

Another exchange of harshly voiced questions from von Kuhner, followed by halting, mumbled responses from Helmuth, and the baron reported, "When they were attacked, he was wounded. Something struck him in the head. He lost consciousness and knew nothing of the battle after that."

Jamie raised a hand and started to brush aside the thick, brown hair above Helmuth's left ear. Helmuth flinched and started whining like a trapped animal.

"I won't hurt you," Jamie told him. "You're going to be all right now, Helmuth. You're among friends."

Helmuth recognized his name, if nothing else, and took some reassurance from Jamie's calm, steady voice. He allowed Jamie to push the hair aside and explore the side of his head above the left ear.

"I thought I spotted something here," Jamie said to the others. "He's got a scar where a rifle ball must have struck him. It had to have glanced off instead of penetrating. If it hadn't, he'd be dead, but it was enough to knock him out cold. The Blackfeet must have thought he was dead."

Preacher put in, "He's mighty lucky they didn't come along afterward and cut his throat, just to make sure he was finished off. That's what they'd do most of the time."

Von Kuhner said, "The wound must have bled so much that he appeared to be dead beyond any doubt. Head wounds usually bleed excessively."

"That's true," Jamie agreed. "Ask him what he remembers after that."

Helmuth took them all by surprise by saying, "I . . . I can tell you. *Ich sprechesie Englisch. Ein bisschen.* A little."

"Well, all right, then, old son," said Preacher. "Tell us what happened."

"It has been so long . . . I could not remember . . . at first . . . how to speak . . . either in *Deutsche* . . . or English. But now . . ." Helmuth cleared his throat. "It is starting to . . . to come back to me. If I could have . . . another drink . . . ?"

"All right," Jamie said. "But only a little one."

Once again, he allowed Helmuth to take a couple of swallows, then pulled the bottle away. Helmuth took a deep, shaky breath, then resumed the story.

"When I . . . woke . . . I was alone . . . except for . . . the dead. My friends . . . among the other servants . . . the soldiers . . . the Americans . . . all dead."

"The entire party was wiped out except for you?" asked Sutton. That was the information they had come to find.

Helmuth was far from finished. He shook his head, the movement slow and weak, and went on. "No. When

I felt . . . strong enough to do it . . . I looked at all the bodies. Some . . . were not there."

Sutton looked quickly at Jamie. "The Blackfeet took prisoners."

"That's what it sounds like," Jamie said. "Who was missing, Helmuth?"

"Graf . . . Graf von Eichhorn."

"Earl Peter von Eichhorn, as we'd call him," Sutton said. "The leader of the expedition."

"That is correct," von Kuhner confirmed.

"Anybody else?" Jamie said to Helmuth.

"My . . . my lord . . . Baron von Stauffenberg . . . and three ladies . . . Countess von Falkenhayn . . . Countess von Arnim . . . Countess von Tellman . . ."

Von Kuhner muttered something that sounded like a curse, no doubt thinking about the fate of those women if they were taken captive by the Blackfeet.

"I did not see . . . the ladies' maids . . . either," added Helmuth.

"Did any of the Americans survive?" Jamie asked.

"I . . . I do not know . . . I was not . . . well-acquainted . . . with any of them . . ." Helmuth paused. "But I do not recall seeing . . . the leader of . . . the American soldiers . . . or the man called . . . Herr Coburn."

"Reese Coburn," said Preacher. "The head guide, wasn't he?"

"That's right," Sutton said. "So, Coburn may have survived, too, as well as Lieutenant Barton?"

Helmuth shook his head again and said, "I did not . . . see their bodies. I do not know . . . if they lived. But I do know . . . about the ladies . . . They are alive. I have seen them . . . many times." He looked around at the men encircling him. "They *still live.*"

Chapter 31

Excitement gripped the men at Helmuth's words.

Jamie knelt beside him and asked, "How do you know that for sure, Helmuth? Where have you seen the women?"

"At . . . at the savages' village," the half-wild man replied.

"You know where it is?" Preacher asked.

Helmuth's head bobbed tentatively. "Y-yes. I have been there. Not . . . not *in* the village. I am afraid." His gaze dropped to the ground as if he were ashamed. "The savages would kill me, and I am afraid."

"Hell, old son, any man with any sense'd feel the same way," Preacher assured him.

"Why don't you go on with your story?" Jamie wanted to get a better feeling for just how coherent Helmuth was, how well his brain was working, before he accepted at face value anything the man had to say.

"Yes. I saw the bodies . . . around the wagons, saw that so many were . . . were dead. They frightened me, and I wanted to get away from there. And my head hurt . . . so bad."

"From gettin' grazed by that rifle ball," said Preacher.

"But even though I hurt . . . and was afraid . . . I knew I would need food. I searched among the wagons . . . took all the supplies I could carry—"

Von Kuhner barked something in German.

Helmuth cringed as if the baron had struck him. "*Nein!* I was not . . . was not a grave robber. Those poor people were not buried . . . and nothing in the wagons could help them anymore. But I thought it might keep me alive."

"Hold on," Jamie said. "The Blackfeet didn't loot the wagons and then burn them?"

Helmuth shook his head. "No, the . . . the wagons were still there. They took away the horses and mules . . . but left the wagons."

Jamie and Preacher glanced at each other.

"That's a mite odd," Preacher said. "Most times, Injuns'll strip the canvas off a wagon, since they can make use of it, and then burn the rest, just outta sheer meanness."

"Maybe they were in a hurry for some reason," Jamie said. But he agreed with Preacher that what Helmuth had just told them sounded strange. Figuring that out could wait until later, though. He told Helmuth to continue.

"I am not a terrible person," Helmuth said with a sullen glance toward von Kuhner. "I simply wanted to live. I found cloth in one of the wagons and bound the wound on my head. Then I took the food I could carry and went to look for shelter."

"Why didn't you stay with the wagons?" asked Lieutenant Curry.

"I thought about it, but"—a shudder went through Helmuth's cadaverous frame—"all those bodies were there. I could not . . . could not stand the thought of spending the night so close to them."

"A decent man would have buried them," snapped von Kuhner.

"I thought about it," Helmuth said again. "I meant to . . . bury them. I told myself . . . I would come back the next day . . . and do that . . . after I had rested. I *did* go back, sometime later. I do not know . . . how long. But the bodies were . . . gone."

Of course they were, thought Jamie. Wolves and carrion birds would have taken care of them. The idea repulsed him, yet he couldn't bring himself to think too badly of Helmuth because of what had happened. The man had been injured and far, far out of his element.

"I suppose you found a place to get out of the weather?" Jamie asked.

Helmuth nodded. "Yes, I went higher into the hills. There was a cave . . . I had seen the men make fire using flint and a knife, and I had brought both things with me from the wagons . . . I stayed there for"—he sighed—"I do not know how long. Time meant nothing to me. For days . . . weeks . . . maybe longer . . . I was sick . . . I imagined the wild animals came and . . . and danced for me . . . They spoke to me . . . Told me I was one of them . . ."

Quietly, Preacher said, "He was outta his head with fever, more 'n likely, Jamie."

Jamie nodded. "That's what it sounds like to me, too."

Helmuth eyed the bottle of schnapps that Jamie had set aside. "Could I . . . if I could have another drink . . . ?"

"One more little one," Jamie told him.

He didn't have to take the bottle away. Helmuth took one swallow of the liquor and then handed the bottle back to him.

"The time came when I was not as sick." With practice talking to other people again, and the bracing effect of the schnapps, his voice had grown stronger. "I was hungry, so I went back to the wagons. But the rest of the food was either gone, stolen by animals, or spoiled. I had to find things I could eat . . . roots, plants . . . Some of it made me sick, but none of it killed me. I . . . I learned how to catch rabbits. At first, I cooked them, but . . . I was too hungry, and it was too much trouble . . ." He shuddered again.

Jamie felt a mite like shuddering, too, at the thought of this wreck of a man gnawing on raw, bloody rabbit carcasses.

"Ever since then, I have lived in the forest. I have learned how to avoid or hide from the animals that might harm me. The bears, the mountain lions, the wolves . . . they have not troubled me." Helmuth glanced around slyly. "I hide from the savages, too, but sometimes, when I cannot stand to think I am the only one of my kind left in the world, I steal close to their village and watch them. That is how I . . . I saw the ladies. Their maids, too. They all live as savages now. I think . . . I think I saw my master, too. Baron von Stauffenberg. He was with Countess Katarina."

"So one of the noblemen is alive?" Von Kuhner's voice was like a lash.

Helmuth flinched at the sharp words. "I . . . I am not sure! I think I saw him . . . but he was not like he once was, when I knew him. The countess led him by the hand . . . she treated him as if he were a child." Helmuth shook, and tears ran down his cheeks. "The poor baron! What have the savages done to him?"

Jamie didn't know, but he was beginning to accept Helmuth's story. A handful of survivors from the attack were still alive. Or at least . . . they had been. There was no way of telling how time worked in Helmuth's hardship-ravaged mind. Years might have gone by since he'd actually seen anybody else from the Prussian expedition.

Jamie leaned closer and said, "Helmuth, it's been five years since the Blackfeet attacked you and the others. Have you been living out here in the wilderness by yourself for all the time?"

"I was alone." Helmuth's voice was utterly sincere. "Nobody here but poor Helmuth."

"He's lost his mind," von Kuhner said callously. "We can put no stock in anything he says."

"Well, he's here, right in front of us," said Preacher. "He had to have survived somehow. And if he did, I reckon some of the others could've, too."

"Not necessarily. There is no reason this man could not be the only survivor," the baron said.

Jamie nodded and said, "I reckon that's true, Baron, but we came all this way to find out."

"Of course. And we must take advantage of this opportunity to discover the truth. Kurtz!"

Helmuth looked up. At the tone of command in the baron's voice, instinct and almost-forgotten habit made him respond, *"Ja, mein herr?"*

"Can you take us to the village of those savages, the place where you saw the others?"

"Oh, jawohl, mein herr." Helmuth nodded. "I know how to get everywhere in these mountains now." He looked at Preacher. "You and your *hund* tried to catch me. But I got away!" He began to laugh, a low cackle that gradually built in volume.

Preacher reached down and closed a hand to Helmuth's shoulder to stop the sound. "Yeah, you done a mighty fine job of givin' us the slip, fella. You know your way around these parts, all right. I'll give you credit for that."

"You never would have caught me . . . none of you would have ever known I was there . . . except I smelled your food, and I was so hungry. I knew better than to come into your camp, but . . . I was so hungry."

Jamie knew that had to be true. Eating roots and whatever small game he could catch had kept Helmuth alive, but only barely. Anybody could tell that by looking at him. Jamie figured he had been starving for something else, too.

Human contact.

"All right, here's what we're going to do," Jamie said. "Helmuth, we'll fix some food for you. Real food, but not too much of it to start with. I figure after all this time, if you eat too much it'll make you sick. But we'll give you food and some blankets, and you can get some rest. You won't have to run away from us anymore. We're your friends." He thought about the bit of German he had picked up from being around the Prussians and added, *"Verstehen sie?"*, asking Helmuth if he understood.

"Ja, ich verstehen." It was hard to tell under all that beard, but Jamie thought Helmuth smiled. "You are . . . friends."

"Lomax," Jamie went on, "I'm putting you in charge of our new friend here. You stay with him. Keep an eye on him. Make sure he's all right."

Lomax frowned. "You mean make sure he don't run away again?"

"I mean take care of him," said Jamie. "We're all on the same side." He patted Helmuth on the shoulder. "Friends."

"Ja," Helmuth said.

Jamie caught the eyes of Preacher, Colonel Sutton, and Baron von Kuhner. The four men moved away, over by the campfire out of earshot.

"The man may be delusional," von Kuhner spoke up before Jamie could say anything. "Going through such ordeal may have left him insane."

"Maybe," Jamie allowed. "But if he's not loco, he can lead us to Stone Bear and those captives, if they're still alive. One way or another, first thing in the morning I intend to find out."

Chapter 32

Helmuth didn't try to get away during the night. In fact, once he had eaten a biscuit, he dropped off into a sound sleep, fueled by the schnapps and utter exhaustion.

Roscoe Lomax kept an eye on him, anyway, just in case. Now that they had found a survivor from the ill-fated expedition, they didn't want him slipping away again.

He might just be the key to completing their mission successfully.

Nothing else disturbed the peace and quiet, and when they were all awake in the morning, Jamie went to Helmuth and asked, "Do you feel up to showing us where that Blackfoot village is?"

Helmuth, who was sitting on a big slab of rock, had a tin cup of coffee in one hand and a flapjack wrapped around a piece of salt pork in the other. His mouth was full, and he had to chew and swallow before he was able to answer Jamie's question.

He didn't meet the big frontiersman's eyes as he said, "If they find out you are in their land, they will kill you. If I am with you, they will kill me."

"We're not going to let that happen, Helmuth."

"I have stayed alive for a long time. So long. I do not wish to throw my life away now."

"You said yourself that you've been to the village," Jamie pointed out. "You saw the captives there. You want to help them, don't you?"

"The savages frighten me," whined Helmuth.

"I know. They're scary folks. They frighten anybody who's got any sense. But we're your friends, and we'll be there to protect you and help you if there's any trouble. We'll make sure you're far away if anything like that happens."

Jamie wasn't going to make promises he couldn't keep, but he meant every word of what he said to Helmuth. The man had been through a great deal already. Jamie had no desire to add to Helmuth's hardships. However, if there were white captives in Stone Bear's village, he wanted to rescue them. "How about it, Helmuth? Can you do it?"

Helmuth sighed and said, "I . . . I will try. I will show you where the village is. But I will not get too close!"

"Fair enough," Jamie told him with a nod of acceptance.

When he consulted with Preacher and Colonel Sutton about the plans for the day, the colonel asked, "Should some of the men stay here to maintain the camp?"

Jamie thought about it and then shook his head.

"It's a good place, but we'd better stay together. Even if we can get those captives away from the Blackfeet without being discovered right away, which is pretty unlikely, they're bound to notice before too long that the prisoners are gone. When that happens, they'll be after us, and you can't hide the trail of a group this big."

"Besides," added Preacher, "we're liable to need every

gun we've got. The chances of sneakin' those folks outta Stone Bear's village without bein' caught are pretty slim."

"So you believe we'll have to fight his entire band," said Sutton.

"Maybe," Jamie said. "But we're a good-sized force, almost seventy men. Stone Bear may not have any more warriors than that. Like I said before when we had that run-in with the Sioux, the trick to winning against the Indians is to make pushing a fight too expensive for them."

"What we'll do," Preacher said, "is get close to the village and then have most of the men hunker down somewhere that can be defended. Jamie and me, maybe Lomax and a few others, will get a closer look at the village and grab those prisoners if we can. Then we'll all have to light a shuck outta these parts as fast as we can. We'll probably have a runnin' fight with the Blackfeet for a spell, too."

The colonel sighed and nodded. "Nothing is easy out here on the frontier, is it?"

"If it was easy, it wouldn't be worth it," Preacher said.

They broke camp and moved out a short time later. Helmuth, who seemed very uncomfortable on horseback, rode between Jamie and Colonel Sutton. Preacher was up ahead with Lomax.

Before leaving, Helmuth had talked for a while with the mountain man, describing the area where Stone Bear's village was located and the route they would have to take to get there. Preacher, who had been in these parts years earlier, claimed to have a pretty good idea of where he was going.

Jamie didn't doubt that for a second. You could drop

Preacher down in almost any trackless wilderness . . . and he would have a pretty good idea where he was going.

Baron von Kuhner hadn't objected when Sutton told him their plans, but he urged his horse up alongside Jamie and spoke across him to Helmuth in German. Helmuth muttered an answer.

Colonel Sutton said, "Since both of you men speak English, perhaps it would be better if you conducted your conversations in that language, Baron."

"I will speak how I wish, Colonel, but I assure you, this servant and I are not conspiring against you."

"I didn't think you were, but whatever you've got to say might have a bearing on our mission."

"I was merely asking him what sort of shape the ladies appeared to be in the last time he saw them," von Kuhner explained. "I am concerned about their welfare, of course."

"Of course. What did you tell the baron, Helmuth?"

"The ladies were alive," Helmuth answered in a surly tone. "They were dressed like Indians. Their hair was slicked down with something."

"Bear grease, more than likely," said Jamie.

"They looked like Indians. I thought they *were* Indians, at first. But Countess Katarina's hair is too light for her to be a savage. And then when I looked closer, I recognized her, and the others, as well." Helmuth shook his head. "They all looked much older than they should."

"They've probably had pretty hard lives. The Blackfeet regard white captives as slaves. Sometimes they'll take a female prisoner as a wife, or take a boy into the tribe to raise as a warrior, but those instances are rare. Mostly they just work them so hard and mistreat them so much that slaves don't live long. If all those survivors are still alive after five years, they're either mighty lucky or mighty determined."

"I find it difficult to believe that pampered aristocrats could endure such hardship," von Kuhner said.

Jamie looked over at him. "I thought you were one of those aristocrats, Baron."

"I am, but I am a Junker! A member of the warrior class. I live for strife and struggle." Von Kuhner scowled. "Having weaklings in charge is one reason our glorious German Empire has declined. Too many concessions have been made in recent years. Someday a truly strong leader will take the reins once more, and our homeland will again be what it once was."

Jamie had a hunch von Kuhner considered *himself* "a truly strong leader" and believed that he, or someone like him, ought to be running things. Political wrangling on the other side of the world was none of Jamie's business. All he cared about was doing what they had set out to do. Listening to the baron's arrogant ranting just put a bad taste in his mouth.

"Well, I reckon we'll find out how the survivors are doing once we get there," he said. "After talking to Helmuth, Preacher figured we ought to reach the Blackfoot village by nightfall. That'll give him a chance to get in there and see for himself what the situation is."

"What? You mean inside the Blackfoot village itself?"

Jamie grinned at von Kuhner. "It sure won't be the first Blackfoot camp Preacher's slipped in and out of. Get him to tell you the story sometime about why they call him the Ghost Killer."

Von Kuhner snorted. "I have no interest in stories. Only in finishing the job I have come to do."

"That's good," Jamie said. "I reckon that one way or another, this mission isn't far from over."

Following Helmuth's directions, Preacher led the group through winding valleys, over hogback ridges, and through rocky badlands. Their route tended generally higher and higher in elevation, and in some places, they could pause and look back over breathtaking vistas of miles and miles of wilderness spread out below them. The sky was so clear and blue it almost hurt the eyes to look at it for too long.

First thing that morning, the air had been cold enough to make a man's breath fog in front of his face, but by mid-morning it was just crisp and cool, and it stayed that way until late afternoon when the wind picked up and added an extra chill to it.

During one of the pauses to rest the horses, Preacher went to Jamie and said, "Snow by mornin'. Question is, how much and how long will it last?"

Jamie nodded solemnly. "I thought the same thing. Can smell it on the air. I don't reckon we're in for a blizzard, though. Probably just a few inches."

"I hope you're right. Although a nice little blizzard'd make it harder for them Blackfeet to trail us once we've grabbed the captives."

"Make it harder for us to travel, too," Jamie pointed out. "We might wind up getting snowed in somewhere and freezing to death."

"Well," said Preacher, "it's gonna do what it's gonna do, and it's up to us puny human bein's to cope with it as best we can. That's always the way life goes, ain't it?"

They started up another long ridge. Helmuth looked more worried behind the bushy beard as he said, "The village is not far now. On the other side is a trail that leads down into a small valley where a stream runs. The Blackfeet live there. The forest is so thick you cannot see the lodges until you are almost in the village."

"Good," Jamie said. "Those trees will give Preacher plenty of cover."

"They will catch the man you call Preacher and kill him," warned Helmuth.

"Not likely. You don't know Preacher."

"You do not know these savages. They are evil. They cannot be defeated."

"You're wrong about that, too. And for your information, *mein freund*, I've fought plenty of Indians and know them pretty well, including the Blackfeet."

Helmuth shook his head. "Your accent when you speak my language is terrible."

That made Jamie chuckle. "You talk better English than I talk Deutsche. I won't argue about that."

A short time later, he called a halt and gathered Preacher, Colonel Sutton, Baron von Kuhner, and Roscoe Lomax together to discuss the situation. *It feels like a council of war*, Jamie mused.

Probably because that might well be what it amounted to.

"I think we should stay here until after dark," he began. "Then most of the men can move up to the ridge crest without taking a chance on the Blackfeet spotting them."

"While you're doin' that," said Preacher, "I'll go over the ridge and down into Stone Bear's village. I should be able to get amongst the lodges without bein' spotted. If I can, I'll find the captives and get 'em out of there. If I can't do that, I can at least locate where in the village they're bein' kept, so we'll know more on the next attempt."

"Just do not allow the savages to discover you," von

Kuhner said. "That will ruin everything. If they know we are nearby, they will be ready for us. We won't even be able to take them by surprise if we attack them."

"We're not going to attack them if we can help it," Sutton said. "We didn't come here to start a war with the Blackfeet. The less bloodshed, the better, as far as I'm concerned."

Von Kuhner's lip curled in a sneer that revealed what he thought about the colonel's approach, but he didn't say anything else.

"I'm comin' with you, ain't I, Preacher?" asked Lomax. "That's what you and MacCallister said earlier."

"That's right. I'll be the only one goin' into the village, at least startin' out, but you and a couple more men will be close by in case I need a hand. Colonel, if you'd pick out a couple of good boys—"

"I would like for Feldwebel Becker to accompany you," von Kuhner broke in, causing the others to look at him in surprise.

After a moment, Preacher responded, with an unusual amount of diplomacy for him, "I ain't so sure that's a good idea, Baron."

Lomax wasn't so diplomatic. "Becker," he repeated, sounding like the name tasted bad in his mouth. "He don't need to come along. Not hardly."

"I realize the two of you have clashed in the past, Herr Lomax," von Kuhner said, "but nevertheless, I feel that a representative of the German Empire must be present when these captives are recovered . . . if they are." His broad shoulders rose and fell in a shrug. "Besides, his services as a translator may be required."

"Maybe that fella Helmuth could come along," Lomax suggested. "He's the one who's been here before, after all."

Jamie said, "No, I promised him he wouldn't have to go near the village. Baron, are you saying you don't think any of those captives will speak English?"

"How would I know, one way or the other?" Von Kuhner spread his hands. "It seems possible to me that, by now, after five years of living among the Indians, they may not be able to speak *any* language other than the grunting and jabbering of the savages."

That was possible. Sometimes captives forgot their native tongues and had to learn them all over again. Their language usually came back to them, but it could take a while.

Jamie's forehead creased in thought for a moment before he said, "I suppose you've got a point, Baron. And Becker's a fighting man. We know that."

"I still don't like it," said Lomax, "but I'll go along with whatever you decide, MacCallister."

Preacher said to von Kuhner, "Make sure Becker knows that I'm in charge and he'd damned well better do as he's told. If he can do that, I reckon he can come along."

Von Kuhner nodded. "Very well. I shall make certain he understands. When will you be leaving to make your approach to the village of the hostiles?"

"A couple of hours after it gets good and dark. Stone Bear and his people won't be expectin' any trouble. Thanks to Helmuth, we found the village quick enough so there's a good chance the Blackfeet ain't got wind yet of us bein' in these parts. They'll all be good and asleep." The mountain man grunted. "That's the plan, anyway. But we'll see how the hand plays out."

Chapter 33

In addition to Preacher, Lomax, and Becker, two of the dragoons were chosen to go on the scouting mission: a grizzled, middle-aged corporal named Conroe who had never aspired to any higher rank because of his hatred of responsibility, and a young private named Willis who came from the backwoods of Tennessee. He had grown up skulking through the woods after game, he told Preacher, so he knew how to be quiet and how to shoot.

"That'll do, boy," the mountain man said. "Just listen to what I tell you, and you'll be fine."

The full group of rescuers made a cold camp, of course. Close to the village, they couldn't afford the smell of smoke drifting to the Blackfeet. Instead, they gnawed jerky and biscuits and waited.

Preacher and Jamie sought out Helmuth, who sat on a log, hugging himself against the cold and rocking forward and back in a steady rhythm.

"Helmuth," Jamie said gently, "we just want to make sure what Preacher will be looking for. You said there are seven white captives in that village, three ladies and their maids, plus a baron. Is that right?"

"*Ja.* Countess Katarina, Countess Marion, and Countess Joscelyn. Countess Katarina's maid is named Gerda. I liked her. She was my friend. I . . . I don't remember the names of the other two. And Baron von Stauffenberg, my master. The poor baron." Helmuth lowered his voice to a whisper. "From what I saw, I don't think he's right in the head anymore."

Jamie and Preacher glanced at each other in the gathering shadows. They hoped Helmuth was right in the head— at least, enough so that he wasn't completely wrong about what they would find in the Blackfoot village.

"Can you tell me what they all look like?" asked Preacher. "Or the way you remember 'em, anyway. After all this time bein' slaves, they may have changed a lot."

For the next few minutes, Helmuth described the Prussians to the best of his recollection, veering off a few times into stories about things they had said or done in the past. Jamie and Preacher gently steered his memories back on track.

When they had gotten all the information out of him they could, Jamie clapped a hand on the man's bony shoulder and said, "Thank you for helping us, Helmuth. We have a better chance of rescuing those captives now than we would have had without you."

"I hope you save them," Helmuth said. Then he looked up at the two frontiersmen. "But even if you do . . . after all this time, won't they be more Indian than white?"

"That's been known to happen," Jamie admitted. "But I've got a hunch that what those folks want more than anything else is to go home."

"I hope so." Helmuth added wistfully, "I would like to go home, too."

"Maybe you will, before too much longer," Jamie told him.

A short time later, the entire group moved higher on the ridge, stopping just before they reached the crest. Jamie and Colonel Sutton went with Preacher's smaller detail to the top of the slope, where they all knelt behind some brush and looked down into the valley on the other side.

Full night had fallen, but a quarter moon and millions of stars provided enough illumination for the men to make out the valley's general outlines.

Clouds had blotted out stars far to the north as the storm bringing the snow Jamie and Preacher had smelled approached at a steady rate. The wind wasn't blowing hard where the men were, but it would pick up in the next couple of hours.

As Helmuth had said, the forest was thick with towering pine, spruce, and fir trees growing close together on the slope leading down into the valley. Underbrush clogged the spaces between the trunks, preventing the men from seeing any fires in the village below, but wood smoke carried to them on a vagrant breeze. That gently moving air also brought the sound of dogs yapping.

"I'd planned to go with you," Jamie said quietly to Preacher, "but the colonel wants me to stay here with him and the rest of the bunch."

"And that's a good idea," said Preacher. "No sense in riskin' the Blackfeet catchin' both of us. If ol' Stone Bear grabs me, I'll feel a heap better knowin' you're still on the loose to pull my fat outta the fire, Jamie."

Jamie grunted and said, "Let's just hope it doesn't come to that."

Becker said, "It's almost pitch black down there. How will we see where we're going?"

"Don't worry about that," Preacher told him. "I can see well enough to get us there. You and these other fellas will wait in the brush while I sneak into the village. If we're lucky, that's all you'll have to do. But if I yell for help, you'd best come a-runnin'."

"*Jawohl.*"

"That means yes, don't it?" Preacher waved a hand. "Never mind. You boys ready to go?"

"You think it's dark enough?" asked Lomax.

Preacher eyed the sky and said, "We could wait for the moon to go down, but by then the night'd be half over. I'd rather make our move now. If we can sneak the captives out and get away from here, we can put some distance behind us 'fore the Blackfeet even know they're gone."

"All right," Lomax said. "I'm ready."

Mutters of assent came from the two dragoons. Becker said, "*Ja, das ist gut.*"

Preacher took that to mean he was ready to go, too.

The mountain man shook hands with Jamie and Sutton and said, "See you fellas later."

"You'd better," Jamie told him.

The five men started down the far side of the ridge as Jamie and Sutton withdrew down the near side to rejoin the others. Dog slipped alongside Preacher like a shadow.

Becker said, "That *hund* is coming with us?"

"That hound, as I think you just called him, is the best scout west of the Mississippi. He can see better, hear better, and smell better than me, and since *I'm* the second-best scout west of the Mississippi . . ." Preacher left the rest of it unsaid and let the other men draw their own conclusions.

When Becker didn't respond, Preacher went on. "All right, no talkin' from here on out. Those damn Blackfeet have pretty good ears, too. Just keep an eye on me and watch what I do."

"It is too dark to keep any eye on anything," Becker grumbled.

"No talkin'," Preacher repeated. "Do the best you can." He let Dog lead the way.

The big cur was skilled at picking the best route. He even seemed to take into account that the humans were bigger than he was and made allowances for their size.

Some small noises were unavoidable, but nocturnal animals were abroad in the forest, too, and Preacher hoped if the Blackfeet heard anything, they would figure it came from varmints moving around.

And they wouldn't be far wrong where Becker was concerned, thought Preacher. He didn't trust the big Prussian soldier.

They didn't get in any hurry as they descended toward the village. Stealth was more important than speed. Later, it might very well be the other way around.

Eventually, they reached the bottom of the slope. The brush thinned. Preacher reached back and put an arm across Lomax's chest to stop him. Lomax turned and brought the man behind him to a halt, and that man passed it on until Becker, who was bringing up the rear, stopped, too.

Preacher put his mouth close to Lomax's ear and breathed, "Hold everybody here. Dog and I will go into the village and try to find the captives."

Lomax didn't say anything, but Preacher's head was close enough to the bullwhacker's that he felt the brim of Lomax's hat brush his face as Lomax nodded. Preacher reached down, touched Dog lightly on the head, and drifted forward to the edge of the brush. Man and cur stretched out full length on the ground to study the scene in front of them. Dappled shadows made them virtually impossible to see, even if someone in the village happened to be looking in their direction.

Preacher couldn't see all the lodges from where they were, but he could see enough to estimate that approximately eighty of the dwellings were scattered on the creek bank. The village stretched for more than two hundred yards along the stream.

On the far side of the creek, the band's pony herd grazed in a large meadow. The horses were spread out, and it would take a while to round them all up. That was a point in favor of the rescue party.

Embers in some of the cooking fires still glowed faintly, but none of them were actually burning. Thick, gloomy shadows covered the entire village. Preacher lifted his head to glance up at the sky. Clouds were starting to obscure the moon. It was fixing to get even darker, which Preacher didn't mind a bit.

After a few minutes of study, he started crawling, following the line of the forest's edge. Dog bellied along beside him. They couldn't sneak up to every lodge in the village and call softly to its inhabitants, hoping to find the white captives that way. One mistake would be enough to ruin everything if they did that.

But Preacher had narrowed down the most likely lodges where the slaves were kept—farthest from the creek, on the roughest ground, and near the area where the Blackfeet dumped human waste, offal, bones that couldn't be used for anything, and other garbage. He followed his nose as he crawled toward that handful of lodges.

If so much time hadn't gone by, Dog might have been able to identify the captives by smell. After five years, though, their scent would be the same as their captors, a mixture of smoke, buckskin, bear grease, and unwashed flesh.

Preacher hoped that by eavesdropping, he might overhear the prisoners talking together in their native language. There was also a possibility that guards still watched the lodge where they slept, although again, after so much time, Stone Bear might not deem such a precaution to be necessary.

Slowly, carefully, Preacher and Dog approached the rear of the lodge the mountain man figured was mostly likely to house the captives. Fifty feet of open space lay between the trees and that lodge. Preacher and Dog took fully half an hour to cover the distance.

At last they were very near the back of the lodge. Preacher was able to reach out and grasp the dwelling's hide wall. He pushed closer and lifted the hide a few inches, just enough to put his ear next to the opening and listen.

He heard deep, regular breathing. People were asleep in there. Somebody shifted around restlessly. As slaves, the captives would be worked so hard that exhaustion probably claimed them every night as soon as they stretched out on their buffalo robes. At the same time, aching muscles made it hard to sleep soundly.

Minutes dragged by before he heard someone inside move around again, and a sleepy voice muttered, *"Mein Rüchen schmerzt! Verdammt* Blackfeet!"

Preacher recognized the Prussians' language instantly. He had a hunch some of what the woman said might translate as *damn Blackfeet* or something close to that.

"Tut mir leid, Gerda," another woman replied.

To Preacher, her tone of voice sounded sympathetic. What really mattered, though, was the name the second woman had uttered. According to Helmuth, Countess Katarina Falkenhayn's maid was named Gerda.

That confirmed he had come straight to the lodge he was looking for. Some might consider that an incredible stroke of luck, but actually, it was more a matter of instinct and the ability to make a highly educated guess about where the Blackfeet would keep captives they had enslaved.

He wasn't a bit surprised he had found the right place.

Lifting the hide wall a little more, he moved closer . . . and remembered Helmuth had said some of the ladies spoke English. He just hoped they hadn't forgotten how during their captivity.

Preacher was just about to call softly to them when a cold, hard wind hit and rattled the lodge's hide covering. At the same moment, a shot roared and a scream ripped through the night, both coming from the spot where he had left Lomax, Becker, and the two dragoons in the forest.

Chapter 34

Roscoe Lomax figured that he was in charge of the small group of scouts once Preacher had moved off toward the Blackfoot village. After all, he had more experience on the frontier than any of the other three men.

Of course, Becker, being the arrogant, surly Prussian son of a gun he was, probably believed that *he* was the boss of things. He would find out just how wrong he was if he tried throwing his weight around, thought Lomax.

Apart from an occasional *woof-woof* from a bored dog or an outburst of snapping and snarling as some of the curs got into a scrap, the Blackfoot village was quiet. That silence started to get on Lomax's nerves after a while. He couldn't see Preacher and Dog anymore, hadn't been able to follow their progress for more than a moment after they left. The uncertainty of not knowing where they were or what they were doing gnawed on Lomax's guts.

Finally, Becker crawled over next to him and whispered, "Shouldn't he be back by now?"

"Quiet," Lomax breathed. "Preacher said no talkin'."

"Something must have happened to him."

"Naw, he's just bein' careful. Just be patient, blast it.

Preacher'll be along directly." Lomax wished he felt as confident as he tried to sound.

On the other hand, if the Blackfeet *had* stumbled over Preacher, a great commotion would have ensued. The mountain man wouldn't let himself be killed or captured quietly. Lomax didn't doubt that for a second. The fact that they hadn't heard any sort of ruckus was actually a good thing.

Becker moved back to where he'd been crouching in the brush, behind Lomax and the two dragoons. Lomax wished the Prussian would just settle down. It wouldn't take much to set off the dogs in the village, and once that happened, the barking would roust out some of Stone Bear's warriors to have a look around and see what was going on.

Lomax wasn't sure what warned him. Maybe he heard movement again, or maybe it was just instinct. But he pushed up from where he had been lying on his belly and turned his head to look behind him.

A dark shape loomed over him. A man grunted with effort as he struck.

Lomax threw himself to the side.

His eyes were adjusted to the darkness, but shadows were thick under the trees and onrushing clouds had swallowed up the moon and most of the stars as a cold wind sprang up, so he still couldn't see very well. He heard something strike the ground where he had been only a second earlier.

"What the hell are you—" Before Corporal Conroe could finish that startled question, a shot roared, slamming shut like a gate on any more words.

In the bright orange glare of the flame that erupted from

a pistol's muzzle, Lomax saw Conroe jolted backward by the lead ball that smashed into his chest at close range.

In that same muzzle flash, Lomax saw Feldwebel Becker rip his saber from the ground where he had just tried to skewer the bullwhacker. The just-discharged pistol was in his left hand, the saber in his right as he whirled around.

Private Willis lunged at him, exclaiming, "You fool! You'll—" He screamed as Becker rammed the saber into his belly with so much force that it went all the way through and the bloody point ripped out of his back.

Lomax pushed himself onto hands and knees and dived at Becker, tackling him around the knees. The feldwebel bellowed a German curse as he went down, his saber lodged so securely in Willis's body that it was pulled out of his hand as he fell.

Lomax had no idea why Becker had gone loco, killed the two dragoons, and tried to kill him, all while raising such a ruckus that it was bound to wake up the whole Blackfoot village. Lomax didn't *care* what Becker's motive was. He was just so mad he wanted to beat the Prussian's head in and hammer wild punches to his face. The attack was so swift and ferocious Becker couldn't fend off the blows.

However, Becker wasn't the only enemy Lomax had to worry about. Shouts came from the Blackfoot village. Even in his rage, he heard them and knew that Stone Bear's warriors would be on top of him in a matter of minutes. He smashed his fist into Becker's face again and felt the Prussian go limp underneath him—out cold.

Lomax took his only chance to get away, and leaped to his feet, grabbed the rifle he had dropped, and dashed into the woods as howling figures ran from the village toward the trees. As he rushed through the shadows, hoping he wouldn't dash his brains out on an unseen tree limb, he heard gunfire from the other side of the ridge.

All hell was breaking loose over there, too.

After Preacher and his four companions left the main group, the soldiers, American and Prussian alike, settled down to wait while their commanders stood near the crest and talked quietly. The Prussians kept to themselves, as usual, and therefore, by necessity, so did the American dragoons.

Helmuth sat by himself on a rock, not really part of either group. His head was down and he muttered constantly to himself, but nobody knew what he was saying.

In answer to a question from Baron von Kuhner, Jamie said, "If Preacher comes back with those captives, we'll head back the way we came, making as little noise as we can. Once we're out of earshot, we can mount up in the dark and ride like hell . . . or as much like hell as possible in terrain this rugged."

"In other words, we will not be able to put much distance between ourselves and our pursuers, even under the best of circumstances," von Kuhner said.

"Not as much as I'd like," admitted Jamie. "But we'll do what we can. Luck may be with us. You never can tell."

"A strong man makes his own luck," snapped von Kuhner. "That is what too many of my countrymen fail to understand."

Jamie didn't feel like arguing with the baron, and besides, there was some truth to what he had said. A man had to be strong to survive on the frontier. Jamie supposed it was the same way in the German Empire, even though

Europe supposedly was civilized. From what he had seen
of Europeans, that veneer of civilization was actually pretty
thin. Most men, no matter where they came from, were
either barbarians at heart—or they didn't last very long.

Colonel Sutton said, "What if Preacher locates the
captives tonight but isn't able to rescue them?"

"I've been thinking about that," Jamie said. "Probably
what we'll have to do is come up with some sort of distraction to get Stone Bear and most of the warriors away
from the village—" He stopped short and his head jerked
up in alarm as a gunshot blasted on the other side of the
ridge, followed a heartbeat later by a scream of agony. He
started to utter a startled exclamation, but before the words
could emerge from his mouth, shots thundered on his side
of the ridge, too.

The gunfire came from the area where the soldiers had
settled down to wait. Jamie whirled in that direction, and
in the flickering muzzle flashes that came from two dozen
pistols, he saw the Prussian troops on their feet, mowing
down the American dragoons. The first volley had come
from the Prussians' rifles, a withering hail of death that
had scythed through their unsuspecting American coun-
terparts. Rather than reloading, the Prussians had dropped
their empty rifles and yanked out pistols to continue their
killing spree. Each man must have had two revolvers
hidden under his uniform. They poured out a tremendous
amount of bullets. Taken completely by surprise, dragoon
after dragoon fell to this well-planned, treacherous attack.

Outnumbered as they were, it was the only way the
Prussians could hope to win—by striking swiftly and
savagely with utter ruthlessness, killing as many of the
Americans as quickly as they could.

Only one man could be behind it: Baron Adalwolf von Kuhner.

Jamie swung toward him, palming out the Walker Colt. He eared back the hammer as the gun came up. No matter what else happened, he was going to blow a hole in that so-called aristocrat.

Unfortunately, Jamie couldn't pull the trigger. Von Kuhner had already grabbed Finlay Sutton and jerked the colonel in front of him as a shield. The Prussian pressed the razor-sharp blade of his saber against Sutton's throat, hard enough that the cold steel drew a trickle of blood. The dark trail was thin enough that most men wouldn't have noticed as it crawled over the colonel's flesh.

Jamie did, and knew how close to death Sutton was.

"Lower your gun, MacCallister," ordered von Kuhner, "or I'll cut the colonel's throat. You, too, Lieutenant."

Curry had drawn his revolver, as well, but the barrel sagged at von Kuhner's threat.

"Don't listen to him, either of you," Sutton forced out through clenched teeth. "Kill him! Kill this double-crossing snake!"

The thunderous gunfire had begun to taper off and came to a stop completely, leaving the echoes to roll away across the rugged terrain. The night wasn't silent, though. Wounded men groaned, gasped, and cried.

Jamie hadn't lowered his Colt. It was still trained on the shadowy shape formed by von Kuhner and Sutton standing so close together.

"You kill the colonel and you'll be dead a split second later," said Jamie. "I reckon you know that, von Kuhner."

"Yes, but your friend will still be dead." Von Kuhner laughed. "I do not think you want that, MacCallister. You are too weak and soft to stand and watch him die, just so you can shoot me."

"K-kill him—" Sutton urged again. His voice choked off as von Kuhner dug the blade harder against his throat. The trickle of blood grew wider.

"Drop your guns, both of you," von Kuhner said. "I will wait no longer."

Sutton managed to say, "Tom, I order you—"

"I'm sorry, Colonel," Curry said as he bent slightly to drop his pistol on the ground. "I'm going to have to dis-obey you."

"A wise decision, boy," said von Kuhner. "Now, draw your saber and throw it down, as well. And MacCallister, I'm tired of waiting for you to drop that gun."

"Take it easy," Jamie said. He lowered the Colt's hammer and dropped the weapon on the ground at his feet. He could still make a grab for it if he got the chance.

"That knife of yours, too."

Jamie slid the knife from its sheath and dropped it next to the Colt. Curry had tossed his saber on the ground next to his pistol.

"Excellent." Von Kuhner eased off a little on the saber pressed to Sutton's neck. "Now you, Colonel. I want you disarmed as well."

"You'll never get away with this," Sutton said as von Kuhner used his free hand to take the colonel's revolver and saber and toss them aside. "I don't know what kind of double cross this is, but you've overplayed your hand. You should have made your move before we got here."

"Then I would not have known what I need to find out," said von Kuhner.

Jamie said, "You know, in just a few minutes, Stone Bear and all his warriors are going to come boiling over the top of that ridge, and they'll be looking to kill every white man they see."

"Are you so certain of that, MacCallister? Are you willing to wager your life on it?" Von Kuhner laughed. "Oh, wait. You already are."

Jamie didn't know what the baron meant by that, but he was all too aware that the situation had spiraled out of control.

And it was his fault, he told himself. He had never liked or even trusted Baron von Kuhner, but he hadn't imagined the Prussian was capable of this level of perfidy.

Such thoughts served no purpose, though. He had to figure out a way to turn the tables back on von Kuhner before it was too late.

It might be too late already. Despite being outnumbered, with surprise on their side the Prussian soldiers had been able to wipe out a large part of Colonel Sutton's command. One of the men kindled a fire, and as the flames began to climb higher, their hellish glare revealed dozens of dragoons sprawled on the forest floor in limp attitudes of death.

It had been a slaughter.

The survivors, most of them wounded, were huddled together under the guns of von Kuhner's men. Even though there were still more of them than Prussians, they weren't capable of putting up much of a fight.

Jamie hadn't heard any more gunfire from the other side of the ridge after that first shot, which had been followed immediately by a scream. He didn't know if Lomax and the two dragoons who had gone with him were still alive, or if Becker had killed them. Considering the double cross von Kuhner had pulled, it seemed pretty safe to assume Becker had been in on the plan—whatever it was.

And Jamie had no idea what had happened to Preacher, but he found it hard to believe that Becker could ever get the drop on the mountain man.

Von Kuhner transferred his saber to his left hand and used his right to draw his revolver. He kept it pointed in the general direction of Jamie, Sutton, and Curry as he ordered, "All of you, step back away from those weapons. Move over there next to the others."

"I'm telling you, you've made a bad mistake, Baron," Jamie said. "You'll need every fighting man you've got once Stone Bear gets here."

"We'll know soon," von Kuhner said, smirking in the glow from the fire. "I believe he's coming now."

Jamie looked up at the ridge crest. Buckskin-clad figures swept over it, some carrying rifles, some armed with bows and arrows. The firelight didn't reach far enough for Jamie to make out the details right away, but he had no doubt who was approaching. That was confirmed as the Blackfeet stalked toward them warily.

At least the warriors hadn't attacked yet, although that surprised him. Maybe they were just curious about the commotion that had rousted them out of their robes and blankets. An Indian could be more unpredictable than usual when something piqued his curiosity.

One of the warriors moved out a little in front of the others. Tall, lean, with a dignified bearing, he carried himself with an air of command that told Jamie he was Stone Bear, even though he had never set eyes on the chief before. Stone Bear held a single shot rifle and looked ready to use it.

As if that potential threat didn't bother von Kuhner at all, the baron walked toward the Indian, pistol held down at his right side, saber on his left. He called in English, "Stone Bear, my old friend! It is good to see you again."

Stone Bear stopped where he was, frowned at von Kuhner, and said, "I remember you. You are the one who called himself . . . baron?"

"That's right." Von Kuhner half turned to indicate Jamie and the others with a sweeping gesture of his saber. As flakes of snow began to swirl down and dance around, borne on the strengthening wind, he went on.

"And I have brought you more white men to kill!"

Chapter 35

The first shot was still echoing through the night as Preacher jerked up the hide wall at the back of the Blackfoot lodge, hoping the captives were all together and at least one of them remembered how to speak English. "Ladies!" he said as he thrust his head and torso into the lodge and pushed himself up on his left hand so he could beckon with the right. "I'm a friend! Come with me!"

A couple of them cried out in surprise.

In the dim glow from the embers of the fire in a circle of rocks in the center of the lodge, he saw several figures sitting up in their robes. "Come on!" he urged them. Casting his memory back to what Helmuth had said, he added some names. "Katarina! Gerda! Marion! Joscelyn! I've come to help you. We need to get outta here now!"

One of the women thrust her robes aside and scrambled toward him. She spoke, swiftly and urgently, to the others in German.

"Let's go, let's go!" Preacher held the hide wall up so the women could crawl under it.

At first he thought the woman who'd responded to his urging was the only one who was going to escape. Then, as her words continued to lash at them in their native tongue, the others started to move, too. One by one, all six crawled out the back of the lodge.

One of them cried out in fear at the sight of Dog, who had risen to all four legs.

The first of the ladies whirled and clamped her hand across the other one's mouth. "Quiet, Gerda! We must not draw their attention!"

"Don't worry about Dog," Preacher assured them as he let the hide drop. "He's friendly, too."

The woman who had silenced the other one clutched Preacher's arm and said, "Walter! We must get Walter before we flee."

That would be the baron Helmuth had talked about, the fella he used to work for. Preacher said, "Where is he?"

"There!" Her finger stabbed toward the neighboring lodge.

Preacher felt cold, wet kisses against his leathery cheeks. It had started to snow.

The air was also full of barking and strident yelling as commotion raced through the village. Preacher heard more shots, a nearly continuous wave of them that rolled like thunder across the valley. Something had gone badly wrong with the rescue attempt, but he still had a chance to let the captives get away.

"You ladies run for the woods," he told them as he surged to his feet. "I'll get Walter."

"I must come with you," the woman said. "He'll be afraid and won't listen to you or cooperate unless I'm there to help him."

"All right. Come on."

The other captives made it upright and stumbled toward

the trees. Preacher and his companion turned toward the neighboring lodge.

A shape loomed up to Preacher's left, rushing toward them. Even in the bad light, Preacher knew it was a Blackfoot warrior, probably coming to check on the captives after hearing voices back here.

As soon as he realized they were escaping, he would let out a yell, so Preacher struck first, yanking his knife from the sheath at his waist and lunging with such speed and ferocity the man didn't have a chance.

Preacher buried the blade in the warrior's throat, cutting off any outcry he might have made. The cold steel grated on bone as it found the Blackfoot's spine and sheared through it. The warrior collapsed instantly, falling against Preacher, who stepped back and let his enemy crumple to the ground. Blood gushed from the ruined throat as Preacher pulled the knife free.

The few desperate, blood-choked gurgles the warrior made as he died couldn't have been heard more than a few feet away—and nobody in the village was interested in such things at the moment, anyway. The shooting and yelling elsewhere had all the Blackfeet in an uproar.

Preacher swung back to the woman and made a guess as he grasped her arm. "Are you Katarina?"

"*Ja*. Yes. How did you know?"

"Never mind that now. Let's get Walter."

They hurried toward the other lodge, Preacher keeping an eye out for more guards. Katarina led the way, circling toward the front of the dwelling. She thrust the hide entrance flap aside and called softly, "Walter! Walter, come here!"

A frightened voice responded, "Mama?"

"He thinks you're his ma?" Preacher said as he stood close beside Katarina, watching for threats.

"His mind is not right. It hasn't been since he was hurt badly, five years ago." A bitter note entered her voice. "When we were attacked and brought here."

A stocky figure shuffled out of the shadows inside the lodge and spoke in German. Katarina said something meant to be reassuring, then she took Baron Walter von Stauffenberg's hand and led him out of the lodge as if he were a child.

"We can go now," she told Preacher breathlessly. Then she paused and quickly said something else to Walter. Preacher didn't understand any of it except for the name Reese.

Reese Coburn, he recalled, had been part of the original Prussian expedition, hired as a guide.

"Are you talkin' about Reese Coburn?" he asked Katarina. "Is he still alive, too?"

"Yes," she said. "But I don't know where he is."

Walter babbled something, and Katarina went on. "Neither does he."

"Well, we ain't got time to look for him now," said Preacher. "Hang on to Walter, and let's go." He hurried them toward the trees where the other women had disappeared.

The shooting on the other side of the ridge had stopped. Preacher paused just inside the tree line and looked back at the village as snow continued to fall intermittently. He heard enough noise to know some of the Blackfoot warriors were swarming up the ridge toward where all the gunfire had been going on.

They were headed right toward Jamie, Colonel Sutton, and the rest of the bunch. Preacher knew something bad had happened over there. Either some other warriors had surprised his friends . . . or that blasted Baron von Kuhner had double-crossed them for some reason the mountain man couldn't understand.

The more he thought about it, the more likely that possibility seemed to him. It was hard to take Jamie MacCallister by surprise, but a man he considered an ally might—just might—have been able to get away with it.

Dog whined at Preacher's side.

Preacher nodded. "Yeah, I know," he told the big cur. "We get to round up them women and get 'em to some place safe."

However, he vowed to himself that as soon as he had done that, he was coming back to find out what had happened, and to give Jamie a hand if there was any way he could.

If he wasn't too late . . .

Jamie's jaw clenched tightly as he heard von Kuhner's greeting to the Blackfoot chief. Obviously, von Kuhner and Stone Bear knew each other, and the only way that was possible was if the baron had had something to do with the attack on Peter von Eichhorn's expedition five years earlier.

The idea that von Kuhner could have been a double-crossing snake back then didn't seem all that far-fetched to Jamie.

For a long moment, Stone Bear just stared at von Kuhner. Tension stretched out the time. The Blackfoot warriors, at least thirty of them that Jamie could see in the firelight, were ready to fight. Rifles were raised to shoulders, and arrows were nocked on bowstrings.

The Prussian soldiers had reloaded their revolvers, though, and were also prepared to go to war.

Jamie and the other prisoners were between the two groups, where any outbreak of hostilities would shred them first.

Stone Bear made a curt gesture to his men, and they lowered their weapons.

Von Kuhner did likewise with the Prussians, and grinned at Stone Bear. "You look well, old friend."

"We are not friends," Stone Bear replied. "You traded with us. Gave us guns and supplies to help you betray your own people. We could never be friends, white man."

Von Kuhner's jaw tightened angrily, but the baron kept a close rein on his temper. "Then perhaps we can trade again—these prisoners for your assurance that you kept your word to me."

Stone Bear cocked his head slightly to the side. "My word? I made no promise to you, except to let you live." The chief sneered. "And here you are, still breathing."

"You said those prisoners I turned over to you would lead short, painful lives with the Blackfeet. You were supposed to kill them after you'd kept them as slaves for a while!"

Stone Bear regarded him solemnly for a couple of seconds, then shrugged. "They are good slaves. Why would I kill them? You may have believed that would be their fate, but I never promised you that would happen."

"We had a bargain—"

"And again, I kept my end of it. You are alive."

Colonel Sutton leaned closer to Jamie and whispered, "Are you hearing all this?"

"Yeah, I'm afraid so."

"Von Kuhner was behind that attack five years ago! From the way he's talking, he even took part in it."

Jamie nodded and said quietly, "Yeah, that's the way it sounds to me, too."

The baron continued to Stone Bear. "When rumors reached me that white captives had been seen in this region, I believed they could not be true. I knew all the prisoners I left with you should have been dead long before now. But I had to be sure. That is why I've come here. And now you tell me . . . that it *is* true? They still live?"

"Not all of them," replied Stone Bear. He looked like he was getting annoyed. "All the women are alive, and two of the men."

"Von Eichhorn?" The sharp tone of von Kuhner's voice as he asked the question made it clear which of the captives was most important to him.

"Dead," Stone Bear said flatly. "Long ago."

Von Kuhner nodded, clearly relieved. "Good. Then he will never stand in the way of my ambition. All the others must die, too. I cannot take the chance that any of them might ever return to Prussia and tell the truth of what happened."

"You cannot tell me what to do, white man," Stone Bear snapped. "I am the chief here. My word is what will be done."

"Then let me have them, and I'll take care of it myself."

A shrewd look came over Stone Bear's face. "And what will you give me in trade if I return the captives to you?"

"More captives," von Kuhner answered instantly with another wave of his sword toward Jamie and the other prisoners. "All these white men to torture and kill. They will provide great sport for you and your people. They are soldiers, the sort of men who, sooner or later, will come out here to wage war on you and your people and drive you from your land."

Stone Bear let out a contemptuous snort. "That will never happen! The whites cannot conquer the Blackfeet, no matter how many soldiers they send."

Stone Bear might want to believe that, thought Jamie, but it was pretty unlikely. There weren't enough Blackfeet, or enough warriors from all the other tribes, to win in the long run. Eventually, they would all be vanquished and civilization would stretch all the way from one side of the continent to the other.

Whether or not that was a good thing was open for debate, and honestly, Jamie didn't know which side of the argument he would come down on.

Not that any of that mattered. The only important thing at the moment was the dangerous predicament he and his surviving allies found themselves in.

As that thought crossed his mind, he wondered about one of his allies in particular.

"Preacher," he muttered to himself, "where in blazes *are* you?"

Chapter 36

Preacher had to take hold of Katarina's arm to guide her through the dark forest. She gripped Walter's hand with her other as they followed Dog, who picked out a path for them with his keen-eyed gaze.

"Dog, find them other ladies," Preacher ordered in a whisper. "Find!"

The big cur's nose dropped lower to the ground as he searched for the scent.

"Who are you?" Katarina asked Preacher, keeping her voice down so it couldn't be heard very far off.

"A friend," he told her. "Call me Preacher. I'm here with some other fellas who've come to get you away from them Blackfeet." He didn't add that some of those other men probably were dead now, based on the shooting he had heard on the other side of the ridge.

Not Jamie, though. He couldn't imagine Jamie MacCallister being dead, no matter what kind of low-down double cross Baron von Kuhner might have pulled.

Preacher indulged his curiosity and asked Katarina, "Do you happen to know a gent name of Adalwolf von Kuhner? Calls hisself a baron?"

A sharply indrawn breath told him she recognized the name, all right. "That man—" she started to exclaim.

Dog stopped short and made a little noise in his throat.

Preacher heard somebody else draw in a quick, deep breath and figured whoever it was planned on screaming. He let go of Katarina's arm and sprang forward. When he bumped into somebody in the darkness, he reached out to where he thought the person's head ought to be, and clapped his hand across the woman's mouth before she could make a sound.

"Don't yell!" he told her. "I won't hurt you. You're all right. Katarina, tell them—" He hung on tightly as the woman in his grip struggled to get free. Those struggles came to an end as Katarina loosed a swift torrent of German words.

"If I let go of you," he said to the woman he held, "you promise you won't start caterwaulin'?"

Katarina hesitated a little over the unfamiliar word then figured the essence of it and translated that, too.

After a moment Preacher felt the woman nod and took his hand away from her mouth, hoping she would remain quiet. When she did, he unwound his other arm from around her waist.

"Are they all here?" he asked Katarina. "Did they manage to stay together?"

She spoke, and a chorus of voices answered. Turning to Preacher, Katarina said, "They're all here."

"Are any of 'em hurt?"

Again, German words went back and forth. To Preacher, most of it sounded like somebody clearing their throat, but he supposed it all made sense to the women.

"Marion and Ingeborg tripped and fell while they were

running," reported Katarina. "They're shaken up, but not actually injured."

"Well, that's good. Gettin' you gals outta that Blackfoot village without anybody gettin' killed or even hurt bad is a heap more luck than we had a right to expect." Of course, they were still a long, long way from being safe, he thought, but he kept that bleak assessment to himself.

The fleeing women had stopped in a small hollow ringed by trees. Some of them were still panting as they tried to catch their breath after their desperate flight.

Preacher could make out their vague shapes as they stood nearby. "All y'all sit down and rest for a spell. Dog'll let us know if any varmints come skulkin' around."

"You speak very . . . colorfully," Katarina told him before she translated what he had just said.

Preacher chuckled. "I never had much education, except in the school of stayin' alive."

"The most important lesson of all."

"Most of the time, yeah. You and Walter sit down and rest, too."

"What about the Blackfeet? Their village is still very near."

"I reckon they're busy with other things right now." Preacher had a hunch Stone Bear and his warriors had hurried over the ridge to find out what all the shooting was about over there. It was possible the captives' escape hadn't even been discovered yet.

Meanwhile, he wanted to take advantage of this brief respite to maybe clear some things up. "A few minutes ago, when I mentioned Baron von Kuhner, you acted like you recognized the name," he said to Katarina.

"Of course I recognize the name. That monster!"

Standing so close to her Preacher felt a shudder go

through her. "I ain't arguin'. I never cared for the fella, myself. But you're gonna have to explain why you think he's a monster."

"Because he's responsible for the deaths of many innocent people . . . and for the five years of hell the rest of us have gone through!"

That was enough for Preacher's nimble brain to make a leap of logic. "Von Kuhner was to blame for your bunch gettin' jumped by the Blackfeet all those years ago," he guessed.

"Worse than that." Katarina drew in a breath. "He and men working for him . . . mercenaries with no loyalty to anyone except him . . . actually carried out the attack. They slaughtered many of our companions and then handed the rest of us over to Stone Bear."

"You know this for a fact?"

"I know our original captors were white men." Quickly, she filled him in on the chain of events, starting with the attack on their camp and ending with their five years of captivity in Stone Bear's village.

"I knew there was something familiar about the voice of the man who spoke to me while I was blindfolded. Finally, it came to me where I had heard it before. I had met Adalwolf von Kuhner several times in the past at various parties and functions."

"You were friends?" asked Preacher, astonished.

"No! Never friends. Mere acquaintances." Katarina shuddered again. "The man is a brute and a boor. One time, he made a very improper suggestion to me— Never mind. I am certain he was the one responsible for what happened, even though I never actually laid eyes on him that time."

"I'll take your word for it. He seems like the sort of hombre who'd do somethin' like that."

"But I do not understand," said Katarina. "You say he came to this place . . . with you? Why would he do that?"

Preacher explained how the government of the German Empire had requested aid from the United States in finding out what had happened to Peter von Eichhorn's party, and how the expedition headed by Colonel Finlay Sutton had come to Blackfoot country.

"But that makes no sense," Katarina protested. "Von Kuhner would never want us found. That would ruin all his plans, the reason he wanted us dead in the first place. He is ambitious and believes that *he* should sit on the throne someday. Peter would have stood in the way of that, so von Kuhner seized the opportunity—our trip to America— to get rid of him."

The theory she had just laid out made sense to the mountain man. He speculated. "Von Kuhner must have figured that, even though you were still alive when he turned you over to Stone Bear, you wouldn't live very long as slaves of the Blackfeet. If those rumors of white captives in these parts reached him, he could've gotten worried and figured he'd best find out for sure who was still alive . . . and dispose of you for good." Preacher shook his head. "No offense, but it would've made a heap more sense for him to make sure all of you were dead the first time, instead of countin' on Stone Bear to finish the job for him."

"But you see, that is exactly the sort of vicious cruelty I would expect from Adalwolf von Kuhner. He wanted those of us who survived the initial attack to suffer greatly before we died. Especially the ladies. I'm certain I'm not the only one who ever rejected his crude advances. And

Peter, who was his real target, did in fact die less than twenty-four hours after we reached the Blackfoot village."

"Sounds like von Kuhner's even worse 'n I figured he was."

"He is a monster," Katarina said again. "If I ever get the chance, I will kill him myself."

"Let's not get ahead of ourselves," Preacher said. "I'm more interested in gettin' you ladies outta here, and in findin' out what happened to my friends. It's lookin' more and more like all that shootin' we heard a little while ago was von Kuhner double-crossin' 'em."

"Yes, he's certainly capable of that."

"So now that you've rested a spell, we're gonna start workin' our way along this ridge, and then we'll go up and over it and look for a place the rest of you can hole up while I come back and find out what happened."

Katarina clutched his arm. "No! You must keep us with you. You . . . you cannot leave us alone."

He felt her trembling again.

"You do not know how hard I have worked . . . how difficult it was . . . to keep all the others alive . . . to keep them from giving up . . ." She sobbed a broken little sound.

Preacher put his arms around her and drew her tightly into a comforting embrace. He patted her on the back and said quietly, "You've done just fine, ma'am. You've done more 'n anybody could've ever expected from a . . . a . . ."

"A spoiled, pampered countess?" She laughed a little through her tears and hugged him around the waist. "It's all right. I . . . I know what most people would think of me, especially you egalitarian Americans."

"I don't rightly know what that word means," he told her, "but this is one American who thinks you've done a mighty fine job of survivin'. Now you've got to do it for a while longer, because I don't plan on lettin' that skunk von Kuhner get away with what he's done."

"No. He cannot get away with it. If we need to hide so you can go after him, I . . . I suppose we can do it."

"That's the spirit," said Preacher. "Come on."

The snow had started to fall harder while they were talking. Clouds of the white stuff swirled in the air, began to pile up in places on the ground, and catch in the branches of the trees.

That was all right with Preacher. It would serve as a distraction for the Blackfeet and also help hide the tracks he and the ladies and Walter left as they tramped through the forest with Dog in front of them on the scout for trouble.

The weather might be a problem in other ways, though. Since they'd been asleep under bearskin robes, the ladies had dashed out of that lodge dressed only in buckskin dresses, and without the leggings and moccasins they usually wore. Their bare feet were in danger of freezing, and the rest of their bodies would be chilled clear through. At the very least, he needed to find a spot where they would be out of the wind.

Worry over the fates of Jamie, Colonel Sutton, and the others—even Roscoe Lomax—gnawed at Preacher's mind. He wasn't given to brooding, so it didn't distract him from what he needed to do, but the feelings were still there.

There hadn't been any shooting behind them for a long time. The fight was over, and that was worrisome, too.

A few times, the other ladies started to whine and complain, but Katarina shut that down in a hurry. She spoke to them in a sharp tone of command, and even though

Preacher didn't know what she said, it was effective. The ladies quieted down and kept moving.

When they had followed the ridge for a mile or so, he had them turn and start up the slope. Too long since he'd been through there, he didn't remember all the physical features in the area. He would have liked to find a cave but didn't know if any were nearby.

The climb was hard on the ladies, but with urging from Katarina, they made it. Some of them even helped the others, taking their arms to brace them as they struggled upward. In the dark, Preacher didn't know which were countesses and which were servants, and supposed that didn't matter anymore. The hardships of the past five years would have obliterated those sorts of distinctions. They had all been slaves together.

At last they reached the top, he allowed them a few minutes to rest again. He moved a few feet away and stood silent and motionless with Dog beside him, as his senses reached out into the night, searching for any indications the Blackfeet might be nearby looking for them.

Not seeing, hearing, or smelling anything unusual, Preacher had just started to turn back toward Katarina and the other ladies when Dog growled softly beside him. Preacher paused, his right hand dropping to the butt of the holstered Colt on that side.

A tall, whipcord-lean shape stumbled out of the shadows and rasped, "D-don't shoot! I'm a friend."

"Reese!" Katarina exclaimed. She rushed forward as Reese Coburn stepped out of the night and wrapped his arms around her.

Chapter 37

The Blackfeet herded ten prisoners over the ridge and down the slope to the village: Jamie, Colonel Sutton, Lieutenant Curry, and seven of the dragoons. Three of the soldiers had minor wounds, and somehow the other four had come through the murderous attack unscathed.

Another eight soldiers had survived the ambush by von Kuhner's men, but they were more badly wounded. The Blackfeet made short work of them after the others left, quickly slitting throats while laughing and joking about what they were doing.

But Jamie knew what was going on, and white-hot rage burned inside him.

Those killings were that many more marks in the ledger against von Kuhner, he reckoned. That many more scores to settle. But von Kuhner had piled up so many crimes already, it didn't really matter. He could only die once.

Jamie intended to make sure that happened. It might take a while, but he'd see to it. There was a little matter of staying alive to attend to, as well as keeping as many of his companions alive as he could. He told them quietly, "Play along with the varmints . . . for now. It wouldn't take much to set Stone Bear and his warriors off on a killing spree."

Sutton said, "We have to get out of this, Jamie. Our government needs to know what von Kuhner has done, and so do his own people."

"He'll get what's coming to him, don't worry about that."

Several large fires had been kindled in the Blackfoot village. The snow, which was falling heavily, hissed when it landed in those flames. The light from the blazes spread over the whole village, giving the women and children and older warriors who had been left behind a good view of the prisoners as they were brought in.

Shouts of excitement and anticipation filled the night air. Soon, the blood of their enemies would be spilled, and the screams of white men would echo across the valley. The Blackfeet were eager to get started on their cruel sport, although probably they would wait until morning.

Jamie thought the young dragoons looked terrified as they shuffled along through the lane that opened in the ravening crowd. They had good reason to be afraid. Their chances of escape were very slim, and would have been non-existent except for one thing.

Preacher was still out there somewhere. Jamie believed the mountain man was alive and working to help them until he saw with his own eyes proof otherwise.

Von Kuhner and the other Prussians came down to the village, too, but they stayed well away from the prisoners and stuck close to Stone Bear so the rest of the Blackfeet wouldn't get carried away and come after *them*, too. Jamie saw von Kuhner talking to Stone Bear, and then the chief waved one of his warriors over to him and spoke sharply.

The warrior hurried away, heading toward some lodges

at the edge of the village. He looked into one of those lodges, then jerked back from the entrance as if in surprise.

Jamie watched with increasing interest as the man practically ran over to the neighboring lodge and jerked the entrance flap aside. He disappeared inside the dwelling, only to burst back out a moment later, running and yelling toward Stone Bear and von Kuhner.

The Blackfoot warriors escorting the prisoners stopped short, clearly surprised and alarmed by what they were hearing. The prisoners halted, too, once their captors quit prodding them with lances. Stone Bear spoke swiftly with the man he had sent on that errand, then turned and said something to von Kuhner.

"Gone?" the Prussian exclaimed as his face flushed in the firelight. His voice was loud enough for Jamie to hear him plainly as he went on. "How can they be gone?"

"We will find them—".

Roaring curses in German, von Kuhner interrupted him then demanded in English, "How could you let them escape?"

"You are the one to blame," Stone Bear snapped back at him. "We knew nothing of you being nearby, and when that shooting started, we had to see if it was a threat to our village. Those slaves are gone because of *you!*"

Jamie leaned closer to Sutton and whispered, "Hear that? Sounds like the survivors from that first bunch have gotten away. But I don't reckon they did it on their own."

"You mean . . . ?"

"I mean I'd bet a hat it was Preacher who got them out," said Jamie, "and that goes right along with what I thought earlier. Preacher's still on the loose, and some of the men who went with him could be, too."

Sutton looked like he wanted to appear hopeful, but he

couldn't quite pull it off. "Even if that's true, what can a handful of men do against all these savages?"

"When one of them is Preacher, you'd be surprised." Something else had occurred to Jamie, something he didn't mention to Sutton or the others because he wasn't sure whether it meant anything. Preacher and the men who had gone with him to rescue the captives weren't the only ones unaccounted for tonight.

Immediately after von Kuhner's double cross and the ensuing slaughter, and ever since then, Jamie had seen no sign of the half-wild Helmuth.

Katarina stepped back from the gaunt, long-bearded, shaggy-haired Reese Coburn. She touched his chest lightly as if she still couldn't quite believe he was there. "Reese, how . . . how did you get away?"

"Well, with all that commotion goin' on," drawled Coburn, "I figured it was the best chance I'd get to make a break for it. Shoot, maybe the *only* chance I'd ever get. Stone Bear had a fella watchin' me, but I jumped him. All this time, I never gave 'em a lick of trouble, so he wasn't expectin' any from me." Coburn paused. "I got my hands on his knife, and that was all it took."

He didn't elaborate, but he didn't need to. Preacher had never met Coburn, but he knew the fella had had a reputation as a veteran frontiersman before he'd disappeared five years earlier. He wasn't surprised Coburn had been able to dispose of his guard and escape from the Blackfoot village.

The mountain man stuck his hand out and said, "Coburn, they call me Preacher. I'm mighty glad to meet you."

"Preacher," Coburn repeated with a note of awe in his

voice as he gripped the mountain man's hand. "You're just about the most famous fella west of the Mississippi, 'cept for Jim Bridger, Kit Carson, and Jamie MacCallister. And I ain't sure but what you're more famous than even them."

"No point in arguin' about who's more famous. We're all in good company. I'm glad you made it outta there safe, Coburn . . . but the job ain't finished yet."

Coburn cocked his head slightly to the side in puzzlement. "Didn't you come to rescue us? I ain't sure how you found out about us, but right now the most important thing is gettin' these ladies back to somewhere safe—"

"Not until I find out what happened to the friends of mine who came with me," Preacher broke in. "You just mentioned one of 'em. Jamie MacCallister."

"MacCallister's here?" Again, Coburn sounded a little awed.

"So is Baron Adalwolf von Kuhner," Katarina added.

Coburn shook his head. "Sorry, I don't know who that is."

"The man responsible for everything that happened to us."

"Is that so?" Coburn's voice hardened. "In that case, I wouldn't mind meetin' up with this von Kuhner hombre."

"You're gonna have to wait your turn," said Preacher. "Come on. I was lookin' for a place these ladies could fort up for a spell. While we're doin' that, I'll tell you how all this hell-raisin' got started."

The group continued on through the darkness, unable to move very fast because of the rugged terrain. Preacher got to the point in the story where he and Jamie and the others had encountered Baron von Stauffenberg's former servant, who he hadn't mentioned before, and Katarina exclaimed, "Helmuth! But that's impossible. He was killed in the attack. I saw him shot in the head. He fell and didn't move again."

"That rifle ball just creased him and knocked him out," Preacher said. "Von Kuhner's men should've finished him off, but likely they figured he was dead, too, just like you did, ma'am. But he survived, and he's been livin' in the woods by his ownself ever since."

"The ghost of the forest," Katarina said as she lifted a hand to her mouth. "It must have been poor Helmuth!"

"The ghost of the forest?"

Coburn said, "Yeah, I've heard the Blackfeet talkin' about that. They used to catch a glimpse, ever' now and then, of some weird figure in the woods. They never could catch it or even get a good look at it. They decided it must be some sort of evil spirit. Some food would be missin' from time to time, and they said the ghost of the forest took it. The squaws would scare the little ones into be-havin' by tellin' 'em if they weren't good, the ghost of the forest would get 'em." Coburn laughed. "It was ol' Helmuth all along! Good for him. I'm glad to hear he's alive."

"Well . . . I don't know if he still is. There was a lot of shootin' earlier. I don't know who lived . . . and who died."

"It's too bad he ain't here," mused Coburn. "If he's been livin' on his own around these parts for five years, he prob-ably knows ever' good hidin' place."

"Yeah," Preacher agreed, "but for right now, we'll have to get along without him, I reckon."

They were about two miles away from the Blackfoot village, Preacher estimated, when they came to a narrow ravine with a tiny stream flowing along the bottom of it. Preacher almost stepped into the yawning emptiness, but Dog sensed it and warned him with a growl and a push of his nose against the mountain man's leg.

Once Preacher knew the ravine was there, he was able to see into it and studied it for a long moment before saying, "This wouldn't be a bad place to hide. That creek I can hear down there might flood at other times of year, but not now with winter settin' in. Let's see if I can find a place where the ladies can climb down."

The snow had started falling harder. The wind still blew, but it hadn't increased in force, so it wasn't a blizzard, just a fairly heavy snowstorm. The snow might drift some in the bottom of the ravine, but Preacher didn't think it would be a problem.

After a while, his search turned up a place where the slope was gradual enough to be handled, as long as the ladies were careful climbing down. Coburn volunteered to make the descent first to be sure it was all right. He took one of Preacher's Colts with him in case he ran into any trouble, and Preacher stayed at the top to guard against anything up there.

Eventually, everyone was at the bottom of the ravine. Preacher guided them along it until he came to a spot where the bank had enough of an overhang to provide at least a little protection against the elements.

"A fire's risky," he said, "but I reckon you ladies must be about froze by now, so we got to take the chance."

He found enough dry brush, and dead grass for kindling, to get a small blaze going with flint and steel. The women huddled around it so tightly for warmth that their bodies blocked most of the glow from the flames. The smoke still drifted up, though, and it represented the greatest danger if the Blackfeet already had search parties out.

Even though he hated to leave them there, Preacher knew he had to go back to the Blackfoot village. He had to find out what had happened to Jamie . . . and the others. If possible, he would slip into one of the lodges and steal some robes and blankets for the ladies, otherwise they might not survive the cold. At least they had Reese Coburn to look after them while he was gone.

Preacher told Coburn, "You hang on to that revolver. I'm headin' back to Stone Bear's village."

Katarina put a hand on his arm and said, "Do you have to go, Preacher?"

"I got friends who probably need my help," he replied. "Don't worry. I won't do nothin' foolhardy."

Reese Coburn gave him a look that said the man didn't believe that at all. "I wish I could come with you. Whatever you do, you'll be facin' mighty steep odds."

Preacher grinned. "Wouldn't know any other way to go about it." And that was the truth. "Come on, Dog."

In a matter of seconds, both of them vanished into the still-swirling snow.

Chapter 38

Even at night, in the middle of a snowstorm, Preacher and Dog had no trouble retracing the steps that had taken them from the Blackfoot camp to the primitive shelter of the ravine. They had just reached the ridge overlooking the valley in which the village lay when Dog stopped suddenly and growled. Preacher reached down and felt the hair standing up on the back of the big cur's neck.

He dropped to one knee next to Dog, put an arm around his neck, and whispered, "What is it, old son? Blackfeet?"

Instead, a muttering apparition came stumbling out of the snowfall and nearly tripped over them.

Preacher surged to his feet, grabbed the figure, and clapped a hand over the man's mouth. Taken by surprise, Helmuth tried to jerk away and then began writhing and struggling madly when he couldn't.

Preacher had heard what he was saying and recognized the language as German even though he didn't understand the words. That and the figure's shape, gaunt yet bulky at the same time because of the bearskin garment, had told him who he and Dog had just run into in the snowstorm.

"Helmuth!" Preacher said as he bent his head closer.

"Helmuth, stop fightin', damn it! It's me, Preacher. I'm your friend, remember? Helmuth!"

The urgent repetition of the man's name finally got through to him. His struggles lessened and then stopped altogether. He stood there, breathing hard, as Preacher hung on to him.

"Now, I'm gonna take my hand away from your mouth, and you ain't gonna yell, right?" It seemed to Preacher like he was spending an awful lot of time asking that question tonight. He was getting tired of it.

After a moment, Helmuth nodded. Preacher lifted his hand from the half-crazed fellow's mouth.

As Helmuth had promised, he didn't shout, but he did ask, "Where are the others? Did you rescue them?"

"I got 'em away from the Blackfeet, and they're in a safe place," Preacher told him. "As safe as I could find for 'em under the circumstances, anyway. I'm on my way back to Stone Bear's village, and you're comin' with me." Even in the thick, snow-shrouded darkness, Preacher could see the whites of the man's eyes as he reacted to that statement.

Helmuth cringed away from him. "No! I . . . I cannot go there. It's too dangerous!"

"I'd take you back to where the gals are if there was time, but I got to find out what happened to Jamie and the others. And I don't want you wanderin' around out here by yourself. Ain't no tellin' what sort of mischief you might get into, even if it was by accident. So you're coming with me where I can keep an eye on you."

Helmuth shook his head stubbornly. "I won't, I won't—"

Dog growled.

Helmuth stopped talking and gulped then he moaned and said, "Don't make me go back to the village."

"You don't have to go into the village itself, I reckon.

I'll leave you on the ridge. But you'll have to stay put until I come back for you. You got that?"

Helmuth put his hands on his head, and instead of answering directly, he said, "All that shooting . . . it was so loud. And there was blood everywhere. All those men died."

"What about Jamie?" asked Preacher. He tried to keep his voice calm and not let Helmuth hear the urgency he felt. "Did you see what happened to him?"

"Who?"

"Jamie MacCallister. The big man who's my friend. The one who isn't a soldier."

"I . . . I do not know. I don't remember. I don't think I saw . . . what happened to him. The men in the tall hats started shooting . . . and I ran. I wanted to get far away from there. They were doing bad things."

That was sure as hell the truth, thought Preacher. He believed that Helmuth didn't know what Jamie's fate had been. To find that out, he was going to have to venture into the Blackfoot village, more than likely.

Helmuth started to sob. Preacher patted him awkwardly on the shoulder and said, "Hang on, old son. I know you've been through a bunch of mighty bad trouble, and you just want to be done with all of it. So do I. The sooner I find out what I need to know, the sooner we can both get outta here. So come on. It'll be all right."

Helmuth sniffled, but after a moment, he drew the sleeve of his bearskin garment across his face and then nodded. "All right. I will go with you. But I will not go into Stone Bear's village."

"That's fine. Just do what I tell you, and you'll be fine."

"What did you say your name is?"

"Preacher," the mountain man replied.

"That is a strange name."

Preacher chuckled. "When we get outta this mess, I'll tell you the story of why folks started callin' me that."

Jamie and the other prisoners were prodded into a single lodge. It was crowded with all ten of them, but at least they were together and the body heat they gave off helped warm the air inside the lodge.

"I've been thinking," Jamie said quietly to Colonel Sutton and Lieutenant Curry. "Outnumbered the way we are, it seems like there's only one way we're getting out of here . . . and that's if the Blackfeet let us go."

"They're not going to do that," Sutton said.

"They might . . . if I challenge Stone Bear to single combat with all our lives as the stakes."

Lieutenant Curry said, "I don't see how that would work. Even if you kill Stone Bear, won't some other warrior just take over as chief and order that all of *us* be killed?"

"That could happen," Jamie admitted. "But an Indian's word means a lot to him, Lieutenant. That's why they get so upset when we break treaties right and left. They don't like being lied to, and they don't like lying. If Stone Bear agrees to the deal, he'll insist that all his warriors agree to it as well. And there's at least a chance that if they do, they won't go back on it."

Sutton shook his head. "That will never work. Von Kuhner won't allow Stone Bear to agree to such a bargain."

"The baron might try to talk him out of it," Jamie said, "but from what I've seen, Stone Bear might agree just *because* von Kuhner tried to talk him out of it. Those two may have worked together in the past, but it doesn't seem to me that they get along all that well."

"I don't know . . ." Sutton shrugged. "You might be on to something, Jamie. At any rate, I don't have any better suggestions to make."

"Neither do I," added Curry.

"The Blackfeet won't do anything until morning," Jamie said. "I'll ask to talk to Stone Bear and put my proposition to him. I think he'll take me up on it."

"And if he doesn't?"

"Then we'll probably all be dead by tomorrow evening. But one way or another, I intend to die fighting."

Reese Coburn turned quickly and raised the gun in his hand. "Who's there?"

"Rest easy," said Preacher as he stepped out of the thick shadows at the bottom of the ravine. He made a bulkier shape than usual because of the load he carried in his arms. "It's just me. I've brung some things from Stone Bear's village . . . and brung a friend, as well."

Another tall, bulky figure followed Preacher and Dog under the bank's slight overhang.

Katarina stepped hesitantly toward the newcomers and said, "Helmuth . . . ?"

"Countess," Helmuth said. "It is good to see you again."

She threw her arms around him, heedless of the robes he was carrying. "All these years, I believed you were dead. I am so sorry you were abandoned."

"He wasn't exactly abandoned," Preacher pointed out. "Everybody figured he was dead. If things hadn't happened that way, there's a good chance he wouldn't have survived this long."

"That's true," Helmuth said. He seemed a little more rational, now that he was among other human beings and

Stone Bear's village was a couple of miles away. "So many of the others died."

The other women crowded around, each of them hugging him in turn. The barriers between aristocrats and a former servant were gone.

Preacher and Helmuth passed around robes, leggings, and moccasins to the half-frozen women, who pulled them on gratefully and wrapped the robes around themselves.

Katarina asked, "Where did you get these?"

Preacher chuckled. "This is the stuff that belonged to you ladies. I figured that since you'd escaped, the Blackfeet wouldn't be watchin' the lodge where you'd been stayin'. I was right. It was easy to slip in there and gather up these things. Luckily, they hadn't cleaned nothin' out of there yet."

"What about your friends?" Coburn asked. "Did you see them?"

Preacher's voice grew solemn as he said, "I caught just a glimpse of 'em as they were bein' herded into one of the lodges, but that was enough to tell me Jamie's still alive. I knew he would be. Looked like him, Colonel Sutton, Lieutenant Curry, and a few of the soldiers survived von Kuhner's ambush. That lodge where they're bein' kept is right in the center of the village, and Stone Bear posted a dozen guards around it. No way for me to get to it."

Coburn sounded wary as he said, "You brought somethin' else back with you."

"Yeah, I did." Preacher picked up a bundle he had set aside earlier while they were handing out the clothes and robes. He untied the strip of rawhide he had tied around several bows and passed them out to the women as well.

"What am I supposed to do with this?" Countess Marion von Arnim said.

"You've been around the Blackfeet for five years, ma'am. I reckon you've seen them usin' bows plenty of times." Preacher unslung a quiver that was slung over his shoulder. "I've got a couple dozen arrows here. Gathered 'em from here and there in the village, along with the bows, in the hope that they wouldn't be missed too soon."

"Wait a minute," said Coburn. "You expect these ladies to attack the Blackfeet with nothing but some bows and a handful of arrows each? No offense, Preacher, but that's loco!"

"I don't figure they'd win any real battles, no. But spread out on that ridge, they might be able to make the Blackfeet believe we've got a bigger force on our side than we really do. When I give the signal, you'll all fire an arrow down into the village. You don't have to hit nothin', just show Stone Bear that you're there."

"And what will that accomplish?"

"I'm hopin' it'll make 'em hold off from killin' me when I walk in there, bold as brass."

Katarina gasped, "Why in the world would you do that?"

"Because I'm gonna challenge Stone Bear," Preacher said. "A fight to the death with your lives, and the lives of Jamie and the other prisoners, ridin' on the outcome."

Chapter 39

By the time the storm came to an end not long before dawn the next morning, it had dumped a foot of the white stuff on the mountainous landscape. As winter weather went, that was fairly mild. Considering that, according to the calendar, it was still autumn, it was a significant snowfall, even though the later ones would be worse.

The temperature was well below freezing, causing Jamie's breath to fog in front of his face as he was led through the village toward Stone Bear's lodge. He glanced along the creek where von Kuhner and the rest of the Prussians had made camp a short distance from the Blackfoot lodges.

Near the tents, several of the soldiers stood guard with rifles in their hands. The men looked nervous, as well they might. Knowing the Blackfeet outnumbered them, if the Indians decided not to honor the truce, the white men wouldn't have much of a chance, even well armed as they were. The best they could hope to do was inflict considerable damage on the Blackfeet before they were all slaughtered.

Von Kuhner emerged from one of the tents, with Feldwebel Herman Becker following him into the frosty morning. Jamie's eyes narrowed at the sight of Becker. He'd wondered what had happened to the man. The fact that Becker had rejoined his countrymen might mean something about Preacher's fate.

Stone Bear pushed aside the entrance flap of his lodge as the warriors brought Jamie to a stop in front of the dwelling. The chief regarded Jamie coldly and said, "I am told you wish to talk to me, white man. Have you come to beg for your life?"

"No," said Jamie. "I want to find out what yours is worth to you."

Stone Bear scowled at him. "What do you mean by that?"

"I'm challenging you, Stone Bear. Fight me, man-to-man, just the two of us. If you kill me, you can do whatever you want to the other prisoners."

"I can do whatever I want to the other prisoners anyway," Stone Bear pointed out.

As if he hadn't heard the chief, Jamie went on. "If I kill you, all of us go free, including the captives you had from before, the ones von Kuhner turned over to you five years ago. You haven't found them yet, have you?"

The angry flash in Stone Bear's eyes told Jamie he had guessed correctly.

Stone Bear said dismissively, "They are helpless slaves. Even if we do not find them . . . we have not searched for them yet . . . they will die. They will freeze to death or be eaten by wolves."

"Sounds like you don't value them very highly. You wouldn't have a lot to lose, would you? Other than your life, of course."

"You cannot defeat me," Stone Bear snapped.

"Prove it."

Stone Bear sneered. "This is just the sort of trickery I

expect from white men, who lie every time they take a breath."

"No tricks," Jamie insisted. "Just a plain, simple challenge. My life against yours, with the fate of all those others added into the bargain."

Moving closer as Jamie spoke, Baron von Kuhner was near enough to hear that last, straightforward declaration. He hurried forward and exclaimed, "No! Do not agree with him."

He had reacted to the challenge just as Jamie expected him to. Whether or not that worked to the prisoners' advantage remained to be seen, but Jamie didn't figure the revelation would be long in coming.

Stone Bear's cold eyes flicked toward the Prussian. "You do not give me orders . . . Baron." The chief's use of the title was full of contempt.

Von Kuhner flushed angrily, but he made a visible effort to control his emotions and said, "This man and the others with him should all be killed. They cannot be trusted. Once they're dead, you should hunt down the others and kill them, too." In an attempt to sound reasonable, he added, "This course of action will be best for both of us, Stone Bear."

"The slaves who escaped are no threat to me. This one"— Stone Bear nodded toward Jamie—"looks like a formidable foe. There would be much honor in defeating him."

"But don't you see, he's counting on you feeling that way—"

Stone Bear slashed the air with his hand and said, "No one makes decisions for me! I do what I want, and now I will—" He stopped short as cries of alarm and surprise went up from some of the warriors gathered around his lodge. His eyes widened as he peered over Jamie's shoulder.

That reaction made Jamie swing around to find out what in blazes was going on. He couldn't have predicted the new development, and yet once he saw it, he wasn't the least bit surprised.

Tall, straight, and unafraid, Preacher strode through the Blackfoot village toward them with Dog pacing along beside him. The big cur's teeth were bared in a snarl as his massive head swung slowly from side to side.

Becker charged forward with his hand going to the saber at his side. Several of the Blackfoot warriors leaped to bar his path, reaching for their knives.

Von Kuhner flung out a hand and called, "Becker, no!"

At the same time, Stone Bear spoke curtly to his men, who, with obvious reluctance, didn't draw their blades. As a result, Becker was surrounded by tense warriors, gripping his still scabbarded sword's handle while staring in hatred at Preacher.

Other warriors tried to block Preacher, but Stone Bear ordered them to stand back.

The mountain man walked up to the gathering in front of Stone Bear's lodge, grinned, and said as if he didn't have a care in the world, "Mornin', Jamie."

"Morning, Preacher," Jamie replied. "Have a good night?"

"Tolerable."

"What are you doing here?"

Still grinning, Preacher said, "Why, I came to see if ol' Stone Bear here would be willin' to fight me, man-to-man."

The chief said, "You come here alone to make this foolish challenge?"

"Oh, I never said I was alone." Preacher lifted his arm and dropped it again in an obvious signal, and a flight of arrows soared out from hidden bowmen on the ridge, arching over the village and dropping from the overcast sky, causing several of the warriors to leap aside hastily to avoid the missiles.

"I've got plenty of warriors up there ready to join in this fight if they have to," Preacher said. "But I'd rather settle things just between the two of us, Stone Bear, like honorable men."

"You can't do that," Jamie said.

"And why in blazes not?"

"Because Stone Bear is going to fight *me*."

Preacher's grin widened. "Well, I'll swan. I remember my old pard Audie, who used to be one of them professors, sayin' that great minds think alike. I reckon you and me got great minds, Jamie."

"Stop it!" von Kuhner burst out in utter exasperation. "Stop this foolishness!" He pointed at Preacher. "Another enemy has placed himself in your hands. Kill him! Kill them all! Or else—"

"Or else what, white man?" Stone Bear cut into the Prussian's rant, phrasing the question in a low, dangerous voice.

Von Kuhner swallowed. "It is the only thing that makes any sense. They are here. You want them dead. Kill them. It is as simple as that."

"It seems that *you* are the one who wants them dead," Stone Bear observed. "Their fates mean little or nothing to me."

"Sure wish you'd let me fight him, Jamie," Preacher said.

Stone Bear snapped, "I have not agreed to fight either of you. Why would I agree to such a bargain?"

"Because your honor has been challenged," Jamie said, "and we both know you're an honorable man."

Silence stretched for several long, tense seconds, then Stone Bear nodded and said, "It is true I am an honorable man . . . and a great warrior. If I fight you . . . either of you . . . you will die."

As Preacher shrugged, Jamie said, "I'll take that chance."

"You." Stone Bear's eyes were dark slits as he stared at Jamie. "How is it you are called?"

"MacCallister. Jamie Ian MacCallister."

Stone Bear's nostrils flared slightly as he drew in a breath. Clearly, he had heard of Jamie.

"And I'm called Preacher," the mountain man put in, "even though you didn't ask me."

At the mention of Preacher's name, all the Blackfeet within hearing reacted. He was a legend among them—and not a good one. The Ghost Killer, the White Wolf . . . they had many names for him, all representative of the fact that he and the Blackfeet had been at war with each other for many, many years.

Finally, Stone Bear said, "To be the warrior who killed Preacher would be a very great honor. But MacCallister challenged my courage and skill first. I must fight him."

Jamie nodded emphatically. "I'm glad to hear you say that, Stone Bear. You agree to the terms I mentioned earlier?"

"No!" von Kuhner cried.

Stone Bear ignored him and said solemnly, "I agree, MacCallister. If you defeat me, you and all you claim as friends will go free. None of my people will harm you as you leave our hunting grounds, or elsewhere."

"Your warriors will abide by that bargain?"

Stone Bear called sharply in the Blackfoot tongue, and one of the warriors responded, trotting over to join them. He and Stone Bear spoke for several moments. The warrior nodded solemnly.

"This is my brother, Beaver Tail," Stone Bear said to

Jamie. "He will be chief if I die. He knows the bargain and will abide by it. Is that agreeable to you?"

"Of course," Jamie answered without hesitation. "I know the brother of Stone Bear will be just as honorable as he is."

"Very well. The bargain is struck."

Obviously furious, von Kuhner said, "This is a mistake, Chief. You cannot trust these men."

Stone Bear regarded him coolly. "From what I know of this business, the only one who has proven himself untrustworthy is you." He turned away from von Kuhner in dismissal and raised his voice, speaking to his people.

They headed for the snowy bank of the creek, where they drew back and formed a circle to wait for the combatants.

Stone Bear stalked toward the makeshift arena. Jamie and Preacher followed at a more leisurely pace.

Jamie asked quietly, "Who's really up there on that ridge?"

"Those six gals, Reese Coburn, and ol' Helmuth." The mountain man chuckled. "Not much of a war party, is it? But that's what we've got."

"If I can kill Stone Bear, maybe we won't need one."

"Not to deal with the Blackfeet, maybe, but there's one other problem we've got to consider." Preacher rubbed his chin. "Even if the Blackfeet are willin' to let us go, von Kuhner ain't. He's gonna do his level best to kill us all . . . and Stone Bear didn't promise not to let him."

"Yeah, well, you might be right," said Jamie. "But we can only stomp one snake at a time."

Chapter 40

Stone Bear walked around and kicked snow out of the way, clearing an area where he and Jamie could do battle. Several warriors joined him in the task. Satisfied, he faced Jamie and asked, "How would you fight, MacCallister? Knives? Tomahawks?"

"How about both?" Jamie suggested.

Stone Bear's dark eyes glittered with anticipation. He jerked his head in a nod and motioned to one of his warriors. The man stepped forward and offered his own knife and tomahawk to Jamie.

"I'm much obliged to you," Jamie told the warrior as he took the weapons. He studied them, weighed them in his hands, then nodded and told Stone Bear, "These'll do."

The chief had drawn his own knife and tomahawk. He raised them in front of him, then made a beckoning gesture with the knife.

Jamie glanced at Preacher and said, "If I don't make it out of this, you know what to do."

"Damn right. Von Kuhner?"

"Yep."

Preacher nodded. If Jamie failed and was killed, all their

lives would be forfeited, but Baron Adalwolf von Kuhner would die first. Preacher was damned fast on the draw and could put a ball from that Colt on his hip through von Kuhner's head before anybody could stop him.

With the knife in his right hand and the tomahawk in his left, Jamie advanced toward Stone Bear.

The fight erupted with blinding speed. Stone Bear lunged, sweeping the tomahawk at Jamie's head, but it was just a feint. At the same time he sent a low, wicked thrust with the knife at Jamie's midsection.

Jamie didn't bite on the feint. He leaned back to avoid the tomahawk and twisted aside so that Stone Bear's knife missed him. His tomahawk swept down and cracked across Stone Bear's forearm as the chief tried to snatch it back out of the way.

If the head of Jamie's tomahawk had struck Stone Bear's arm, it would have broken the bone and inflicted a terrible wound. As it was, only the wooden handle hit the warrior's arm, but that was enough to make Stone Bear grunt in pain and drop the knife. He threw himself backward as Jamie tried a backhanded blow to the head. Stone Bear's feet slipped on the thin layer of snow left on the ground, and his legs went out from under him. He landed hard on his rump.

Jamie rushed but didn't commit himself fully, which was a good thing because Stone Bear rolled out of the way and came up swiftly, lashing out with the tomahawk in what could have been a disemboweling swipe if it had landed. Jamie pulled back and kicked Stone Bear's fallen knife well out of the circle.

Shouts of disapproval came from the Blackfeet at that tactic, but no one moved to interfere. Stone Bear had lost his knife fair and square, and Jamie had every right to deprive him of the weapon for the rest of the fight.

The chief didn't appear to care. Sneering, he slowly circled Jamie. "I have no need of a blade to kill you, white man," he taunted.

Jamie smiled. "If you're trying to prod me into throwing away *my* knife, I reckon I'll hang on to it for now."

Stone Bear's sneer turned into a growl as he launched another attack, slashing back and forth with the tomahawk so fast the eyes of the watchers could barely follow the strokes.

Jamie dodged some of the blows, blocked others, and forced Stone Bear to break off his attack and give ground when the tip of Jamie's blade raked across his ribs and drew blood. The watching Blackfeet roared angrily again. So far, Jamie had the edge in the deadly contest.

All that mattered was the final outcome, though, and that was still very much in doubt. One slip, one wrong move, and Jamie would be finished.

But the same was true for Stone Bear.

All Jamie needed was one opportunity.

That came when the two men had been fighting for ten minutes that seemed much longer.

Luck guided Stone Bear's tomahawk in a wild swing that happened to catch the blade of Jamie's knife and knocked the weapon out of his hands. A triumphant snarl twisted Stone Bear's face as he tried to seize the opportunity. He charged in and backhanded the tomahawk at Jamie's head.

Jamie went over backward to avoid the slashing blow and landed in the snow. He drew up both legs and lashed out with a double-barreled kick that caught Stone Bear in the stomach and sent him flying through the air. Both men rolled, came up at the same time, and flew at each other, the wild leap carrying them through the space Jamie's kick had opened between them.

Stone Bear was hurting, and his reactions weren't quite as fast as they had been. He tried to block Jamie's tomahawk with his, but he was a shaved whisker of a second too late.

The head of Jamie's tomahawk struck Stone Bear in the center of the forehead, split his skull open, and buried itself in the Blackfoot chief's brain.

Stone Bear's knees buckled and he dropped, dead before he hit the ground.

A huge, shocked, grief-stricken wail that sounded like one cry came from the throats of the crowd. Several warriors started to step forward, but Beaver Tail's shout stopped them. His face was twisted with emotion, but Jamie saw instantly that he was going to honor the bargain his brother had made with the white man.

"Damn," Preacher said into the stunned silence that fell, "that was some wallop, Jamie."

"Kill them!" Baron von Kuhner screeched. "Kill them all!"

The Prussian soldiers opened fire. Unfortunately, as nervous as they were, they didn't wait for the Blackfeet to get out of the way, and several Indians cried out in pain and collapsed.

With Beaver Tail shouting orders at them, other warriors turned and fell upon the Prussians, who were trying desperately to reload their rifles or haul out the pistols they had used on the American dragoons. Instantly, the village was a bloody, screaming melee.

Preacher grabbed Jamie's arm and yelled over the uproar, "Let's go get the colonel and the rest of the boys!"

Dodging Blackfoot warriors, they raced toward the

lodge where Sutton and the others were being kept, then spotted the American soldiers hurrying toward them.

"Our guards charged off to get in that battle, whatever it is," Sutton explained breathlessly as Jamie and Preacher joined them.

"It's the Blackfeet against von Kuhner and his men now," Jamie said, "and the Prussians are getting the worst of it."

In fact, outnumbered as they were, it was only a matter of time until they were wiped out. Von Kuhner had led those men to their deaths.

With a pistol in one hand and his saber in the other, von Kuhner broke free of the battle. Behind him, Becker was armed the same way as they charged toward Jamie, Preacher and the others, shooting and chopping down any of the Blackfeet who got in their way.

Jamie and Preacher turned to face them.

Becker charged ahead, only to stop short as a shot blasted. He stumbled, dropped his gun and sword, and pawed at the blood-welling hole in his chest. A split second after that shot, von Kuhner staggered as well and looked down at the arrow that sprouted from his chest as if by magic. He swayed as he dropped his pistol and reached up to grasp the arrow's shaft. He was trying to pull it free of his body, then blood trickled from the corner of his mouth and his eyes rolled up in their sockets.

He and Becker hit the ground almost at the same time and didn't move again.

Preacher looked over at Roscoe Lomax, who stood to one side holding a rifle with smoke curling from the barrel. "Well, what do you know?" said the mountain man with a grin. "I wondered what happened to you, Lomax."

"I've been around," the bullwhacker replied. "Just bidin' my time and waitin' for a moment when it looked like I could make a difference. I wasn't gonna pass up a chance to settle the score with that Becker varmint."

Countess Katarina von Falkenhayn, who stood not far from Lomax, lowered the bow she held and stared at the fallen form of Baron von Kuhner. She drew in a long breath, let it out in a sigh, and turned to Preacher. "You had no way of knowing it when you gave me this bow, but when I was growing up, my father spent many hours teaching me archery at our family's castle."

"Looks like you learned mighty well," Preacher told her. He nodded to Reese Coburn, Helmuth, and Walter von Stauffenberg, who came up behind the countess, trailed by the other ladies. "You boys all right?"

"We're fine," Coburn said. "Looks like the fight's about over."

"Yeah," Jamie agreed. He watched as Beaver Tail stalked toward them, a bloody tomahawk in one hand. "And now we'll find out what the Blackfeet intend to do."

They stood shoulder to shoulder—the frontiersmen, the soldiers, the aristocrats, the former servants—all ready to fight and sell their lives dearly if need be.

Beaver Tail stopped and spoke rapidly and angrily in Blackfoot. Preacher and Jamie listened and then nodded. Preacher replied in the Indian tongue. Beaver Tail turned away.

"For heaven's sake, what did he say?" Colonel Sutton burst out.

"He said they wouldn't kill us, but he advised us to get while the getting's good and not waste any time about it, either," Jamie replied.

"Yeah," Preacher added. "There are some long-standin' grudges betwixt me and the Blackfeet, but Beaver Tail's willin' to honor Stone Bear's deal . . . for now. If I ever run into 'em again, though . . ."

Preacher didn't have to finish his sentence. They all knew what he meant.

"We'd better round up our horses." Jamie squinted at the clouds. "I don't think it's going to snow anymore, and the drifts shouldn't be too bad. If we hurry, we'll get you folks back to civilization before you know it."

Six weeks later, Jamie and Preacher stood on a St. Louis dock and watched passengers boarding a riverboat that would take them down the Mississippi to New Orleans. There, the passengers would board a ship that would take them across the Gulf, around Florida, and up the east coast to New York, where another great sailing vessel would be waiting to take them home.

As Marion von Arnim and Joscelyn von Tellman barked orders at their servants while going up the gangplank to the riverboat's deck, Preacher shook his head and said quietly to Jamie, "Sure didn't take long for things to get back to normal with that bunch, did it? Once they got some good food and had a warm bed to sleep in and didn't have to worry about Injuns killin' 'em all the time, them damn aristocrats went right back to actin' like they did before."

"Those two did," Jamie agreed. "I suppose that's just their nature. They want to put everything that happened behind them. Anyway, not all of them are like that." He nodded toward the couple strolling along the dock toward them, arm in arm.

Reese Coburn was still whipcord thin, but he was starting to fill out a little now that he wasn't living as a half-starved slave in a Blackfoot village. Freshly shaved and barbered and wearing a suit instead of buckskins, he looked downright respectable.

Beside him, Katarina was beautiful. She smiled as she looked up at Coburn while they talked.

Behind them came Helmuth and Gerda. Helmuth was even more scrawny than Coburn had been, but like the frontiersman, he'd had his beard and most of his long, tangled hair shorn off. Only part of the time did a crazy expression still lurk in his eyes.

Gerda held Walter von Stauffenberg's hand and led him gently toward the boat. He seemed happy enough, although not really sure what was going on. A poignant reminder of Adalwolf von Kuhner's evil treachery and ambition.

Katarina and Coburn stopped before Preacher and Jamie. She hugged both big men and kissed them on their leathery cheeks.

"Ain't ever' day I get kissed by a countess," Preacher said with a grin. "You probably can't say the same, Reese."

Katarina blushed, and Coburn returned the mountain man's grin as he said, "I reckon there are a lot of ways I'm just about the luckiest fella in the world right now."

"I can't help but wonder how you're going to like Europe," Jamie said.

"We don't have to stay there if he doesn't," Katarina said. "I've told Reese I'm perfectly willing to come back here to live, as long as I can visit my family from time to time."

"And who knows?" said Coburn. "Could be I'll fit right in over there with all those highfalutin' folks." He looked at Katarina. "With your help, of course, Your Countesship."

She laughed, then grew more serious as she asked, "Where's Herr Lomax? I thought he might come to see us off as well."

"He would have," Jamie said, "but he got wind of a

wagon train over at Independence that's heading off to Santa Fe with a load of freight, so he lit a shuck in that direction, hoping to sign on with them before they left. He said to wish you good luck, though."

Preacher said, "You may need it once you get back and tell folks what a lowdown skunk von Kuhner was. I reckon he's probably still got some friends over there who won't take kindly to you spreadin' the news."

"I'm not worried about that," Katarina said. "The truth must come out, no matter what the danger." She looked around at Coburn, Helmuth, Gerda, and Walter. "Besides, I have wonderful friends to help me."

"That's true." Jamie shook hands with Coburn, then took his hat off and said, "So long, ma'am. Have a safe voyage home."

Preacher took off his hat, too, and nodded to her. "Just watch your back trail, ma'am."

"I'll be helpin' her do just that," Coburn promised.

A few minutes later, the riverboat's shrill whistle sounded as the paddles of the big sternwheel began to turn.

Preacher and Jamie watched it move out into the mighty river.

Preacher squinted and rubbed his chin. "You reckon maybe we should've gone with her?"

"To Europe, you mean?"

"Yeah. We could've seen us some o' them castles and things like that."

"You know what I'd rather see? The high country. Mac-Callister's Valley. My wife."

"Well, I don't reckon I can argue with you there. I've seen your wife. She's mighty pretty."

Jamie laughed, and the two men walked back along the dock. They were heading toward home, ready to answer the call of the frontier.

Chapter 1

Danny O'Neil wasn't sure what made him turn back around to face the depot platform. An unshakable premonition of sudden violence?

He'd never felt any such thing before. The sudden stiffening of his shoulders made him turn around and, holding the mail for the post office in the canvas sack over his right shoulder, he cast his gaze back at the train that had thundered in from Ogallala only a few minutes ago.

As he did, a tall man with a saddle on one shoulder and saddlebags draped over his other shoulder, and with a glistening Henry rifle in his right hand, stepped down off the rear platform of one of the combination's two passenger coaches. He was obscured by steam and coal smoke wafting back from the locomotive panting on the tracks ahead of the tender car. Still, squinting, Danny could see another man, and then one more man, similarly burdened with saddle, saddlebags, and rifle, step down from the passenger coach behind the first man.

The three men stood talking among themselves, in the snakes of steam mixed with the fetid coal smoke, until one of them, a tall strawberry-blond man with a red-blond mustache, set his saddle down at his feet, then scratched a match to life on the heel of his silver-tipped boot. The blond man, wearing a red shirt and leather pants, lifted the flame to the slender cheroot dangling from one corner of his wide mouth.

As he did, his gaze half met Danny's, flicked away, then returned to Danny, and held.

He stood holding the flaming match a few inches from the cheroot, staring back at the twelve-year-old boy through the haze of steam and smoke billowing around him. The man had a strange face. There was something not quite human about it. It was like a snake's face. Or maybe the face of a snake if that snake was half human. Or the face of a man if he was half snake.

Danny knew those thoughts were preposterous. Still, they flitted through his mind while his guts curled in on themselves and a cold dread oozed up his back from the base of his spine.

Still holding the match, the blond man stared back at Danny. A breeze blew the match out. Still, he stood holding the smoking match until a slit-eyed smile slowly took shape on his face.

It wasn't really a smile. At least, there was nothing warm or amused about the expression. The man dropped the dead match he'd been holding, then slowly extended his index finger and raised his thumb like a gun hammer, extending the "gun" straight out from his shoulder and canting his head slightly toward his arm, narrowing those devilish eyes as though aiming down the barrel of the gun at Danny.

Danny felt a cold spot on his forehead, where the man was drawing an imaginary bead on him.

The man mouthed the word "bang," and jerked the gun's barrel up.

He lowered the gun, smiling.

Danny's heart thumped in his chest. Then it raced. His feet turned cold in his boots as he wheeled and hurried off the train platform and on to the town of Harveyville's main street, which was Patterson Avenue. He swung right to head north along the broad avenue's east side. He'd been told by the postmaster, Mr. Wilkes, to "not lollygag or moon about" with the mail but to hustle it back to the post office pronto, so Wilkes could get it sorted and into the right cubbyholes before lunch.

Mr. Wilkes always had a big beer with an egg in it for lunch, right at high noon, and he became surly when something or someone made him late for it. Maybe he was surly about the lunch, or maybe he was surly about being late for the girl he always took upstairs at the Wildcat Saloon after he'd finished his beer. Danny wasn't supposed to know such things about Mr. Wilkes or anyone else, of course. But Danny was a curious and observant boy. A boy who had extra time on his hands, and a boy who made use of it. There was a lot a fella could see through gauzy window curtains or through cracks in the brick walls of the Wildcat Saloon.

Wilkes might be late for his lunch and his girl today; however, it wouldn't be Danny's fault. His grandfather, Kentucky O'Neil, knowing Danny spent a lot of time at the train station even when he wasn't fetching the mail for Mr. Wilkes, had told Danny to let him know if he ever saw any "suspicious characters" get off the train here in Harveyville. There was something about the infrequent trains and the rails that always seemed to be stretching in from some exotic place far from Harveyville, only to stretch off again to another exotic place in the opposite direction—that Danny found endlessly romantic and fascinating.

Someday, he might climb aboard one of those trains and find out just where those rails led. He'd never been anywhere but here.

For the time being, he had to see Gramps, for Danny couldn't imagine any more suspicious characters than the ones he'd just seen step off the train here in dusty and boring old Harveyville. They had to be trouble. They sure *looked* like trouble!

As Danny strode along the boardwalk, he kept his intense, all-business gaze locked straight ahead, pinned to the little mud-brick marshal's office crouched between a leather goods store and a small café roughly one block ahead.

"Mornin', Danny," a voice on his right called out to the boy.

Not halting his stride one iota, Danny only said, "Mornin'," as he continued walking.

"Hey, Danny," Melvin Dunham said as he swept the step fronting his barbershop. "You want to make a quick dime? I need to get Pearl's lunch over to her—"

"Not now, Mr. Dunham," Danny said, making a beeline past the man, whom he did not even glance at, keeping his eyes grave and proud with purpose beneath the brim of his brown felt hat.

"Hello there, handsome," said another voice, this one a female voice, as Danny strode passed Madam Delacroix's pink-and-purple hurdy-gurdy house. "Say, you're gettin' taller every day. Look at those shoulders. Carryin' that mailbag is givin' you muscles!"

Danny smelled sweet perfume mixed with peppery Mexican tobacco smoke.

"Mornin', Miss Wynona," Danny said, glimpsing the scantily clad young woman lounging on a boardwalk chair to his right, trying not to blush.

"Where you off to in such a rush . . . hey, Danny!" the girl called, but Danny was long past her now, and her last words were muffled by the thuds of his boots on the boardwalk and the clatter of ranch wagons passing on the street to his left.

Danny swung toward the door of his grandfather's office. Not bothering to knock—the door wasn't latched, anyway—he pushed the door open just as the leather goods man, George Henshaw, delivered the punchline to a joke he was telling Danny's grandfather, Town Marshal Kentucky O'Neil: "She screamed, 'My husband's home! My husband's home!'"

Mr. Henshaw swiped one hand across the palm of his other hand and bellowed, "The way Melvin told it, the reverend skinned out that window faster'n a coon with a coyote chewin' its tail, an' avoided a full load of buckshot by *that* much!"

Gramps and Mr. Henshaw leaned forward to convulse with red-faced laughter. When Gramps saw Danny, he tried to compose himself, quickly dropping his boots down from his desk and making his chair squawk. Looking a little guilty, his leathery face still sunset red around his snow-white soup-strainer mustache, he indicated Danny with a jerk of his hand, glanced at the floor, cleared his throat, brushed a fist across his nose, and said a little too loudly, "Oh, hello there, young man. Look there, George— it's my favorite grandson. What you got goin' this fine Nebraska mornin', Danny?"

Mr. Henshaw turned to Danny, tears of humor still shining in his eyes. "You haven't let them girls over to Madam Delacroix's lure you into their cribs yet, have you, Danny boy?" He was still laughing a little from the story he'd been telling, his thick shoulders jerking.

"No, no, no," Gramps said. "He just cuts wood for Madam Delacroix, is all. His mother don't know about that, but what Nancy don't know won't hurt her—right, Danny?"

Gramps winked at the boy.

"Sure, sure," Mr. Henshaw said, dabbing at his eyes with a red cambric hanky. "First they got him cuttin' wood and then he's—"

"So, Danny boy—what's up?" Gramps broke in quickly, leaning forward, elbows resting on his bony knees. He chuckled once more, the image of the preacher skinning out that window apparently still flashing in his mind.

Danny took three long strides into the office and stopped in front of his grandfather's desk. He drew a breath, trying to slow his racing heart. "You told me to tell you if I seen any suspicious characters get off the train. Well, believe-you-me when I tell you I just seen three of the gnarliest-lookin' curly wolves you'll ever wanna meet get off the train not ten minutes ago, Gramps!"

Gramps arched his brows that were the same snowy shade as his mustache. "You don't say!"

He cut a glance at Mr. Henshaw, who smiled a little and said, "Well, I'll leave you two *lawmen* to confer in private about these curly wolves. I best get back over to my shop before Irma cuts out my coffee breaks altogether." Judging by the flat brown bottle on Gramps's desk, near his stone coffee mug, the two men had been enjoying a little more than coffee.

"All right—see ya, George," Gramps said before returning his gaze to Danny and lacing his hands together between his knees. "Now, suppose you tell me what these *curly wolves* look like and why you think they're trouble."

"One's a tall blond fella, almost red-headed, with crazy-lookin' eyes carryin' one fancy-ass . . . er, I mean . . . a real *nice-lookin'* Henry rifle."

George Henshaw had just started to pull the office door closed behind him when he stopped and frowned back through the opening at Marshal Kentucky O'Neil. O'Neil returned the man's vaguely incredulous gaze then, frowning now with interest at his grandson. Not nearly as much of the customary adult patronization in his eyes as before, he said, "What'd the other two look like?"

"One was nearly as tall as the blond guy with the Henry. He was dark-haired with a dark mustache—one o' them that drop straight down both corners of his mouth. He wore a dark suit with a cream duster over it. The blond fella must fancy himself a greaser . . . you know—a bean-eater or some such?" Danny gave a caustic chuckle, feeling adult enough suddenly to use the parlance used in reference to people of Hispanic heritage he often overheard at Madam Delacroix's. "He sure was dressed like one—a red shirt with fancy stitching and brown leather pants with conchos down the sides. Silver- tipped boots. Yessir, he sure fancies himself a chili-chomper, all right!"

"And the third fella?" the lawman prodded the boy.

"He was short but thick. You know, like one o' them bareknuckle boxers that fight on Saturday nights out at

Votts' barn? Cauliflower ears, both of 'em. He wore a suit and a wide red necktie. Had a fancy vest like a gambler."

"Full beard?" Henshaw asked, poking his head through the front door.

Danny turned to him, nodded, and brushed an index finger across his cheek. "He wore a coupla tiny little braids down in front of his ears. I never seen the like. Wore two pistols, too. All three wore two pistols in fancy rigs. *Tied down*. The holsters were waxed, just like Bob Wade waxes his holsters."

Bob Wade was a gunslinger who pulled through the country from time to time, usually when one of the local ranchers wanted a man—usually a rival stockman or a nester—killed. Kentucky never worried about Wade. Wade usually did his killing in the country. Kentucky's jurisdiction stopped at the town's limits unless he was pulling part-time duty as a deputy sheriff, which he had done from time to time in the past.

He should probably have notified the county sheriff about Wade, but the county seat was a long ways away and he had no proof that Bob Wade was up to no good. Aside from what everybody knew about Wade, that is. And maybe a long-outstanding warrant or two. Notifying the sheriff all the way in Ogallala and possibly getting the sheriff killed wouldn't be worth taking a bullet from an ambush himself, by one of the ranchers he'd piss-burned by tattling to the sheriff.

He was too damn close to retirement and a twenty-dollar-a-month pension for that kind of nonsense.

"The big fella wore a knife in his boot," Danny continued.

"How do you know that?" Gramps asked. His attention

was fully on his grandson now. There was no lingering laughter in his eyes anymore from the story about Reverend Stillwell skinning out Mrs. Doolittle's window. The old laughter was all gone. Now Gramps leaned forward, riveted to every word out of Danny's mouth.

"'Cause I seen the handle stickin' up out of the boot well."

From the doorway, Henshaw said in a low voice, "The knife . . . did it have a . . ."

"One o' them fancy-carved ivory handles." Danny felt a smile raise his mouth corners and the warm blood of a blush rise in his cheeks. "In the curvy form of a naked woman."

He traced the curvy shape in the air with his hands, then dropped his hands to his sides, instantly wishing he hadn't gone that far. But neither of these men chastised him for his indiscretion. They were staring at each other. Neither said anything. Neither really had much of an expression on his face except . . .

Well, they looked scared.

Chapter 2

When Kentucky had ushered his grandson out of his office, assuring the boy that, yes, he would vouch for him to Postmaster Wilkes, about why he was late, O'Neil walked up to one of the only two windows in the small building, the one between his desk and the gun rack holding a couple of repeating rifles.

He slid the flour sack curtain back and peered along the street to his left, in the direction of the train station.

George Henshaw walked up beside him, nervously smoothing his green apron over his considerable paunch with his large, red hands. Henshaw was bald and gray-bearded, with a big walrus mustache even more ostentatious than the marshal's soup-strainer. He also wore round, steel-framed spectacles, which winked now in the light angling through the dust-streaked window.

"You think it's them, Kentucky?" Henshaw asked, keeping his voice low though the boy was gone and none of the four jail cells lined up against the building's rear wall held a prisoner. He and Kentucky were alone in the room.

"Hell, yes, I think it's them," the lawman said, gazing

through the dust kicked up by several ranch supply wagons heading toward the train depot. "Don't you?"

"I don't know. I guess . . . I was hoping . . ."

"We knew they'd be back. Someday. We knew it very well."

"Yes, I suppose, but what are we . . . ?"

Henshaw let his voice trail off when he saw his old friend Kentucky narrow his eyes as he continued to gaze toward the depot. The man's leathery red cheeks turned darker from a sudden rush of blood. Henshaw thought he could feel an increase in the heat coming off the pot-bellied lawman's bandy-legged body.

"What is it?" Henshaw said, his heart quickening. He stepped around behind O'Neil and gazed out over the man's left shoulder through the window and down the street to the south.

Kentucky didn't respond. His gaze was riveted on the three men just then stepping off the depot platform and into the street. They were carrying saddles, saddlebags, and rifles. Sure enough—two tall, lean men and one short, stocky one. Not just stocky. Laden with muscle that threatened to split the seams of Kinch Wheeler's checked, brown wool coat. Sure enough, he had a knife poking up from his lace-up boot with fancy deer-hide gaiters. He'd always been a natty dresser. Wheeler must have walked straight out of the prison gates and over to the nearest tailor's shop. Turning big rocks into small rocks for twelve years had added to Wheeler's considerable girth.

Henshaw slid his gaze to the blond man in the Mexican-style red shirt and flared leather pants down the outside legs of which silver conchos glinted. He lowered his hand from his face, wincing as his guts writhed around in his belly with cold, dark dread.

"Christ," Henshaw said over Kentucky's shoulder. "Those twelve years really screamed past."

"They sure did."

"What do you think they came back for?"

O'Neil gave a caustic snort. Henshaw knew what they were doing back in Harveyville as well as Kentucky himself did.

Henshaw nodded slowly in bleak understanding.

O'Neil turned away from the window, retrieved his Smith & Wesson New Model Number 3 from the blotter atop his desk, and returned to the window. Again, he peered out, tracking the three as they slowly moved up the street toward the office. "Oh, Christ," he said, hating the bald fear he heard in his voice. "They're coming here."

"They are?" Henshaw jerked his head back toward the window and drew a sharp breath.

"Of course they are!"

The three men moved up the middle of the street as though they owned the town. Horseback riders and wagons had to swerve wide around them. One horsebacker rode toward them with his head down as though checking a supply list. He raised his head suddenly, saw the three men heading right toward him, and jerked his horse sharply to the left. He turned his horse broadside and yelled angrily at the three men as they passed. The horsebacker's face was creased with exasperation.

While Kentucky hadn't heard the words, he'd heard the anger in the man's tone.

"Easy, now, Ed," he muttered to the man—Ed Simms from the Crosshatch Ranch out on Porcupine Creek. Noreen must have sent him to town to fill the larder. "Just keep movin', Ed. Just keep movin' . . ."

Ed hadn't been in the country twelve years ago, so he

didn't know about the Old Trouble. Hell, a good two-thirds of the people in Harveyville and on the ranches surrounding it hadn't been in the country back then. They wouldn't know about it, either.

But Kentucky knew. He knew all too well. He knew well enough that beads of sweat were rolling down his cheeks and into his white mustache and his knees felt like warm mud.

He was going to die today, he thought as he watched them come. They formed a wedge of sorts, the tall, blond Calico out front, leading the way, like the prow of a ship cleaving the waters with supreme, sublime arrogance. O'Neil didn't know why Calico's return had taken him by such surprise. He'd known this day had been coming for the past ten years.

Hadn't he? Or, like Henshaw, had he lied to himself, telling himself that, no, in spite of what had happened, in spite of O'Neil himself organizing a small posse and taking Calico's trio into custody while they'd been dead drunk in a parlor house—and in spite of what they'd left in the ground nearby when they'd been hauled off to federal court in Denver—they wouldn't return to Harveyville.

Well, they had as, deep down, Kentucky knew they would.

The three men, as mismatched a three as Kentucky had ever seen—the tall, blond, dead-eyed Calico flanked by the thick-set punisher, Wheeler, and the dark-haired and mustached Chase Stockton, who'd once been known as "the West Texas Hellion"—kept coming. As they did, Kentucky looked down at the big, heavy pistol in his hands.

He broke it open and filled the chamber he usually kept empty beneath the hammer. When he clicked the Russian closed and looked up again, the three outlaws had veered left and were heading toward the opposite side of the street from the marshal's office.

"Look at that," Henshaw said softly, under his breath. "They're going into the Copper Nickel! You got a reprieve, Kentucky. They're gonna wet their whistles before they come over here and kill you!" He chuckled and hurried to the door. "With that, I bid you adieu!" He stopped at the door and turned back to his old friend, saying with an ominous wince, "Good luck!"

Kentucky raked a thumbnail down his cheek. "Why in the hell are they . . ." The light of understanding shimmered in his eyes. Then his eyes turned dark, remembering. "Oh, no."

Norman Rivers set a bottle of the good stuff on a high shelf behind the bar in the Copper Nickel Saloon. He had to rise up on the toes of his brogans to do so, stretching his arm high and peeling his lips back from his teeth with the effort. As he did, his sixteen-year-old daughter, Mary Kate, ripped out a sudden shriek from where she swept the stairs running up the room's north wall, on Rivers's right.

Rivers jerked with a start, inadvertently dislodging the bottle of the good stuff from the shelf. It tumbled toward him, bashing him in the temple before he managed to grab it and hold it against his chest, or it would have shattered on the floor at his feet—four-and-a-half dollars gone, just like that!

"Gallblastit, Mary Kate—look what you did!" Rivers scolded, turning toward the girl as he held a hand against his throbbing temple. "What's got into you, anyway?"

"That damn rat is back! Scared me!"

"Hold your tongue, damn you! You almost made me break a bottle of the mayor's good stuff!"

"Why do you put it up so high, anyway?" the girl shot back at him from halfway up the stairs. She was a pretty girl, really filling out her simple day frocks nicely, and she knew it and was too often high-headed about it. Her beauty gave her a confidence she otherwise did not deserve. She was sweeping barefoot when if Rivers had told her once, he'd told her a thousand times not to come down here without shoes on.

She didn't used to be this disobedient or mouthy. It had something to do with her mother dying two years ago, and her body filling out.

Rivers held the bottle up, pointing it like a pistol at the insolent child. "I have to put it up so high so you don't mistake it for a bottle of the rotgut and serve it to the raggedy-assed saddle tramps and no-account drifters who stop by here to flirt with you because they know you'll flirt back!"

Color lifted into Mary Kate's ivory cheeks, and she felt her pretty mouth shape a prideful half grin. She shook a lock of her curly blond hair back from her cheek and resumed sweeping the steps. "I can't help it if they think I'm pretty."

"I can't help it if they think I'm purty!" Rivers mocked the girl. "He pointed the bottle at her again and barked, "You shouldn't be makin' time with such trash. You oughta at least *try* to act like a lady!"

"You mean like the high-and-mighty Carolyn?" Mary Kate said in a scornful singsong as she angrily swept the broom back and forth across the step beneath her, kicking up a roiling cloud of dust. "Look what it got her!"

"Married to a good man!"

The banker's son, no less.

"Hah!" Mary Kate laughed caustically. "Everbody knows prissy Richard leaves her alone at home every night, to tend those three screaming brats, while he—"

"That's enough, Mary Kate! I told you I never wanted to hear those nasty rumors again. And what did I just tell you? *Get some shoes on!*"

Mary Kate stopped at the second step up from the bottom, thrusting the broom back and forth across the first one and shaking her head slowly, hardening her jaws. "Boy, when I'm old enough and have made enough money to flee this back-water cesspool, I'm gonna—"

She looked up when boots thumped on the stoop fronting the Copper Nickel and three men filed into the saloon—two tall men, one blond and quite colorful in his Spanish-style dress. Mary Kate's father, Rivers, had just seen the trio in the backbar mirror and jerked with such a start that the bottle he'd nearly placed, finally, on the high shelf, tilted forward, slammed into his head—the opposite temple from before—and shattered on the floor at his feet.

Mary Kate looked at her father, who held his head, cursing. Then she turned to the tall, red-blond drink of water standing just inside the batwings. The blond man grinned and winked at her.

Mary Kate brought a hand to her mouth and laughed.

Rivers glared at her, then turned his head slowly to regard the three newcomers. He felt a tightness in his chest, as though someone had punched a fist through his ribs and was squeezing all the blood out of his heart. All three men had their heads turned toward Mary Kate. The blond man was smiling at her. She was smiling back at him, still covering her mouth with her hand.

Rivers did not like the expression on the blond man's

face. Nor on Mary Kate's. At the moment, however, he felt powerless to speak, let alone do anything to break the trance the blond man—*Ned Calico?!*—seemed to be holding his daughter in.

Finally, the shortest of the three, but also the heaviest and all of that weight appearing to be muscle, which the man's gaudy checked brown suit could barely contain, removed his bowler hat from his head and tossed it onto a table. "I don't know about you fellas," he said in a heavy Scottish accent, "but this feller could use somethin' to cut the trail dust!"

He kicked out a chair and glanced at Rivers, who still held a hand to his freshly injured temple. "Barkeep, we'll take a bottle of the good stuff."

That made Mary Kate snicker through her nose.

The tall, blond man in the Spanish-style duds broadened his smile, slitting his flat blue eyes and curling his upper lip, revealing a chipped, crooked front tooth that took nothing away from his gambler-like handsomeness. He switched his gaze to Rivers and said, "What's the matter, apron? Did you hear my friend here? A bottle of the good stuff!"

He stepped forward and kicked out a chair from the table the big man—what was his name? Wheeler? Yeah, that was it. Kinch Wheeler. The third man was Stockton, a laconic, cold-blooded, gimlet-eyed, dark-haired Texan. Rivers hadn't thought of them, he suddenly realized, in a good many years. But for several years after "the Old Trouble," as everyone in town back then had called it, he hadn't been able to get their names . . . as well as their faces . . . out of his head. For years, he'd slept with a loaded shotgun under his bed. Now, just when he'd forgotten them—or hadn't been remembering them, anyway, and having nightmares about them, and when his shotgun was clear over at the other end of the bar—here they were.

One of them, Ned Calico, making eyes at his daughter the same way he'd made eyes at another girl so long ago . . .

And there wasn't a damn thing Rivers could do about it.

"The good stuff—pronto!" barked Stockton, as he stepped up to the table and plopped his crisp black bowler down beside Ned Calico's and Kinch Wheeler's. He scowled across the room at Rivers. His face was broad, dark, and savage, his hair long and oily. Time had passed. Twelve years. There was some gray in the Texan's hair, and his face, just like the faces of the other two men, wore the dissolution of age and prison time. But here they were, looking really no worse for the wear.

For the prison wear.

And now, sure as rats around a privy, all hell was about to break loose.

"That man there," said Ned Calico, leaning against his elbow and pointing an accusing finger at the barman, "is either deaf as a post or dumber'n a boot!"

"I got it, I got it," Mary Kate said, walking toward the bar with her broom and scowling bewilderedly at her father, who was just staring in slack-jawed shock at his customers.

"No," Rivers said, finally finding his tongue. "No, I, uh . . . I got it."

Mary Kate stopped near the bar, scowling at him, baffled by his demeanor.

"No," said Ned Calico. "Let her do it." He looked at Mary Kate again and smiled his devil's smile. "I like her. She's got a way about her, I can tell. Besides that, she's barefoot an' she's pretty."